BENEDICT'S COMMANDS

BOOK 4 IN THE BRIDAL DISCIPLINE SERIES

GOLDEN ANGEL

Copyright © 2017 by Golden Angel LLC

All rights reserved. This book or any portion thereof may not be reproduced or used in any manner whatsoever without the express written permission of the publisher except for the use of brief quotations in a book review.

Printed in the United States of America

Cover art by Wicked Smart Designs
Edited by MJ Edits

~

Thank you so much for picking up my book!

Would you like to receive a free story from me as well? Join the Angel Legion and sign up for my newsletter!

ACKNOWLEDGMENTS

I have a lot of people to thank for helping me with this book. Marie for all her help with editing, catching small errors, and the continuity issues that I occasionally struggle with (I swear, she remembers all the things that I can't). Karen for catching my lack of commas and commas in the wrong places, mixed-up words, and my overuse of certain words and phrases. Katherine, for her ever-lasting support, encouragement and suggestions. Michelle for her comments, questions, and suppositions, which always end up changing the way the plot and character development flows. And Sir Nick for providing the much-needed male perspective, requests for clarification when my writing is confusing, and making me aware of continuity issues.

My husband, for his constant love and support.

As always, a big thank you to all my fans, for buying and reading my work… if you love it, please leave a review!

A LISTING OF CHARACTERS, TITLES AND RELATIONSHIPS

Philip Stanley the Marquess of Dunbury married Cordelia Astley, the Dowager-Baroness of Hastings

Lady Gabrielle Astley – stepdaughter to Cordelia Astley, now ward of the Marquess of Dunbury

Hugh Stanley, Viscount Petersham, married to Irene, cousin to Philip Stanley

Edwin Villiers, Lord Hyde, married to Eleanor (sister to Hugh)

Thomas Hood, eldest son of Viscount Hood

Walter Hood, second son of Viscount Hood

Felix Hood, youngest son of Viscount Hood

Isaac Windham, Duke of Manchester

Benedict Windham, brother to the Duke of Manchester

Arabella Windham, sister to the Duke of Manchester

Christopher Irving, Earl of Irving, married to Marjorie Irving

Wesley Spencer, Earl of Spencer, married to Cynthia

Alex Brooke, Lord Brook – heir to the Marquess of Warwick, married to Grace

PROLOGUE

Warmth surrounded Christina's body, making her feel cocooned. Safe. It was a feeling she quite liked. When the large male body shifted behind her, turning onto his back, she lost her little cocoon, rousing her from sleepy drowsiness to full wakefulness. She'd always been a light sleeper.

Opening her eyes, she turned to face her lover; her body curled up to his, her head nestled into his shoulder.

Benedict Windham was an incredibly handsome man. His mahogany hair curled around the strong features of his face - his high brow, Roman nose, full lips, and a masculine jawline that her fingers had traced many times. With his broad shoulders and muscular build – the man had no need of padding beneath his garments - he was the kind of rake many ladies of the *ton* sighed over.

And for the past month he'd been her lover.

She'd led him on a bit of a merry chase before succumbing to his seductions. After marrying the first young man to court her turned out to be such a disaster, Christina now required the gentlemen who pursued her to work a little harder to gain her favors.

Benedict Windham, brother to the Duke of Manchester and the titular Marquess of Dearborn until his brother produced an heir, had been quite fervent in his pursuit. Last month, Christina had finally allowed herself to be seduced. She'd been a bit hesitant initially - her physical reaction to him had been almost overwhelming, reminding her too much of her initial reaction to her late husband.

But she was glad she'd finally given in.

He was the most demanding, exciting, and satisfying lover she'd ever had.

Listening to his heartbeat, Christina slid her fingers down the center of his chest, through the curls of his hair. Grumbling in his sleep, he turned his head towards her, a faint smile curving his lips. Christina knew from experience it took quite a bit to wake him.

Once she'd managed to get his whole cock in her mouth before he'd completely come awake. He'd let her suck him dry before turning her over his knee for 'impudent perversity,' spanking her bottom a bright pink before taking her from behind, continuing her spanking all the while. She'd nearly passed out from the pleasure when he'd finally allowed her to press her fingers to her clit and rub herself to orgasm as he plowed her from behind. His dominance and sexual control over her was as arousing and exciting as it was frightening. Christina struggled with giving over so much control to him, although somehow the struggle also made both of them more excited by each other.

Compared to her husband's disinterest in lovemaking once he'd taken her virginity, Conyngham's skilled but indifferent pleasure-giving, and Haversham's eager but often uninspired maneuvers, Benedict was by far her favorite lover. He was the one who had taught her the ecstasy of combining pleasure and pain, who had shown her the joys of being bound and helpless to questing hands and lips, and he was the only man whose orders she'd ever obeyed - at least, as long as his orders were part of their bed play.

Not only that, but outside of the bedroom, he was thoughtful, generous, and actually interested in what she had to say. They discussed everything from books to politics to art, and he was just as happy walking with her in Kew Gardens as he was taking her to a play at St. James'. They both adored Oscar Wilde's works, although neither was opposed to a night of Shakespeare, and Benedict had even snuck her into bawdier entertainments like gaming hells and masquerades while wearing a hood and a mask. She hadn't been the only lady thus attired, which had given her greater confidence about attending, even as she'd thrilled to the illicitness of the experience.

He made her feel alive in a way she hadn't since before her marriage.

Which was why she had to give him up.

Just the thought of it made her heart ache, and that's how she knew it was time. Already she'd stayed with him longer than she should have, even though it had been a rather short amount of actual time together. But Christina measured her relationships by the quality of her feelings, not the length of time spent in them.

Despite the lesson she should have learned after her husband's betrayals, she was still far too emotional. She struggled with separating the physical from the emotional, although with Benedict the struggle was far greater than she'd been prepared for. By now she would have thought it would be easier.

The moment she'd felt a stir of jealousy at the thought of another woman with Conyngham or Haversham she'd ended the amorous part of the relationships immediately. She'd felt rather possessive of Benedict from the very beginning, which was part of why she'd been so hesitant to become involved with him. Still, the love-making had been worth it... so far.

But now, the very idea of not being with him tore at her. Thinking of him with another woman was enough to make her chest feel as though it was about to burst from the pain.

She'd held on for too long, telling herself that she would end things before Christmas; her reasoning being she would have the whole holiday and several months to compose herself and wrangle her wayward heart back in line before she would have to face him again during the Season. By then he would probably have found a new lover, and she would have control over her emotions again, so it wouldn't bother her to see him with someone else. The same way she'd felt about Conyngham and Haversham. A bit of wistfulness that their time together was over, a touch sad, but certainly not hurt - no jagged edges of betrayal and no hours of sobbing tears that did nothing to ease her misery. The lack of deep emotion was what Christina desired above all else - passion, mutual enjoyment, and then a quiet parting with no pain on either side.

Despite the shortness of their affair, she'd become far too attached to Benedict. She wanted to spend more time with him, she wanted to make excuses... which was why she needed to cut herself off from him. Because she was too close to falling in love with him and she would never - ever - make such a foolish mistake as loving a rakish gentleman again.

It was her great misfortune that rakish gentlemen also seemed to be the only kind of man which she was attracted to.

Sighing, Christina forced herself up from his bed. He would wake to find her gone, as she sometimes was wont to do. Benedict was quite a heavy sleeper, especially after a night of passion. She still throbbed between her legs from his lovemaking and her breasts were deliciously sore from his rough handling as she eased on her corset and dress. The soreness of her bottom would probably linger for several days as well.

She needed to return home, to finalize her packing, and depart from London. She'd decided to spend the Christmas holidays in Bath again. The town was rather insular, which she appreciated. There would be enough social gatherings to entertain and distract her, and yet still give her time to mend her broken heart.

Hesitating in her dressing, Christina looked at the sleeping figure in the bed.

Yes, perhaps her heart was breaking a bit.

She was certainly making the right decision.

How much worse her heart would hurt if she tried to hold on to him, if she let herself truly feel something for him. Benedict was worth a little bit of heartbreak, and she certainly did not regret her time with him, but a greater heartbreak? No man was worth going through that again.

Steeling herself, Christina averted her eyes from the bed as she finished dressing. Walking out of the room without looking back was even more of a chore. Leaving his townhome, the house they'd always met at to indulge in their passions, she felt like Sisyphus, but the boulder she was pushing was her own desire to turn back around, climb back into his bed, and pretend nothing had changed.

But she could not allow herself to do so. She had to leave to protect herself.

When she returned to London she would be over this affliction of her heart. She would greet Benedict as a friend, the same way she had Conyngham and Haversham after those affairs had ended. And then she would find a new lover. As would Benedict, if he didn't already have one by the time of her return.

Ignoring the pang in her heart at the thought - as that pang only strengthened her resolve - Christina exited the house, sure it was for the last time.

~

DEAREST BENEDICT,

Our time together has been a wonderful interlude for the little season, but, alas, all good things must come to an end. I will be spending my holiday away from the capital. I hope you will not hold it against me that I left without saying a proper goodbye; I've never been very good at farewells and I find it easier to take my leave with a note.

I have so enjoyed your company, and I hope, if our paths should cross next Season, that we shall meet as friends.

All my best,

Christina

The paper was soft from being re-opened and re-folded over and over again; Benedict had lost count how many times he'd re-read his lover's dismissal since he'd received it. Often enough he'd memorized the words, and yet he found he couldn't bring himself to dispose of the letter. Nor even set it aside. He kept it in his jacket pocket over his heart, and his valet knew better than to suggest it be consigned to the flames.

Soft footsteps approached the door to the library where he was currently hiding away, and he hurriedly re-folded the note for the umpteenth time and replaced it in his pocket just as the double doors opened. Looking up from the comfortable leather chair he was currently reclining in, he smiled with some relief as he saw his sister-in-law rather than either of his siblings or any of their guests.

Lydia, his sister-in-law, was a sweet, easy-to-get-along-with, calm woman who had had a rather hard time of it the past few years. Her stepfather had behaved in a very unfatherly manner towards her, causing her to become desperate enough to trap Benedict's brother into marriage in order to escape her childhood home. Now the man resided in Bedlam, after drink and grief over Lydia's mother drove him mad (at least, the rest of them could only assume those were the causes of his insanity), and she and Isaac had fallen quite in love. She was a wonderful wife and sister-in-law, and a much-needed restraining influence on Arabella, the youngest of the Windham clan.

Always a lover of the Yuletide, upon discovering Lydia hadn't experienced a real Christmas since her mother had passed away several years prior, Arabella had turned into a whirlwind of plans, decorations, and (according to Isaac) forced participation. She'd driven Isaac quite batty until he'd written to Benedict, begging him to return to the estate and rescue him from Arabella's holiday mania.

"What are you doing tucked away in here?" Lydia asked with a small smile. Her honey-blonde hair was swept back in a loose bun, tendrils escaping to frame her lovely face. The sky-blue dress she was wearing skimmed her curves, silver trim bringing out the astonishing grey color of her eyes.

"Hiding from my sister?"

Lydia's soft laughter was more sympathetic than mocking as she moved to the chair across from him and sat down. She was moving just a touch gingerly, and Benedict knew she and Isaac must have had a very... rousing evening the night before. While he'd occasionally ribbed his brother for their shared bedroom proclivities, Benedict would never embarrass his sister-in-law by showing any notice of his knowledge.

"She and *my* sister are directing the hanging of mistletoe in the ballroom," Lydia said, eyes sparkling. She leaned to the side, resting her chin on her elbow, openly studying him. A little wrinkle formed in her brow and she looked rather nervous, catching his curiosity as she began speaking. "Benedict… I know we do not know each other well yet, but from the little I saw of you before you went back to London… well, I do not wish to pry but you seem to have returned to us rather troubled. After the great service you did me, if there is anything I can do for you…"

The great service had been overseeing her stepfather's move to Bedlam, of course. After the man had run both mad and criminal Benedict had taken him to London to have him admitted, as well as to facilitate the passing of the man's Earldom onto his heir. As the Duke of Manchester's man-of-business, as well as personally eager to return to town to court Christina, Benedict had been all too happy to assist in the matter.

Still, Lydia's delicate offer was not unappreciated and might actually be quite helpful. There were not many women Benedict could truly feel comfortable speaking too candidly on the subject. He did not count any women as close friends, nor could he speak with his sister about his former lover. Actually, he could not do so with Lydia either, at least not in explicit terms, but he could certainly be more frank with her than with Arabella.

"I am just troubled by… well, a woman, let us say," Benedict said with a slightly bitter smile. "I do not wish to be indiscreet or tax your sensibilities."

"Oh no, of course," Lydia said, raising the hand on her lap to open it in understanding, gesturing for him to continue. "If you would like to speak in the most general terms, I am sure I can extrapolate from there."

"I find myself in a position I am unaccustomed to," he confessed, leaning back and looking up at the ceiling. He found it was a bit easier to speak if he wasn't looking directly at his sister-in-law's clear grey eyes, which could be a little too knowing at times. "There is a woman I cannot get out of my mind, and yet she no longer wishes to continue our relationship in the way which we were conducting ourselves. I have never before been troubled when parting with a – a lady... but I miss her." He paused and then added, rather wistfully, "I had actually considered inviting her here, to Christmas."

"That does not sound very discreet," Lydia observed, sounding rather amused. He didn't dare turn his head to see her expression, as he already felt far too vulnerable. "Nor as though you wished to continue your relationship in the manner it had been previously conducted."

"No. It does not." He tapped his fingers against the armrest of the chair, feeling rather jittery all of the sudden. "I had not decided to do so... It was just a thought I had. But I was not ready to make such a definite declaration."

Because doing so would have been tantamount to moving their relationship from clandestine lovers to a more socially acceptable one; in which case marriage would be the clear goal. Clear not just to himself and Christina, but to Society as a whole. It was the only scenario in which inviting her to Christmas with his family wouldn't cause a scandal.

He hadn't thought he was ready for marriage, but he hadn't been ready for their relationship to end either. Especially not so rudely cut off without even a discussion or proper goodbye. She'd left his bed and him simultaneously, without any warning. Had she been upset over a lack of discussion about their future? Had he been taking her for granted? Or had it been a play for attention? None of his suppositions felt right.

"It seems to me, perhaps your indecision is your larger problem," Lydia said thoughtfully. "If you value your relationship with a woman, you must show her. If you can no longer continue on as before, then you must decide what kind of change you would like to make to your relationship. Decide what you want and then move forward from there."

Now he did turn his head to look at her, a teasing smile curving his lips. "As you did?"

"Well, I was rather successful," she replied, a bit sheepish at the reminder of how she'd decided she wanted to marry and had trapped Isaac into it. Although, Isaac had planned to marry already; he'd just thought to have a say in his bride. "Even if events did not play out entirely as I planned." Her smile brightened. "However, I certainly cannot complain about the outcome."

Very true.

Benedict was immediately sunk deep into contemplation. Obviously sensing his preoccupation, Lydia stood, stepped forward to drop a kiss on the top of his head and left him to his thoughts.

All he had to do was decide what he wanted.

And then move forward from there.

CHAPTER 1

The matrons and misses of the *ton* swirled and stuttered in their movements and conversation, the equivalent of Society tripping over itself. To anyone accustomed to the ebb and flow of a ball, it was clear something was amiss - a shark had entered the waters. Lady Christina Rowan, the Marchesse of Stanhope, turned her head towards the staircase of the Wutherings' ballroom, to see whose presence had caused the disturbance. Beside her, the Countess of Marley was also leaning forward curiously.

Daphne and Christina had been friends long before Daphne had married the Earl of Marley and they kept very few secrets from each other. So Daphne's reaction to the latest arrival to the ball was very similar to Christina's.

"Bloody hell." Daphne breathed out the words almost like a supplication, her soft voice reaching Christina's ears but no one else's. Which was just as well, since her husband would have a very stern reaction to hearing his wife swearing. "Is that who I think it is?"

Christina couldn't bring herself to answer as brown eyes, dark with emotion, scanned the ballroom and somehow managed to unerringly seek her out. Her body pulsed, her core tightened, and her breath caught. The time in Bath hadn't been nearly as effective as she'd thought it would be.

She'd missed him.

Thought about him.

Daily at first.

But she'd managed to put those thoughts aside. Convinced herself her emotions had faded. Told herself she was remembering him as more than he was. Finally, eventually, she'd begun smiling with nostalgia. A bittersweet smile.

Bittersweet was an emotion she thought she would be able to handle when they met again.

Now, watching him descend the staircase, bittersweet was the last thing she was feeling. There was a roaring sound in her ears - she'd entirely missed him being announced. Her heart was pounding so fast it felt as though her corset could barely contain it.

His brown hair waved away from a stern face and her fingers itched to run through the strands. The dark navy superfine of his coat was neatly fitted to his body, accentuating the broad shoulders she'd spent so much time clinging to and the narrow waist her legs had spent so much time wrapped around. Well, when her limbs hadn't been tied down.

Arousal, need, want, desire, yearning...

The sudden rush of emotions made her feel alive again, as though she'd been a seed buried underneath the earth through winter in Bath, and now that she was back in London for spring, he was both sun and water and she was coming awake again.

It made her sick.

Panic welled.

If only he wasn't headed directly towards her, every eye flitting between him and where his relentless gaze had landed - on her. If only she could disappear, gather her defenses, and return to the battlefield. If only she could have time to grapple with her emotions, tuck them back where they belonged...

He shouldn't even be here, she realized, her fingers gripping the fan in her lap so hard that the delicate wood creaked. An unwed gentleman of his stature, appearing at a ball this early in the Season? It wasn't a roaring she was hearing in her ears, it was the whispers of the excited *ton*. Murmuring mamas, thrilled debutantes, already thinking to get their hooks in him.

Her stomach churned with sickness for an entirely different reason as jealousy speared her.

Run... she should run to Bath... but if she did so now, with nearly every eye upon her, with the way Benedict was looking directly at her, walking straight to her... it would be a scandal. Assumptions would be made. True assumptions, but still. She might not be able to make an easy return to polite society.

Although, assumptions were already going to be made, she realized, as Benedict Windham - with every eye on him watching to see exactly who the Marquess of Dearborn, brother to the Duke of Manchester, was so intent on speaking with - came to a stop in front of her chair and bowed. Beside her, Daphne tittered with a delight Christina couldn't match.

"Lady Christina," he said, making her want to reach out and slap him for the blatant indiscretion as he practically announced their close relationship to the eager ears crowded around them. While using her Christian name in such public surrounds would be entirely appropriate if they were close family friends or some such, using it here hinted strongly at intimacy between them. As soon as she'd separated herself from him, she'd forced herself to think of him as Dearborn rather than Benedict, although even before she'd left his bed she would never have referred to him by his Christian name in public nor encouraged him to do so. "I request a spot on your dance card."

When she stared up at him, too stricken by conflicting emotions to move, it was Daphne who responded.

"*Lady Stanhope* is a widow, Dearborn, she doesn't have a dance card," Daphne said, emphasizing Christina's title, although the gleeful merriment in her voice undermined any kind of real rebuke. Christina silently cursed her overeager friend.

While she loved Daphne dearly, the dratted woman had become a romantic after falling in love with her own husband, and she was determined to see Christina find the same "blissful marital happiness." Christina, on the other hand, while thrilled her friend's marital circumstances had turned out very differently from her own, had no interest in falling in love again.

Ever.

And especially not with a man like Benedict.

The smile curving across his face at Daphne's response was more than a little triumphant, but didn't quite reach his eyes. His brown eyes, which had always been so warm, were now turbulent with emotions. She wanted to look away, but it was as though he'd trapped her with his gaze somehow and she could barely even blink.

"Well then," he said, his voice almost a purr as the first quivering notes of the violin were sounded, "I shall claim *this* dance for my own."

He held out his hand.

Christina stared at the proffered hand as though it were a viper about to strike. For him to come swanning into the ball, a ball no man would attend without good reason, and come directly to *her* with such focus... the *ton* would be talking about this for days. It had all the makings of a scandal in progress. But if she didn't take his hand, it would mark an immediate scandal. No lady, even a widowed Marchesse, publically refused the brother of a Duke something as simple as a dance without social repercussions.

Daphne elbowed her in the side and Christina jumped a little, finally jolted into movement.

She swore she felt her entire body heat when her fingers touched his, despite the gloves which prevented skin to skin contact.

CHRISTINA WAS SO PALE, Benedict was almost concerned. He'd almost wavered from his course, but... once set, it had been impossible to divert from unless he wanted to create even more speculation. And he was well aware he was already creating quite a bit. However, the current gossip he was stirring supported his cause.

He'd heard the adage "absence makes the heart grow fonder," but he hadn't realized its truth until he'd been without Christina. During their time apart he'd thought of little but her, had dreamed of her nightly, and had come to the realization that - for the first time in his life - he'd truly fallen in love. While he remembered being in love when he was younger and more inclined to such soft feelings based on his attachment and pleasure with a woman, this was different. For one, he was much older and jaded. For another, the emotions had crept up on him slowly; he hadn't even realized how much he cared for her until he'd thought he'd lost her.

She brightened his days and his nights, but it wasn't just her beauty or her body that he'd missed. He'd missed her conversation, her quick wit, her flashing smile, even her tiny spurts of temper. He'd missed her presence by his side, the way she leaned into him when they stood beside each other, and her hand on his arm when they walked. Several times a day he'd had a thought he wanted to share with her, a humorous moment he knew she would have appreciated, and he'd missed her with an ache that only grew with each passing day, rather than abating.

So his return to London didn't mark his pursuit of just returning her to his bed, rather he had much more honorable intentions.

Intentions he'd just informally announced to the *ton* by arriving at one of the earliest balls of the Season - an event gentlemen such as himself usually avoided - and made a beeline straight to her. When other rakish gentlemen heard of his determined interest they would heed it as the warning it was. The ladies of the *ton* were already tittering, whispering behind their fans as he escorted Christina to the dance floor. Some looked disapproving - Benedict recognized the jealous glances for what they were - while quite a few of the youngest set, those who were getting their feet wet in Society by attending tonight's soiree, looked thrilled. Probably by either the implied romance or seeing for themselves the moment which would be gossiped about all week.

As Christina turned to face him, he was relieved to see her cheeks had become quite pink as they'd walked. She wasn't nearly so pale now. In fact, she looked more incensed than anything else.

"What. Are. You. Doing?" she hissed the words at him, her fingers delicately placed in his as they began to move in the complicated steps, sliding in between other dancing partners.

Benedict would have preferred a waltz, especially for this conversation, but a smaller event at the beginning of the Season, such as this one, with so many debutantes who had not yet been to Almack's to receive permission to engage in the dance was unlikely to play the music for one.

Which meant his appearance and immediate pursuit of Lady Christina Rowan was probably going to be the most interesting thing to happen tonight.

"You look lovely, this evening," he said, rather than answering her, letting his eyes rove down her body. The violet silk hugged her curves becomingly, the neckline dipping low to reveal an expanse of creamy décolletage, inviting a man to imagine what the gown hid from his eyes.

"Thank you, my lord," Christina bit out the words primly, too polite to ignore the compliment even though she obviously wanted to. Hearing her call him 'my lord' rather than by his name only made him more resolute to break down the wall she'd erected between them. "Again, I inquire, *what are you doing?*"

"Isn't it obvious?" he asked, with a teasing mirth he didn't actually feel. "I'm dancing with you."

The dance took them apart for a moment and then they came back together again.

"You know that's not what I meant," she hissed at him.

Strangely, the more upset she became, the calmer he felt. He'd wanted to disrupt her equilibrium, the way she had his when she'd deserted him before Christmas, and it appeared he had. If she truly hadn't cared about him at all, he wouldn't have been able to do so.

"Why did you leave me the way you did?" he countered, his voice slightly deeper. The calm settling over him allowed him to feel more in control, the part of him which craved domination coming to the forefront - a part of himself which he'd often indulged with her.

She reacted to his tone of voice, blinking rapidly, taking in a breath... he'd never used his deeper, more authoritative demeanor outside of their amorous encounters before.

"I was going away for the holiday, it seemed best to take my leave with as little fanfare as possible," she said, trying to appear confident, although her voice trembled and gave her emotions away. She was uncomfortable and trying to hide it, feeling vulnerable and trying to ignore it.

"Without notice? Or a proper goodbye?" he asked, his anger and indignation starting to rise again at his remembered concern for her and then his realization of the deliberation of her actions. Christina's cheeks paled and then flushed as he continued. "After all we shared together-"

"My lord," she said sharply, struggling to keep her voice low. "This is hardly the proper surrounds for such a conversation-"

"You are correct," Benedict responded, rather grimly.

Fortunately, the dance had taken them to the French doors leading to a large terrace overlooking the gardens. Directing their movements to the edge of the dance floor, Benedict placed her hand on his arm, leading her towards the outside. Most of their audience would assume they desired a breath of fresh air, perhaps that conversation interested them more than a dance. There would be speculation by some parties, of course, but Benedict would keep their encounter completely above board - in public.

He felt her fingers tense on his arm, and covered them with his other hand, giving her no chance to try and slip away from him. Not again.

FEELING FAR MORE breathless than the dance should have made her, Christina allowed herself to be drawn out to the terrace. She told herself she was allowing him to do so, although the truth was, she wasn't sure she could stop him. Part of her didn't even want to.

Even as she felt compelled to run, to guard her wayward heart, she also wanted to cling to these moments with him, to savor every second she was the center of his attention. A desire she fought against, knowing full well how such dangerous emotions could hurt her. Still, she let him draw her into semi-privacy, steeling herself for the moment when she must give him a verbal *conge*, as he had apparently not been satisfied with a written one.

Not too private, of course. Although widows were allowed far more latitude than debutantes, as they'd already made a stir this evening far too many eyes would be watching them through the doors for her to behave anything less than circumspectly. She wanted no part of malicious gossip or - worse – aggressively importuning rakes, which meant keeping her good reputation. A reputation which he'd already imperiled by approaching her in the manner he had.

Several other couples were strolling through the well-lit gardens, and a small group of gentlemen were on the other side of the terrace involved in some kind of discussion. They were far enough away for privacy of conversation, but close enough there would be no blemish on her reputation. Also, close enough to deter any sort of theatrics on either her or his part, she hoped.

She didn't quite know what to expect from him or what he wanted; she'd been thrown decidedly off-kilter by his appearance tonight as well as his single-minded focus on her. Addressing him directly had only served to cause her further aggravation, so now she kept her lips pressed firmly shut, waiting for him to speak.

The Marquess led her to the marble balustrades overlooking the gardens, the lights below twinkling like stars fallen to earth, while the rich fragrance of the flowers wafted upwards in a heady perfume. Christina took a deep breath, willing herself to calm despite her pounding heartbeat and her hyper-awareness of Bene- the Marquess' closeness. She had to muster her defenses, already it was becoming hard to keep her distance from him - not just physically, but emotionally.

She would not let herself start referring to him so familiarly again, not even in her own mind. It would be far too easy to forget herself, slide back into intimacy with him - not just in a physical manner - and find herself back where she'd started when she'd ended their affair. Perhaps worse than where she'd been; and there was no retreating from the Season, she'd have to stay in town and watch as he found another lover, all while trying to mend a re-broken heart.

Keeping her hand on his arm, denying her the opportunity to draw away from him, he turned his body slightly towards her, studying her expression in the light coming from the house. With the practice of many years, Christina kept her face carefully blank.

"You left," he finally said, the two words an accusation. "Not only did you leave, you snuck away while I was still abed, and left nothing but a cold note."

"It was not a cold note!" she protested. She wanted to protest his accusation of sneaking, but truthfully *sneaking* had been exactly what she'd done. Even if she didn't like to think of it as such. "It was just... just a note. And I did say I'd like to remain friends."

"But I would not."

Christina flinched, but his hand kept hers on his arm, not allowing her any room to retreat. Her chest ached suddenly, and she felt cold and empty inside at the thought of Benedict out of her life forever. *Dearborn.* If they weren't even to be friends, then she certainly needed to keep herself from thinking of him intimately. She'd had a difficult enough time doing so when she thought some ember of their relationship might survive.

But if he didn't want to be friends... what was he after?

Revenge?

Scandal?

He hadn't seemed the type, but perhaps she had misjudged him. Perhaps her note had angered him to the point of unreason. Although he did not have a reputation of being an angry ex-lover, it wasn't as if she knew exactly how his previous affairs had ended.

For the first time, fear slid through her.

"What do you want?" she whispered, watching his face for some clue, some hint as to his disposition.

But his face looked as though it had been carved from granite - at least what she could see of it. It did not escape her notice that he'd positioned them so the light from the candelabras in the house would allow him to see her, whilst his expression was mostly shadowed. Christina trembled, feeling so very cold, except for those parts of her he was touching directly. If he wasn't so formidable, if she wasn't so unsure of his agenda, she might have leaned into him, seeking warmth and reassurance.

Unfortunately, those days were past, because she herself had ended them.

"I want what I've wanted since I met you," he said, his voice low, ominous. Not quite a threat, but certainly not reassuring. "I want you."

Christina licked her lips, hating the part of her which still thrilled to his words. She pushed the sudden surge of arousal away. While her body and heart might betray her, her mind had been made up.

"I've already given you your *conge*, my lord," she said quietly, trying to tug her hand away from his. "Please accept it gracefully."

"Explain why. Please." Even in the darkness, she could see his hard eyes flicker, a note of pleading in his voice. She'd reduced him to nearly begging... and the revelation made her heart hurt.

"I... I..." She took a deep breath, words failing her as she searched for the correct ones. She leaned towards him, drawn in by his very presence, trying to see more of his expression. Now, out here, with just the two of them, he seemed almost vulnerable. "I..."

"Christina? Oh, there you are." Daphne's voice floated through the air, full of curiosity and expectation.

Turning, Christina saw her friend coming onto the terrace, escorted by her handsome husband. The Earl of Marley was tall, with dark brown hair and dark brown eyes, which he set off admirably in his dark green jacket and amber waistcoat. Christina had always found him to be rather imposing, but he softened noticeably in his wife's presence. They had not begun as a love match, but they had certainly become one after their wedding.

His attention was on the Marquess, rather than Christina herself, studying him intently for some reason. Perhaps he saw the Marquess as a kind of rival? Seeing them sizing the other up was very much like watching two sleek predators meeting for the first time.

Daphne was smiling, but her sharp eyes were taking in the entire scene in front of her, flicking back and forth between Christina and Dearborn. "We're ready to be on our way, would you like a ride home?"

She felt Dearborn's startled reaction, which loosened his grip on her hand just enough for her to take advantage and tug her fingers free. Immediately, she stepped forward, her heart pounding as she retreated from the man behind her.

"Yes, that would be lovely," she said, heart in her mouth.

For some reason, she expected Dearborn to stop her. To say something. But there was no response from him as she followed the Earl and Countess of Marley back into the ballroom. Glancing over her shoulder, she could see Dearborn's form still in the shadows, watching her go.

Even though he wasn't following, Christina didn't dare let herself relax. Since he had not received a satisfactory answer from her, he would approach her again. At least now she had time to try and come up with a more adequate response. And she told herself she was *not* relieved or excited by the idea of him continuing to seek her out.

The glittering throng of the *ton* danced and swirled around her like a mad carousel of color and laughter, with herself trapped at the center. It was an utter relief to make their farewells to the hostess and escape the clamoring ballroom. She felt almost feverish, a touch shaky, after her confrontation with her former lover. Even now her body was hot, thrumming with arousal just from having been in his presence; apparently, her physical response to him was in no way hampered by the anxiety his unexpected appearance had roused.

When Marley closed the door to the carriage behind him, settling into the seat beside his wife, Christina let out a sigh of relief. In the

GOLDEN ANGEL

close confines of the carriage, hidden from view, knowing she need not declare her emotional vulnerabilities this evening at least, she felt safe again.

Across from her, Marley raised his eyebrow. "Should I have a word with Dearborn, Lady Christina?"

A smile curved her lips at the protective manner in which he asked. In many ways, Marley reminded her quite a bit of Dearborn. Both authoritative males, strong-willed, protective, and used to getting their own way.

"No, thank you, my lord," she said.

She told herself it was the tiny niggling of guilt which made her feel as though she had to face the Marquess again, not her own desire to see him. While she'd felt a moment's fear when confronted by his anger, she didn't believe he would hurt her. The man wanted an explanation, which was not entirely unreasonable. He also wanted her, which he couldn't have, but hopefully if she gave him the explanation he desired he would desist in trying to extend their relations.

The thought made her chest tighten in unhappiness, but that was the course she had chosen. It was the sensible course, designed to protect herself.

"Well, I thought he was rather dashing," Daphne said, grinning widely, as her husband gave her a wry look.

"I thought he was rather awful," Christina said, frowning at her friend. "People will be gossiping about us horribly if he is not careful."

"They already are," Daphne said, although she sounded delighted rather than horrified. "Not in a detrimental way to your standing; the ladies are all agog wondering how you managed to secure his notice."

"Not detrimental?" Christina was confused. What other way could there be? A fission of fright went down her back as she realized what else Daphne had said. "They all concluded I have secured his notice for... for..?" They all knew he was her lover? Or they thought he was in pursuit of her now? The gossip would be horrendous!

Both the Earl and the Countess were looking at her now with a touch of confusion.

"Well, yes, of course. What other possible conclusion was there to draw when he arrived tonight, at Lady Spearow's ball of all places, and immediately focused on you? You are an eminently eligible widow and he's brother to a Duke who was fairly recently wed." Daphne mused, cocking her head. "I suppose they think he's following his brother's example."

"They think he means to court me for... marriage?" Christina asked, relaxing back against her seat with utter relief. She didn't know if Dearborn realized how his actions would be interpreted, but such an interpretation would harm neither of them. Not even once she explained and he accepted his *conge*, it would be all too easy to understand why a sudden courtship led to nothing.

"The way he whisked you around the dance floor and then off onto the terrace? Everyone could see how taken he was with you. A man does not behave in such a manner with a potential mistress, only with a woman he is courting. What were you two talking about? He looked like he wanted to ravish you right then and there, no matter who was watching."

The relish with which Daphne made her observation had both her husband and Christina's lips twitching. Due to the circumstances of their friendship, Christina knew quite a bit more about Daphne's and the Earl's unorthodox relationship than anyone outside of their very secretive and clandestine club. They were quite improper on an entirely different level than the erotic pleasures of pain which Benedict had introduced her to, yet Christina never judged them and their own peccadilloes had made it possible for her to feel comfortable confiding in Daphne about the scandalous specifics of her own affair with Benedict. Bloody hell, *Dearborn* not *Benedict. Dearborn, Dearborn, Dearborn.*

It was so much harder to think of him as such so soon after seeing him in the flesh again.

She felt like bashing her head against the carriage door, but surely that would cause comment from her friends.

"Christina?"

"Yes?" Oh, she hadn't answered Daphne's question, having been distracted by her own inner ramblings. "He... wished an explanation for my hasty departure before Christmas." That or he wished for her in his bed again... or both.

Honestly, Christina wasn't entirely clear on what his goal had been. She was overwrought and confused, and her memory of her conversation with him was already muddled in her head.

"That's it?" Daphne was obviously disappointed, making Christina smile wryly.

She didn't want to admit to her friend that Benedict had also said he still wanted her. After all, he'd backed away from that statement, hadn't he? He'd demanded an explanation... but had he indicated he'd leave her alone once he'd received one, or not?

Her head was beginning to hurt as she tried to reconcile the whirling thoughts in her mind with the lingering arousal his presence and touch had engendered. Clearly, she wasn't as beyond her relationship with him as she'd thought. Thank goodness her friends had been there to rescue her, so she could retreat, regroup, and shore up her defenses.

Now she knew he was returned to town and in pursuit of an explanation from her, she could prepare herself. Next time he approached her, she would be ready.

CHAPTER 2

Staying on the terrace as Christina left had given Benedict the opportunity to wrestle his emotions and body back under control. Besides, he admitted to himself, he didn't particularly want to watch her leaving him. *Again.* With no way to stop her. *Again.*

At least, no way which was socially acceptable, although he was fast approaching the point where he might not care about breaking Society's strictures. But Christina would care, and so he was trying to play by the rules. A smile suddenly bloomed, as he remembered her look of shock at his appearance in the ballroom. Yes, playing by the rules did have some benefits. For instance, using her desire to avoid gossip in order to inveigle her into a dance, and then out onto the terrace for some nominal privacy.

It was underhanded, perhaps, but it had worked.

She'd danced with him. Gone outside with him.

Had *responded* to him. So he knew whatever had led to her breaking off their arrangement, it wasn't a lack of attraction to or desire for him. More than once, as she'd looked up at him, she'd tilted her head in such a way that it had seemed like she was asking him to kiss her.

Something which had taken all his self-control not to do.

After all, he was courting the woman he wanted to make his wife. Kissing her on a terrace, under the watchful eyes of the *ton* would guarantee immediate success for his task; however, it would not make for a happy bride. As willful as he was already finding Christina to be, he didn't need to exacerbate her temper.

Returning to the ballroom, he was obliged to dance with three blushing, giggling debutantes before taking his leave. While it would not completely deter the gossips from talk of him and the Marchesse, at least he hadn't singled her out entirely. There would likely be speculation, but he'd also appeased the marriage-minded mamas by literally dancing to their tune.

Really, he'd been giving Christina time to return to her home and he'd had nothing better to do. His friends would not be returning to the ballrooms until a few weeks hence, for the larger events - beginning with the Duchess of Richmond's ball, which was always the first large event of the Season. The debutantes would be expected to have gained some polish during these smaller balls and events before then.

Even his family was not in attendance. While his younger sister, Arabella, remained unwed as she embarked on her second Season, she had no need of practicing her social graces, and therefore would only attend soirees thrown by friends and family before the Richmond ball.

Lacking any of his usual circle, as well as wanting to throw some doubt on his reason for attending this evening, dancing with debutantes had been the easiest way to pass the time without drawing attention. Besides, it was rather expected of him as a gentleman.

Fortunately, there was a small break in the music after his third dance with a milk-and-water miss who was far too young and innocent for him, and Benedict took the opportunity to slip away from the proceedings. The marriage mart of young misses wasn't for him. While he had made up his mind to marry, there was only one woman whom he imagined in the position of his wife.

BENEDICT'S COMMANDS

ONCE SHE WAS in her filmy white night rail, Christina dismissed her lady's maid, Esther. While removing her ballgown had necessitated help, she was desperate for solitude. Sitting in front of her vanity, she began the laborious work of taking down her mahogany curls from the elaborate coiffure she'd worn. Tending to her own hair would have caused a mild murmur of gossip among her peers if they knew, but Christina had always found the process rather relaxing, and there were some nights she preferred to tend to it herself.

Which, of course, made her think of other nights when the hands gently pulling the pins from her hair had been masculine rather than feminine, lips traveling over her shoulders and neck as he'd brushed the sweeping strands aside, even as her hair fell down. Benedict had loved to touch her hair, and she'd loved to let him.

Pushing the memories away, Christina firmed her lips as she picked up her brush.

The memories might remain, but she should not dwell on them. She should be thinking about her future, not her past, and what kind of explanation she could give him which would suffice. Admitting her finer feelings for him, her fear that she had become too emotionally involved with him was right out...

Or was it?

Her brush strokes slowed as she stared at herself in the mirror.

Men, rakes, who preferred inamoratas to marriage... well, they preferred to keep such messy things as emotions from their relations. Anything beyond affection or desire was a deterrent for them, as far as she understood it. While admitting her unreturned feelings for him might be humiliating, it might also be the best way to send him on his way. Perhaps she need not even admit the full depth of the emotions he'd sparked in her, but just admit that she had been *beginning* to feel for him more than was appropriate for an affair. Which was the truth. She just hadn't realized her feelings had gone far beyond that until after she'd broken off their arrangement, however there was no need to admit that revelation to him as well.

It would be hard, embarrassing, even hurtful to be spurned after admitting she had started developing feelings for him... but it would also be better in the long run for her.

If he forced her hand, if he demanded an in-person explanation from her again, she would tell him the why. Hopefully, she would be able to hide her hurt when he agreed with her that ending things before Christmas had been the wiser decision.

Perhaps she should start looking for a new lover immediately. Even if she didn't find one as exciting as him, she could at least put him behind her with a new affair - which would also hopefully be a distraction when he began his own search for a new amour. There were other men among the *ton* with the same domineering attitudes as Benedict, men who were also experienced in exotic bed play... she just had to find one. Daphne might be able to assist her.

Assuming she could thwart her friend's current romantic aspirations for Christina.

The thought appealed.

A new lover.

One with the same command over her body and sensual reactions.

Christina began to fantasize about what such a lover might be like. She already knew she enjoyed being bound, spanked, even strapped on occasion. Benedict had hinted at further decadent behaviors, he'd even enjoyed inserting a finger into her anus more than once, promising her in dark tones that one day he would have her there. The stinging burn and his whispered vows had sent her climax soaring, even as she'd shaken her head in refusal; shocked and tempted by such depravity in equal measure.

Benedict had whispered other perversions they might try... perhaps she could try them with a new lover. Clips for her budded nipples and phallic toys to fill her, small whips meant specifically for her most tender bits, her body entirely at the mercy of her lover as she was bound by all fours to bedposts. The vision rose in her mind, making her more hot and achy than ever, so full of repressed need, she didn't even notice her dream lover had a strong resemblance to the man she was trying to forget.

Letting out a small sigh of pleasure as her brush pulled through the strands of her hair, over her breast, Christina found herself brushing that one spot again... and again... her nipple swelling and tingling under the soft brush bristles as they caressed her night rail. The silky fabric moved against the bristles, stimulating her sensitive bud, and she was reminded of the time Benedict had spanked her lightly, turning her bottom pink, and then rubbed her brush over the tender skin. She'd felt incredibly sensitive afterwards, and he'd sat her down on his desk, spread her thighs, and had her right there, her bottom throbbing against the hard wood he'd purposefully placed her on.

She moaned, leaning back, her breath coming a little faster at the memory. Giving up the pretense of continuing to brush her hair, Christina pushed the heavy strands over her shoulders, arching her back to thrust her breasts up as she moved her brush to her other nipple. The tiny bud tingled under the stiff bristles, softened only by the silky fabric of her night gown, and she pressed her thighs together at the pleasurable sensation.

Although she'd indulged in self-pleasure before, after her marriage and in between lovers, she hadn't been so inclined in months. Not since before becoming Benedict's lover. But now it seemed her libido had reawakened with a vengeance, and Christina felt almost desperate to assuage it.

Jumping to her feet, her nipples and pussy pulsing, she hurried over to her bed, throwing herself onto it as she spread her legs. With one hand, she pushed down the silky fabric of her gown between her spread thighs, holding the brush until she could begin to rub the bristles over the gown again, only this time she was rubbing her aching pussy with the implement. It was entirely wicked, not something she would have ever thought of before, and it felt wonderful.

The bristles, which would have been far too abrasive without the shield of the silky nightgown, massaged her nether lips and swollen clitoris, making her writhe with the sensation. She pressed harder, her free hand coming up to cup her breast, and she imagined what her new lover might think of such wanton behavior... how he might punish her for it... Perhaps by spanking her with the brush she was using so indecently? Turning her buttocks a cherry red, and then flipping her over to spank the lips she was so vigorously stimulating? Wetting the wooden handle in her pussy, like a cock, and pushing it into her bottom before taking his pleasure?

That last wicked thought was nearly enough to make her scream her climax. She moaned, without thinking, picturing the man who would be depraved enough to do such things.

"Benedict..."

No sooner had his name left her lips, but suddenly firm fingers were wrapped around her wrist, yanking the brush away from her throbbing core, and Christina nearly screamed for an entirely different reason.

When Benedict had first scaled the tree closest to Christina's bedroom - at least, what he'd assumed was her bedroom based on the usual layout of fashionable Mayfair houses - he'd planned to jump to her balcony, enter her room, and demand the accounting she'd left unfinished earlier. The plan had lasted all the way up til he'd actually landed on her balcony and looked through the pane glass of her doors.

The sight he'd seen had taken his breath away.

Christina on her back, her knees in the air with her feet on her mattress, one hand rubbing up and down between her thighs. The silky material of her night dress clung to her curves, her pink nipples pressing upwards against it. Her auburn hair flowed across the white pillows beneath her head, making her look like a naughty, virginal wanton.

If he'd been aroused by her this evening, properly attired in her ballgown, that was nothing to how he'd felt glimpsing her in such a shocking tableau. His cock swelled so quickly he felt light-headed, as if all the blood in his body had rushed to the organ and turned it to steel.

Moving quickly and quietly, he'd opened the balcony door,

thankful she'd been distracted enough to leave it unlocked, and nearly unmanned himself as he moved closer and closer to the bed. With her eyes closed, her breathy moans filling the air, it was obvious she was unaware of his presence in her room, making him an unwelcome voyeur... yet wild horses couldn't have torn him away.

When she moaned his name, he couldn't take it anymore.

She was on the cusp of climax, but the rule established between them was that her orgasms, her pleasure, belonged to him.

He wrapped his fingers around her wrist, gently but firmly, and pulled the brush away from the juncture of her thighs. Christina's eyes flew open, wide and terrified, and her lips parted as if to scream... but she just sucked in a breath and froze as her eyes met his.

Instead of a scream, her breath came out on a strangled shriek as she pressed her knees together and tried to roll away from him. Both amused and feeling a bit guilty at having frightened her, Benedict kept his hold on her wrist. The brush waved in the air between them, her fingers still tightly clenched around it, as she settled back against the bed, realizing she couldn't pull free from his hold.

"Be- what are you doing here?" she whispered furiously, amusing him all over again now that her fright had faded. Her cheeks were pink with fury, her eyes glittering with both anger and arousal, and her breasts heaved, nipples rubbing against the silky material of her night rail.

"I'm here to finish our conversation," he said easily, his voice silky with menace, as he sat down on the bed next to her, pressing her wrist down onto the bed beside her head, still holding her brush.

Her eyes widened and her breath caught as she realized the vulnerable position she was in. The erotic position.

Yes, regardless of why she'd left him a lackluster note ending their arrangement, she certainly still felt desire for him - as did he for her. Noting her response to him softened him somewhat. Something had sent her running, both before Christmas and tonight, and as soon as he ascertained what it was, he could fix the problem, renew their relationship, and then marry her so she couldn't leave him again.

"Our... our conversation?" Her voice was breathy as he leaned over her, her body tense in anticipation as his lips brushed very gently across her temple... her cheek... she tilted her head up, offering up her lips, but Benedict pulled away again.

No kisses until he knew what was wrong.

"Yes, love, our conversation," he murmured, bringing his hand up to caress her cheek. Christina's eyelashes fluttered. "About why you left me so suddenly with no explanation and nothing but a note."

Sadly, the reminder brought her back to her senses. She stiffened, no longer looking like a woman ready to be seduced, instead appearing more as a woman on her guard.

Her free hand pushed against his chest, and Benedict allowed her to push him away, giving her more space as he sat up - although he kept her other hand pressed down beside her head, which necessitated leaning partway over her body... but not hovering over her the way he had been before. With her hand still on his chest, she glared at him, but he could still see the arousal simmering in her brandy colored eyes.

"A gentleman would have taken heed of the note," she said accusingly.

Something about her anger seemed false, though, as if she was trying to purposefully arouse her ire to hide other emotions.

A slow smile slipped across his lips, purposefully infuriating. "By now you should already know, I'm no gentleman." Then he let his smile vanish. "And I do require an answer."

"Well you shan't have one." Even as she said the words, Christina wondered what she was doing.

She'd had a plan, had determined the road she was to take, but her shock at Benedict's presence in her bedroom, her body's thrumming need for climax after being denied, and his high-handed behavior... well, it seemed her mouth had run away with her in response. Instead of placating him, she was prodding him; instead of explaining and telling him to go, she was taunting him and guaranteeing he would stay.

As he studied her expression, his eyes half-hooded and far too knowing, Christina felt her heart sink as she realized what she was doing. She was delaying. Putting off the moment when he would turn away from her. Doing exactly what she'd told herself she wouldn't.

But before she could open her mouth and amend her statement, before she could offer the explanation she'd settled upon and ask him to remove himself from her bedroom, she found herself being lifted up and tossed over his knee. Christina let out a little shriek of surprise as he manhandled her, a thrill going through her at how easily he positioned her, the way he often had.

The brush was pulled from her hand as the skirt of her night rail was flipped up, exposing the creamy mounds of her bottom.

"Benedict!"

She shuddered as the bristles rubbed over her skin, sensitizing it as he brushed circles across her bare flesh.

"You've been very naughty, my love," he said, his voice dark with sadistic promise, and she shuddered as her arousal surged hard and fast, shooting through her like a bolt of lightning as her inner muscles clenched in reaction. The ache between her legs bloomed, becoming nearly unbearable, and Christina moaned in response. "I think ten swats for trying to orgasm without my permission, and then we'll return to discussing your note."

A whimper escaped her lips.

Refusing her climax had been one of Benedict's favorite games. He'd touch and caress her, with his fingers and mouth, drive her absolutely wild, fill her with his cock, and require her to beg before he'd allow her to orgasm. She'd loved every moment of it, even as she'd wanted to scream at him for denying her release. Those orgasms, when he'd finally granted them, had been incredibly powerful.

He'd never caught her masturbating though, as she'd never needed to during the time they'd been together. Now, it seemed, his reaction was feeding right into the fantasy she'd been imagining as she'd used the brush to pleasure herself.

SMACK!

The flat hard wood of the brush smacked against her sensitized flesh, where he'd been rubbing the bristles, and Christina squealed in pained relief.

The stinging burn hurt so good, fulfilling an aching need she'd been unable to satisfy after leaving him. She'd even tried swatting herself once, but it hadn't been the same at all.

SMACK!

Tears sparked in her eyes as the brush flattened her other creamy cheek, her body aching with pent-up desire as the stinging burn sent her arousal climbing higher.

SMACK! SMACK! SMACK! SMACK!

Gritting her teeth against crying out, Christina writhed on his lap, unsure if she was doing so from pain or her extreme arousal. Her bottom felt like it was burning from the flurried strikes of the brush, throbbing in time with her pounding pulse.

Benedict's arm pressed firmly against her back, his broad hand pressing down just above the curve of her buttocks and holding her in place. Tears slid down her cheeks as she whimpered, her legs kicking slightly as the brush continued to fall.

SMACK! SMACK!

"Please!" She gasped the word, unsure if she was asking him to stop or to give her more.

Having his hands on her, after months without him - without any man - was causing her senses to go haywire as the sensations rioted through her. She was turning into a seething mass of painful pleasure and raw sensual need.

SMACK! SMACK!

The last two blows landed on the sensitive skin where her bottom met her thighs, and Christina sobbed as her orgasm nearly crested... but there was no more stimulation to send her over the edge. Her entire body was aflame, no matter that it was only her bottom which had been roasted, and all she wanted was for Benedict to set her back on the bed, spread her thighs, and plunge inside of her, filling the emptiness which had ached inside her since they'd parted.

"Are you ready to talk about the letter you left me?"

Benedict's voice was calm, despite the hard rod of his cock digging into her side as he placed his palm on her throbbing, seared cheek. He was always so in control in the bedroom, at least until he'd buried himself inside of her; only then would he allow himself to let loose the reins of his self-control and release all his demons upon her. Christina whimpered at the memories as his hand stroked her hot bottom, her body throbbing and ready for more of his attentions.

While there was still a wary voice in the back of her head trying to remind her to be sensible and to protect herself, it was being drowned out by her shocking arousal, the stinging pain through her chastened cheeks, and the weeks of loneliness without a man's touch. Without *his* touch.

It was madness which would lead to devastation, but oh how glorious the journey would be before she fell...

"No," she said, her voice high and breathy, her bottom wagging in invitation to spank her again.

The dark chuckle she received in response sent a shiver down her spine. "Oh no, love, you'll not receive a punishment you're so obviously desirous of. That wouldn't be a punishment at all."

Christina gasped as something hard pressed into her pussy; not nearly as large as his cock, yet with absolutely no give, it took her a moment to realize he'd just thrust the handle of her brush inside of her. She mewled, both shocked and shockingly aroused by the perverse action, and whined in disappointment as he pulled it out.

The wet tip pressed against the crinkled rosebud of her anus and Christina froze. It was like he'd somehow seen inside her head and was now bringing her depraved fantasies to life. She cried out as the handle of her brush pressed inward, invading her most intimate area, stretching her more than his fingers ever had. The thick shaft of wood only sank an inch into her tight, protesting hole before Benedict halted its movement.

"Why did you take your leave of me so suddenly?" he asked, his voice heavy with repressed emotion and a threat to continue the invasion of her most private area with the hard handle of her brush. Christina gulped. "I can still feel the connection, the desire between us, and I know you do as well. Why did you give me my *congè* so suddenly? Why did you not at least speak with me?"

There was frustration and hurt in his voice, along with his dark pleasure, and guilt swirled into the mix of her emotions. She'd never wanted to hurt him.

"I... I..." She stammered, trying to remember exactly how she'd planned to phrase her explanation, trying to recall the little speech she'd mentally prepared, but her mind was shattered by his shocking appearance, her interrupted orgasm, the throbbing sting of her spanking, and the inner burn from the brush handle stretching her bottom, invading her. "I didn't... I..."

The brush pressed deeper and she squealed as the hard wood stretched her tight channel further, making her feel so strangely full in the most depraved manner imaginable. It burned, it hurt, and she wanted to beg him to stop and take it out even as her body was aflame with a desire to be filled in some manner.

THE WOODEN HANDLE of Christina's brush was about five inches long. Currently, an inch and a half of its stiff length was pressed into Christina's tight rosette, the wrinkles around that tiny hole smoothing slightly as it stretched to accommodate the invasion. Beneath the taut opening's torment and her hot, pink cheeks, her pussy was in full bloom, spread open like a flower and glistening with dew. She was both aroused and alarmed by anal play, something which he used to his full advantage to set her off balance mentally while he pressed her for answers.

He'd found that stimulating her in such a manner brought out her submissiveness quickly and deeply, as giving over control to such an intimate area required a great deal of trust, as well as submission. If he had to, he'd use the entire handle on her bottom and fuck her with it.

"I couldn't stay with you!" she cried out, bucking slightly as she tried to squirm away from the brush. Benedict held her fast, not allowing her to escape its hard prod into her rear channel.

"Why not?" he asked, steeling himself for whatever her answer might be. Considering her reaction to him, he was having trouble imagining what she might say... but whatever her reasons, he was determined to remove them from his path.

"Because I care for you..." She sucked in a breath as Benedict's brow wrinkled in confusion. "Too much, I was becoming too emotionally involved in our affair."

Benedict caressed her bottom, twisting the brush handle to make her moan and shudder. "Sweetheart... I don't see how caring could be a bad thing."

"Because it was too much!" Her distress was real, no matter what he thought, and it was beginning to overcome her arousal. "I did not want to be heartbroken when our affair ended, so I stopped it before I could become more attached to you, and I thought it worked, but now you're here and I don't know what to do!"

His heart nearly stopped when he'd realized she was deadly earnest, but her further reasoning gave him some relief. She didn't want to care because she hadn't realized how his own feelings had become engaged, which was understandable as he hadn't either until she was gone. Now he knew and he could reassure her.

Sliding the brush from her opening, Benedict made soothing, hushing noises as he gathered her up into his arms, cradling her against her distress. The silky fabric of her night rail was soft against his skin as she leaned her upper body into him. Her hot bottom was pressed against the hard ridge of his cock as he arranged her on his lap.

"I'm here because I care as well," he murmured into her hair, dropping kisses along her hairline.

With one arm around her back to help prop her up, he still had a hand free to slide along her hip and down to her hot buttock, squeezing the warm, soft flesh and making her quiver. She was so hot, so aroused, he knew he had to soothe the ache in her body before they could really talk.

Which, incidentally, would soothe the ache in his own body as well.

"Perhaps it's just as well you left me so abruptly," he whispered as he caressed her with one hand, gliding his lips over her neck as she shivered in his arms. "I had not realized how deeply my own emotions had become engaged until you did... let me show you how much I missed you."

"Oh..." She gasped as his teeth scraped over her collarbone, his tongue licking at her skin. "Oh yes..."

That was all the encouragement Benedict required.

CHAPTER 3

*L*ifting Christina up in his arms, Benedict turned to lay her back on the bed. Her eyes were practically glassy with desire as she watched him shrug out of his clothes. Her hands glided up and down her body, and he wasn't sure she was even aware of how she touched herself, waiting for him.

With his breeches still on, he reached out to grab her hand. "I missed your hands. These clever fingers." He kissed her palm and the pad of each finger before moving upward. "This wrist. These graceful arms. This winsome elbow."

Christina blinked at him, dazed with her arousal, but still comprehending of his more playful teases. "My elbows are not winsome."

"They assuredly are," he said gleefully, getting up on his knees so he could hover over her. "Although, I much prefer them uncovered so I may admire them."

Grasping the hem of her night rail, he helped her pull it over her head. As she laid back, he took her by her ankle and lifted her dainty foot to his mouth, giving it the same treatment as he had her foot. "I missed your toes. Your feet. Your ankles."

When his lips reached her knee, she gave a little gasping giggle, as though he'd hit a ticklish spot. Placing her foot back down, he kneeled between her legs, admiring the sight of her laid back against her pillows, completely naked, pussy open and ready for him, pink nipples hard atop creamy mounds. The spanking she'd received would make her bottom sensitive and warm against her sheets in this position.

"Spread your legs, love," he said softly but with authority. "I've also missed seeing you obey me."

A hot blush traveled from her cheeks down her neck as she spread her legs for him, looking almost shy. She'd never been entirely comfortable exposing herself so completely to him, but it seemed their time apart had made her feel even more hesitant about doing so. The slow spread of her legs just made the movements more seductive, more tantalizing, as she laid herself into the wide-spread position she knew he preferred.

"Arms above your head," he purred, his hands going to undo the front of his breeches, finishing undressing while she positioned herself for his pleasure. "Grasp your headboard."

She was completely spread out for him now, her breath coming in hot pants, the mounds of her breasts quivering. Between her creamy thighs the wet, pink flesh of her pussy, fringed with dark curls, beckoned to him; her swollen clit peeked out at him like the tiny nub was inviting him to come play. She was a goddess and a temptation, a sweet treat for him to devour, and his dream come true.

PART of her wondered what on earth she was doing, why she was allowing this to happen...

A very small part, which was quickly drowned out by the raging needs of her body and the yearning of her heart. The problem with denying herself was, deep down, she wanted this. She had still wanted him the entire time they'd been separated, no matter how she'd tried to quash her feelings and stomp out her emotions.

While she may have managed to bank the fires, her emotions had still kindled, ready to be brought back to life, and Benedict's simple words had shattered her defenses and re-lit the embers with all the skill of a blacksmith and his bellows. He was here, commanding and compelling, and she couldn't resist him. She didn't want to.

"OH!" Her entire body spasmed as he leaned over to plant a kiss on her pussy, his tongue flicking out to lick her swollen clit. She felt tears gather at the corner of her eyes as her body responded with intense pleasure to the silken contact. "Benedict, please!"

"Good girl," he said, crooning the words as his hands slid up her inner thighs to her labia, parting the lips so she could feel the cool air of the room wafting over her sensitive flesh. "If you'd called me Dearborn again, I would have had to continue torturing you."

She whimpered as his thumb brushed through her center, gliding over her clit before moving down to her hole, where he inserted the thick digit. It was too short to give her the sensations she craved, teasing her without providing satisfaction, and her grip on the headboard tightened as she fought against the impulse to reach down and touch herself.

"Please, Benedict, stop teasing me!" she begged, writhing for him as he pumped his thumb in and out of her. "You just said you wouldn't continue torturing me!"

"Very well," he said, sliding his thumb away and positioning himself over her. His dark eyes were hot with need, devouring the sight of her as his cock lined up with her pussy, nudging the place his thumb had just occupied. She arched, trying to grind down on that teasing tip, her insides fluttering with the need to be filled. Benedict leaned over her, his hands braced on either side of her, and she could smell the musky sweet scent of her arousal like perfume in the air.

"Tell me you missed me, love."

"I missed you."

The ache in her voice was exceeded only by the ache in her body, the need arching through her... and then his hips thrust forward, his cock splitting her open, and Christina cried out as he filled the emptiness inside of her. He felt so large, so hot, stretching her roughly after weeks of abstinence, and it felt so very, very good.

So right.

When his hands grasped her wrists, pinning them down on either side of her head, she realized she'd been reaching up to touch him. She wanted to so badly, but at the same time, having him hold her in place, keeping her under his control, caused a hot surge of ecstasy to thrum through her. Already she'd been teetering on the edge of orgasm, now it felt like she was pierced with a keen agony that made her want to scream with her unfulfilled need.

Then Benedict began to move.

He thrust hard. Fast.

"Please! Please, Benedict, I need to cum!"

His voice was a growl as he responded. "Cum, love, cum for me."

Now Christina did scream as her long-awaited orgasm rolled through her, making her writhe beneath his hard body, her inner muscles pulsing with the rhythm of his thrusts. Her nipples rubbed against his chest as he moved, abraded by his wiry body hair, her legs moving to clasp him to her as she shuddered with the sweet pleasure. He felt so good atop her, moving so forcefully inside of her, filling her. The heat burned through her body, sending wave after wave of delicious pleasure coursing through her, satisfying the need he'd so skillfully induced.

Benedict lowered his mouth to hers, taking her lips with a slow, drugging kiss as he reduced the rate of his thrusts, slowing his rhythm to take his time. She moaned as she shuddered around him, her body feeling especially sensitive as her climax settled, leaving her feeling mostly satiated... although still aroused as Benedict moved inside her, kissing her like he wanted to drink her. The hands on her wrists gentled and slid away, the pace of their movements becoming more tender as he caressed her breasts and allowed her to reach up and entwine her fingers in his hair.

It was a moment of almost pure sweetness, which pierced straight to her heart, and Christina found herself wishing it could be like this always. As soon as she realized what she was thinking, she began to push at him, her legs dropping away to spread wide open again rather than trying to cling to him.

She broke away from the kiss.

"Do not tell me you've lost your energy, my lord," she said coquettishly, trying to hide her disquiet behind flirtation, not wanting him to see how his love-making was affecting her. With the needy edge of pleasure receding, she was coming back to her senses.

While she did not want him to stop, while she wanted to ensure he found his satisfaction as well, she was also reminded of the need to guard her heart. Perhaps he'd become attached to her as well, but she should not read more into his affection and lust than was there.

She would take tonight, and her future self could make of it what she would... but she did not want to pretend tonight was anything other than lust, passion, and the long absence of each other's company. She didn't even know whether Benedict had taken another woman to bed during their time apart... and she shoved the thought away because it hurt to think of.

Pasting a smile on her face, she arched underneath him, her fingers teasing the hair at the base of his neck where she knew he was particularly sensitive. "Has your stamina deserted you, that you move so slowly?"

"Vixen," Benedict snarled at her.

Sliding from her body, he flipped her over so quickly it took her breath away, setting her on hands and knees before him. Christina loved the way he always handled her so easily, as if she weighed nothing more than a feather, a doll for him to position and arrange. She cried out again as he thrust into her from behind, hard and fast.

If she'd thought a new position, a rougher kind of loving, would dispel the sense of growing intimacy between them, she'd been wrong. He was moving inside of her, filling her, as he leaned over her, cupping her breasts with his hands and kneading them, and every touch set her skin afire. It did not matter that she could no longer see his expression, that he no longer touched her so tenderly, his presence overwhelmed her and even when he pinched her nipples harshly, she could practically feel his pleasure and it affected her deeply.

No, she could no longer touch him, wrap her arms around him... but she still wanted to.

No, he was not kissing her mouth, but his lips still fell on the nape of her neck, the back of her shoulders, and down her back as he took her from behind.

No, his movements were no longer as slow or as tender... but he still filled her, still touched her like he couldn't get enough of her, still pressed himself against her as if he couldn't bear to have space between them.

And she pressed back against him, loving the feel of him surrounding her, filling her, wringing both pain and pleasure from her body. Already his hard thrusts were pushing her towards another orgasm, the pain and pleasure of his hands on her breasts and nipples adding to her growing ardor. Christina was helpless beneath him, writhing on her hands and knees as growing ecstasy wreathed its way around her.

SILKEN HEAT SCALDED Benedict as he slammed against Christina's bottom, the hot flesh of her chastised cheeks heating his belly. She was so supple and tight, her soft cries urging him onwards as he rutted her. This had always been a favorite position of hers - and of his - as it allowed him to molest her unchallenged without actually binding her.

Twisting her nipples roughly, he groaned as her sheath tightened around him in response, massaging his aching length. Already it felt like his balls were fit to burst, but he was holding back his own climax from sheer willpower as he worked her towards her second one. She was already close. He could tell by the quivering in her body, the rosy flush of her skin, the tightening of her inner muscles, and the change in her breath. Benedict leaned back slightly, moving one hand from her breast to the top of her mound, grinning as she let out a high cry as his fingers slid to her creamy slit and pressed against the swollen bud nestled there.

"Again," he commanded. "Cum for me again."

Christina's upper body crumbled beneath the passionate

onslaught, and she began to sob out her ecstasy as Benedict's fingers circled and massaged the tiny, engorged nub of her clitoris. Her pussy spasmed around him, sucking at his cock, and he let out his own shout of pleasure as he pulled free of her body and released his seed over her back.

The white liquid spattered against the pale pink of her skin and the darker pink of her bottom, a satisfying sight.

One day - one day soon - he would not have to use French letters or pull free of the clasp of her body in his release. He supposed he could have begun tonight... but as he hadn't yet spoken to Christina of his intentions, such an act would have been wrong. Groaning, he squeezed his rod with his hand, the last of his seed spurting onto her buttocks as he imagined what it would be like to feel her pussy milking his cock without any barrier.

"Oh..." Christina's soft little sight of contentment made his heart feel light as she slid down onto her stomach, letting him take care of the mess.

Benedict had always insisted on tending to her, allowing her to wallow in the post-coital bliss. For himself, he found caring for his partners extended his feelings of satisfaction rather than interrupting them. He enjoyed wetting a cloth and tending to the aftereffects of their joining, although he did so much more tenderly and lovingly with Christina than he had with any other. With Christina he interspersed strokes of the damp cloth with kisses on her bare skin and small, intimate caresses because he couldn't bear to *not* touch her.

She was so beautiful, so silky soft... and all his.

"Are you going to attempt to spurn me again now?" he asked as he set the cloth to the side. The skin of her back glistened damply in the candlelight before she turned over to face him. The softness of her breasts and belly, the suppleness of her loose limbs, called to him, and Benedict lay himself out beside her, facing her, so he could touch all that delicious softness.

Christina laughed ruefully. "Perhaps I should," she responded, her voice a sultry murmur. "I did not realize it would engender such a passionate response."

"If you do so and then disappear for weeks again, I shall hunt you down and carry you off," he said in warning - and was not entirely joking. "You'll be my princess in a locked room, bound to my bed, and unable to ever escape."

She laughed again, but there was something in her expression - almost like yearning - which Benedict did not understand. Leaning forward, she kissed him gently on the lips, sighing against his mouth as his hand caressed her hip, pulling her to him. It did not matter that he was no longer aroused, he just wished for her body nestled against his, and since she did not even attempt to squirm away it seemed she felt the same.

Her fingers trailed through his chest hair as she pulled her lips away from the kiss, tugging very lightly on the strands in a pleasant manner that would have stirred his arousal if he wasn't already so happily sated.

"And when you tire of me?" she asked, teasingly, although there was an edge to her words. "Would I be set free?"

"No, for I would never tire of you," he said, leaning forward for a kiss - and halting when he saw her rolling her eyes. Benedict frowned. They were only teasing, but still, he didn't like to see such a response. Did she think he was mouthing mere platitudes? Or - worse - was she scornful of such an ardent declaration on his part? "Are you rolling your eyes at me? Do you not believe me?" Silently he also wondered - *do you not want me to keep you forever?*

"I believe men such as yourself say many wonderfully romantic things to appease their lady friends," Christina said. The slight edge to her voice was still there, and now - when he really looked at her - he could see that her smile did not quite reach her eyes.

Something was wrong.

Even though she was snuggled in his arms, even though she hadn't sent him running from her rooms, she was holding herself back from him in some manner. Something had shifted between them, and he didn't like it one bit. He especially didn't like hearing her refer to herself as one of his 'lady friends', as if she were cheapening their relationship and casting herself as one of many.

"You are my only lady *friend*, and I mean every word of it."

"Oh, don't become testy," she chided him, her expression softening just a touch. Her fingers stroked his chest again, almost as if to soothe him. "I was not accusing you of being an unfaithful lover, but I am quite aware of the realities of life and eventually you will tire of me." She sounded determinedly cheerful at the supposition - not as though his eventual tiring of her was something to be desired, just that it was a given and she would make the best of the situation.

Benedict scowled. "Did we or did we not declare our feelings for each other, not half an hour ago in this very room?"

Now her expression flickered to one of surprise and confusion. "Well, I did admit to feeling more than I ought, and, while you were not quite as explicit in-"

"I love you," Benedict declared hotly, cutting her off. "I love you and I want to marry you."

Whatever responses he had imagined, being immediately shoved out of her bed and onto the floor had not been one of them.

~

"OH! I'M SORRY!" Christina cried out, clinging to the edge of the bed as she looked over it to see Benedict in a shocked heap on the floor. She hadn't meant to shove him off the bed, but she'd just reacted so immediately and so forcefully that he'd practically gone flying.

He was already pushing himself into a sitting position as she tried to decide whether to help him up.

"Is that a no?" he asked, in that dry, drawling way that made her want to burst into laughter, but she also saw the flicker of hurt in his dark eyes.

Christina hadn't meant to hurt him - physically or emotionally - even if her actions indicated otherwise. So, she held back her immediate response - *of course her answer was no!* - to ascertain why he would have made such an unexpected declaration.

Declaring his love was logical if he wanted to marry her, since he did not need her money or social position, but why on earth was he speaking of marriage at all? He was several years away from thirty - they both were - and while she was young for a widow, she was quite old for a bride and he was certainly below the age of most grooms! As long as his brother's wife bore an heir to the dukedom, he had no actual need to marry. If he did one day choose to do so in order to have a family of his own, it would be expected he choose a fresh, young bride, not a used widow who hadn't provided her previous husband with any children whatsoever. The thought made her heart ache but...

She forced a smile onto her face anyway, as Benedict stood, sitting back on her haunches. Fortunately, he didn't seem angered at all. While he could be a very strict disciplinarian when they were exploring their erotic pleasures, he could also appreciate the absurd and unpredictable moments of life. It was one of the things she lo- *liked* so much about him. "I should punish you for teasing me by accepting your proposal, and then making you do all manner of groveling to make it up to me when you're forced to recant."

To her surprise, *now* he began scowling at her. His expression would have been much more appropriate when she'd pushed him off the bed! "I am *not* teasing."

The declaration lay heavy in the room, dampening the spirits Christina had tried to summon. Suddenly she felt very strange, very cold, and very vulnerable. She snatched up her sheets, holding them in front of her like the modest maiden she wasn't. Not that she minded his eyes on her naked body, but she felt very in need of some kind of shield.

"Don't be ridiculous," she snapped as her mind whirled, her confusion and disquiet stirring her temper.

He seemed completely serious, and part of her responded with every bit of yearning possible, but the other part of her - the more logical, more cautious part of herself which she'd been pushing aside since he'd appeared in her bedchamber - was crying the alarm. Christina was no longer a giddy girl, taken in by a man's words of love, only to find herself brokenhearted and trapped in a prison of her own naive making. Did Benedict have debts she didn't know of?

Was he trying to escape some kind of unwanted understanding with another lady? She didn't understand what he had to gain by making such an absurd offer, but she understood very well how much it would hurt when he was done playing with her emotions.

Benedict crossed his arms over his chest and Christina found her eyes averting from his hard gaze. Which was just as well; he apparently felt no need to shield his nakedness and right now looking up on him standing so proudly nude in her bedchamber only made her hurt worse. Why did he have to go and ruin everything like this?

She shifted uncomfortably under his stare.

"You can't possibly think to actually marry me," she finally said, unable to hide the bitterness she felt, the resentment at being forced to actually say so.

Christina sat back on the bed, wishing there were a hundred feet between them and quite a few more layers of clothing. Although such superficial means of distancing herself might not have helped very much either, considering the intimacies they'd just engaged in. Even now she could feel the pleasant soreness between her legs and the tingling warmth still lingering along the surface of her bottom.

"More than think to, I am determined to," he said, a hard edge of steel in his voice.

She stared at him, her voice failing her for a long moment. "But *why?*"

He stared at her, just as flummoxed. "Why on earth wouldn't I want to marry you? You're beautiful inside and out, you make me smile, I've never had a lover who completed me so completely, I can talk to you about anything, confide in you, relax with you, and I love you."

"Stop saying that!" Pain seized her chest, making her want to scream. An old pain that was beating at her rib cage and making it hard for her to breathe. She'd honestly never wanted to hear those words from a man again... they'd brought her nothing but misery.

"Stop saying what?!"

"That you love me!" The words were torn out of her, and it was unclear to both of them whether she was making a plea or an order.

Christina gasped for air, clenching her fists in her sheets. Tears stung the back of her eyes, but she ignored them, the same way she ignored Benedict's attempts to meet her gaze. "You don't need to say such things, there's no reason to, even if you wanted to marry me, it would make more sense that you do so because we are well matched socially, and I am an accomplished hostess, and we enjoy the same entertainments, and... and... reasons of that... that nature..."

Her words stuttered to a stop, leaving her feeling breathless all over again, as well as exhausted. Shame washed over her as she was suddenly aware she'd said far too much, shown too much. Her only excuse was he'd thrown her badly off balance.

"Christina," he said, his voice soft and gentle as his hands dropped to his side, as though he wished to appear less threatening. "Is there something you wish to tell me about you first marriage?"

The shame nearly drowned her now, her cheeks blushing and paling by turns as buried emotions rose up and were ruthlessly pressed back down. Still clutching the sheets to her chest, Christina got up and picked up her night rail, pulling it back over her head. She couldn't just keep sitting on the bed, not with all this nervous energy running through her, and she couldn't walk around bare right now... Fortunately, Benedict did not take her movements as an invitation to move towards her.

Facing away from him, she started to pace, staring around her room without really seeing any of it.

"Everyone knows my first marriage was a love match," she said, rather flatly.

"Yes," Benedict replied, his tone bland but tinged with what sounded like jealousy. "Although you did not strike me as the type to forswear future marriage and happiness because your first love perished."

Her laughter was bitter in response. So bitter she could taste it on her tongue as the image of her late husband rose in her mind's eye. George had been handsome, rakish, silver-tongued, and utterly charming. And he'd chosen *her*. Danced attendance on *her*. Wrote sonnets and salacious notes to *her*. Singled her out from all the debutantes and made love to her with all the skill of a gazetted rake who desperately needed a bride with a hefty dowry.

Not that she'd realized his financial situation at the time. As young and naive as she'd been, even if she had known, she might not have cared nor believed any naysayers. Unfortunately, her aunt, who had been chaperoning her Season, hadn't realized the Marquess' situation either, although she may still have supported the match. The title of Marchesse was nothing to sneeze at, after all, no matter how far up the River Tick the Marquess himself was. There had been no sign however; he'd done a marvelous job of hiding his debts from the *ton*. Everyone had believed he'd been smitten with the young Lady Christina on sight and, in doing so, had reformed his rakish ways to marry for love.

And Christina had just happened to have a very generous dowry.

"*Everyone* knows George was killed in an *unfortunate* carriage accident," she continued, ignoring his words.

"Yes," Benedict said, more slowly this time, as if he was uncertain where her train of facts were leading.

"George was..." It was surprisingly hard to say aloud. "George was fleeing his lover's husband when the accident occurred."

A secret. One which she'd never heard a whisper of among the *ton*, to her everlasting relief. Benedict's shocked reaction reaffirmed that it remained a secret.

"His lover..."

"Baroness Mathilde Alvenley," Christina said, her resentment simmering again. The blank look on Benedict's face made it clear he'd never met the woman. Something to be thankful for. After George's death, the Baroness had not been kind in making Christina acutely aware of George's disaffection from his marriage bed to the Baroness'. As if the mere knowledge of why George had been driving so recklessly had not been painful enough. Although the Baron had promised no one would ever know the truth of why George had been driving so recklessly, the Baroness had taken every opportunity to deepen Christina's pain. She was a viper, plain and simple. She'd even sent Christina the love notes George had sent her, the first of which had been dated a mere two months after his wedding to Christina.

They'd been salaciously graphic.

Dealing with the double blows of George's betrayal and death simultaneously had undone something within Christina, broken her in some fundamental way. She no longer had the same hopes and dreams as other women, she only wanted to never be hurt so deeply ever again.

"They'd been lovers for some time before the Baron discovered them. Unfortunately, I was unaware of their relationship until after George's death. The Baron, however, is an honorable man and, not wanting to cause me any more pain once he realized I'd no knowledge of the matter, very kindly kept the truth from ever being known."

In fact, he'd been horrified when he'd realized how innocent she was to their spouses' meetings and how heartbroken. He'd vowed to make it up to her by ensuring George's death would be unblemished in the public eye and no taint would touch her.

Thus, Christina had had the full sympathy of Society during her mourning year and her re-entrance to Society, because of the Baron's success at keeping the secret. If the scandalous truth of George's death had been known, the gossip and censure of the *ton* would have been quite awful, and she well knew it. While she would have still received pity, it would not have been of the supportive kind.

"I have already confessed my feelings for you have deepened, honestly past where I would wish them to be, but when you tire of me, we will be able to go our separate ways. I have no wish to marry again and make such an amicable parting impossible." Not that she would feel particularly amicable when it happened, but she would keep her pride and pretend.

To her shock, Benedict strode forward and took her into his arms before she could stop him, and it was only then that she realized she was trembling. She felt almost sick with all the conflicting strong emotions which had gripped her over the past couple hours, along with the physical exertions. No wonder she felt nearly ill.

BENEDICT'S COMMANDS

It felt good to be in his arms and lean against his strength, a relief to know he wasn't going to abandon her just because she'd rejected marriage. Perhaps he would pull away after this, but at least for this one moment, he was still here with her.

Benedict kissed her on the top of her head and scooped her up in his arms as she let out a little shriek.

"Do not think I have given up, for I have not," he murmured, giving her a squeeze as she started to protest before he placed her down on her bed. "You need rest. But, love, we will discuss this again. I am not your late husband and I will not be painted with the same brush... you will see that soon enough for yourself. I will prove it to you."

She opened her lips to protest again, but he dropped a kiss on her mouth to quiet her, pulling up her sheets over her body as he did so.

"Go to sleep," he ordered, moving away to collect his clothes and redress himself. Christina rolled onto her side to watch him.

She wanted to ask him to stay... but the servants would gossip if they found him in her chambers in the morning. A merry widow's reputation could survive much, but blatant indiscretions would still ruin her - and then she'd have to marry him or become a pariah.

"Go out the side door," she whispered to him, holding the sheets under her chin. There were so many other things she could have said, but somehow she couldn't make the words come. So she just told him how to leave. "Down the stairs, turn right down the hall, and it's at the far end on the left. No one should be in that area of the house at this time of night."

Dressed, he turned to look at her once more. "Those big, sad eyes," he said softly, a rueful smile curving his lips. "I will chase all your sadness away, love, and if I can't, I'll spank it out of you."

The audacious claim made her laugh, the bubbling sound surprising her.

Grinning proudly, Benedict leaned over to claim her mouth with another kiss.

"You're mine, Christina, never doubt it."

With that, he blew out her candles and went to her door, pausing to ensure the coast was clear before sneaking out. She kept listening, but when five minutes went by without any alarm being sounded, she knew he had successfully left the house.

She didn't think she'd be able to sleep at all, but the moment her eyes closed, the deep black pulled her under.

CHAPTER 4

Staring at the hearty breakfast of kippers, sausages, beans, toast, and eggs, Benedict tried to drum up an appetite - like sleep, it eluded him. Every time he closed his eyes, all he'd been able to see was Christina's pale, heart-shaped face, her sad brown eyes, and the pain etched in every line of her body as she'd spoken of her late husband. Not that she'd said much, but everything she'd said and everything she'd left unsaid had weighed her down.

How to overcome her reticence?

It was impossible to think of any other option than overcoming that obstacle, because Benedict could not countenance the idea of marrying any woman other than Christina. Unlike her late husband, he truly did love her. He wanted her by his side for the rest of his life, and he was happy to forsake all other women for her. But how to show her that?

Too bad he couldn't actually spank her until she agreed to marry him. It would certainly be much easier.

Still, Christina was worth every ounce of effort. She deserved it. Benedict would give her everything her late husband hadn't... fidelity, honesty, and loyalty. Unfortunately, since the dead Marquess had couched his own courtship in terms of love, Benedict was unsure how to actually demonstrate his differences from the man. He'd never met the Baron or Baroness of Alvenley either, so he had no idea what further emotional landmines might have been created by the woman's personality.

He'd like to ask for some advice, but doing so could expose the secret Christina had been keeping. Society could turn on a person in an instant, and knowing her purported love match had turned sour would delight the tabbies of the *ton*. The gossip was so very good and the secret successfully kept for so very long.

Which put him in quite a quandary.

"Benedict? Are you unwell?" His sister-in-law's question made him look up from his plate to find his entire family looking at him with concern. Even Isaac, his older brother, had put down his newspaper to focus on Benedict, a slight frown on his face.

These were the people he'd like to ask for advice. His brother, his sister-in-law, and his sister. All of them could be trusted completely, but... even the smallest slip to another trusted party, and so on and so forth... Besides, he wanted them all to meet Christina and welcome her into the family as well, which meant she may one day discover that he'd shared her secret with them.

He didn't need any advice to know such a revelation would go very poorly for him. Perhaps even scupper his plans if he hadn't secured Christina's hand by then.

"Alert the papers, he's been struck dumb," Arabella said, snickering. His baby sister could always be counted on to provide some levity to any situation. "It must be some kind of terrible disease!" Making a face, she leaned away from him. "You don't think it's catching, do you?"

"If it is, I might encourage you to sit closer to him," Lydia teased back gently, causing Isaac to suddenly smile as he gave his wife an adoring look.

They'd been married last summer when Lydia had trapped Isaac into marrying her, but Isaac had still fallen in love with her - especially when he'd discovered she'd only trapped him in order to escape her stepfather. The man had run quite mad and was now occupying a room in an asylum, while Isaac and Lydia were living in happily wedded bliss. The kind of bliss Benedict had found himself envying more and more.

Despite being quiet, sweet, and submissive, Lydia could also be quite stubborn at times, which served her well being married to Isaac, who was as autocratic as his ducal self could manage. She did also serve to soften him a little, and her stubbornness could outmatch his at times. Benedict thought she was a wonderful addition to the family. With her honey blonde hair and grey eyes, she stood out from the Windhams, who were all dark haired and dark eyed, but in personality she fit into a niche they'd desperately needed.

The Windham siblings had been orphaned years ago, their only other direct family member was their Great-Aunt Ida who was quite elderly, tired easily, and had never been the mothering type. In contrast, Lydia had served as mother to her own sister, Amy, after their mother had passed away, and now she brought that warm support to the Windham household. Of course, Isaac didn't see her as a mothering type (except to his own planned brood, which Benedict suspected the first of might already be well on his or her way), but for Benedict and especially Arabella, she was a combination of mother and elder sister.

It was Lydia who ensured they all had proper meals together and enforced a breakfast time, Lydia who checked Arabella's wilder starts (with far more success than Isaac or Benedict had ever had), Lydia who approved Arabella's wardrobe, and Lydia whom Benedict had gone to for comfort after Christina had left him. She'd been a sympathetic ear and very supportive - unlike his brother and sister who had a tendency to tease rather than help.

Her influence was most obvious with Arabella, however. After skirting close to scandal on multiple occasions last Season, and seemingly uncaring at her close brushes with ruination, Arabella was finally settling down. Benedict didn't know if it was because of Lydia's guiding hand or just Arabella's desire to impress her new sister, but it was certainly a welcome change. Arabella was turning into a proper lady, rather than a hoyden who needed to be constantly watched.

Particularly welcome since it appeared he was going to be spending his Season courting Christina, so having to guard his little sister the way he and his brother had done last year would have been a huge hindrance.

"Benedict?" Now it was Isaac's deep voice interrupting his thoughts, making him aware he'd just been sitting there silently with a blank stare on his face rather than answering Lydia.

"My apologies, I've been a bit distracted," he said, trying to decide how much he could tell his family. They all knew about Christina, of course (well, they knew there was a widow he had an attachment to, was planning on pursuing as his wife, and that her name was Christina; obviously he hadn't told the ladies that she had been his paramour), but he hadn't told them where he had gone last night or why. He supposed telling them about attending the ball was harmless enough. "I saw Christina last night."

"What? Where? When? Why didn't you bring us?" Arabella's questions came fast and accusatory as she sat up straight, completely indignant, and no longer the prim and proper lady she'd been presenting to them. "I thought you went to your club!"

Isaac gave him a look, as if warning him not to say anything untoward in front of the women, as if he needed to be told.

"I happened to discover she would be at the Wutherings' ball and so took the opportunity to appear as well," he said blithely, as if his attending the ball - without his debutante sister - was entirely unremarkable.

"We could have gone with you," Arabella said, glaring and pouting at the same time; a skill she had quite mastered, managing to look both threatening and forlorn simultaneously. "Why didn't you tell us? Nothing interesting happened at the Irvings' dinner."

"You wanted to see Gabrielle," he said, which was very true; Arabella had missed her best friend dearly during their months apart, despite a week-long visit after Christmas.

Arabella scowled at him, her expression only smoothing when she caught Lydia giving her a reproachful look. Then she sighed with exasperation. "He's my brother, I ought to be able to harangue him if I want to."

"Of course you may harangue your brother," Lydia said pleasantly. "However, you should be mindful of having an audience, and consider how effective your tactics are." Turning to Benedict, she smiled at him warmly. "Did your meeting with Lady Stanhope not go as you hoped? You do seem a bit downhearted."

Even though she had just admonished Arabella, it was impossible to feel as though Lydia was manipulating him for information - she was far too warm and caring. Although Arabella did watch her closely, and Benedict was aware he needed to be more forthcoming if his little sister was accept Lydia's premise that behaving in a more ladylike manner produced better results than harassing him into submission. The grateful look Isaac shot his wife was nothing less than adoring; no wonder, if she was successfully maneuvering Arabella away from her usual strong arm tactics.

"I made my intentions clear enough, but she says she's not interested in marrying again," he said a bit glumly.

Across the table from him, Isaac raised his eyebrows.

"Why on earth not?" he sounded a bit insulted on Benedict's behalf.

"I would imagine because being a widow brings with it quite a few freedoms, which many women are loathe to give up," Lydia remarked, a bit dryly. Isaac frowned at her and she laughed lightly. "Of course, being married can also give a woman many compensations which I know I, for one, would not relinquish for all the world."

Now both of them were looking at each other with slightly sappy expressions. It was enough to make a man nauseous - mostly with envy, in his case. Arabella looked envious as well, watching the two love birds.

"Maybe you just aren't as good a catch as you think," Arabella teased, turning back to him, obviously trying to dispel the jealousy Lydia and Isaac's loving relationship often engendered.

Benedict glared, more at the memory of Christina's response and pain than his sister's teasing. "Actually, she thinks I'm a wonderful catch."

"Then why doesn't she want to marry you?"

"Because she doesn't want to marry," he snapped, losing his patience, just a little. "It's not specific to *me*."

"Oh. Well, that's something at least," Arabella said. There was an odd note in her voice, but Benedict didn't really have a clue why nor any time to think further on it.

"So what are you going to do?" Isaac asked curiously, finally breaking away from making moon-calf eyes at his wife. "I can't imagine you giving up so easily." He raised his eyebrow sardonically as Arabella smirked. Lydia just smiled encouragingly. She really was his favorite sibling; not actually being related to him by blood gave her a strong advantage in his opinion.

"Of course I'm not giving up," Benedict said vehemently. "I just have to decide what to do next." He exchanged a significant look with his sister-in-law.

THREE WOMEN STARED at the bouquet of flowers Christina had brought with her to Daphne's. It had arrived mid-morning and was the largest, most expensive, and most gorgeous bouquet she'd ever received. The main portion of the bouquet was arbutus, the sweet-smelling fragile flower with white and pink petals must have been hideously expensive as they were not native to England. They must have been grown in a hothouse, after being brought over from the United States. Camellias bloomed in a rainbow of color between the more fragile petals of the arbutus, blue and white violets ringing them, and the entire thing was framed with bright leaves of ivy and tied with a wide violet ribbon.

For those familiar with the meanings behind the chosen flowers, it was a stunning declaration of love, faithfulness, intent to marry, and supplication in a single glorious bouquet.

"Well..." Daphne murmured, still staring at it in wonder.

Daphne's sister-in-law, a sweet young woman with brilliant reddish hair the same color as a sunrise, seemed stunned into silence. Married to Daphne's brother, the Earl of Hastings and one day to be the Marquess of Salisbury, Cecily Stafford was not a close friend of Christina's, but Christina was so out of sorts she didn't care. Besides, the Countess had a reputation for being quiet and composed; she was not the kind of person to indulge in idle gossip. Especially not about a friend of a friend.

"That... is certainly larger than I realized it would be," Daphne finally said, a bit faintly.

Christina had brought the splendid monstrosity in her carriage and sent for a footman to bring it in after her arrival, while she told Daphne and Lady Hastings about Benedict's proposal and her refusal. Of course, since Lady Hastings was there, Christina had not gone into the specifics of the setting of his proposal - although she surely would when she and Daphne were able to speak privately.

"I did tell you," she said, turning her head slightly to look at her friend a bit reproachfully.

"Yes... but..." Daphne gestured at the floral splendor almost helplessly, apparently unable to take her eyes from it. "I thought you were exaggerating, but if anything you understated its proportions."

The three women returned to their mute contemplation until Daphne broke the silence again.

"Last night Benedict proposed."

"Yes."

"You declined."

"Yes."

"And he sent you... *this*."

"Yes."

"Well, what are you going to do now?"

"I don't know! That is why I came to you!" Christina's response was nearly agonized. She truly didn't know what to do; her first reaction had been to flee her house in case Benedict would be following the bouquet's arrival, and her second reaction had been to seek out her bosom friend.

Not only had she come to Daphne, but she'd come before her friend's normal at-home hours. After seeing Christina and the state she was in, Daphne had told her butler that she was *not* at home to any future callers. Of course, Lady Hastings was already visiting and asking her to leave would have been rude; besides, a second, discreet, opinion would not be amiss.

"It's terribly romantic, isn't it?" Lady Hastings said, a bit wistfully, reaching out to stroke one of the ivy leaves. She seemed almost unaware of having spoken aloud, but the wistfulness in her tone tugged at something inside Christina.

From what she remembered, Lady Hastings' marriage had been arranged and she'd never even had a Season as a debutante - although she'd already had one as a married Countess. Her courtship, if she'd had any, would not have been anything like Christina's with George. Not that George had ever sent her such a bouquet, even when courting. He'd sent her a dozen roses, twice a week, before their wedding, which she'd thought incredibly romantic, but compared to this...

It wasn't just the expense, it was the obvious care which had been taken with the bouquet and the message of the flowers. Not to mention the ribbon tying it together, which was the exact shade of violet she loved the most. Benedict was not the type of man to leave such a small nicety to chance; she knew he'd had a hand in every last detail of the stunning array.

Lady Hastings was right. It was terribly romantic.

Just looking at the bouquet stirred all sorts of uncomfortable feelings inside of her; feelings she hadn't had since George. Her stomach felt fluttery, her heart hadn't stopped pounding since the bouquet had arrived, and she wanted to go running to Benedict and cover him with kisses. Alternatively, she also felt sick with the idea of being trapped into marriage again, with the uncertainty of if his love would sustain - not just for weeks or months, but for the rest of their lives.

"Perhaps you should just say yes and be done with it," Daphne said pragmatically, sitting back against the couch with a thoughtful expression on her face. The dark green morning dress she was wearing, set against the cream-colored couch, highlighted her emerald green eyes and jet black hair. On the other side of her, Lady Hastings was also wearing green, but a much lighter shade to go with her pale green eyes and bright red hair, and she had turned to study both her sister-in-law and Christina with a searching look. "Dearborne does not seem the type to give up, especially not when he has made so clear a declaration."

"But I don't want to be married again," Christina said stubbornly, hating the tiny note of indecision in her voice. It was just a small bit of indecision, and she would squash it. "Especially not to him."

"Because you love him," Daphne said placidly.

"Exact- wait, what? No!" Christina floundered at the inadvertent admission, her breath suddenly gone. She pressed her hand over her heart, where it felt as though it was beating so hard it might burst out of her chest.

"Oh my," Lady Hastings said, her voice quiet but clear as she leaned forward in concern. "You've gone quite pale, Lady Stanhope. Are you alright?"

"I- I... yes." Christina took a deep breath - as deep as her corset would allow. She was not going to faint just because Daphne had tricked her into agreeing that she loved Benedict. Daphne smirked back at Christina's glare, unperturbed. "I'm fine. A bit taken aback by your sister-in-law's tricks."

"Her brother isn't fond of them either," Lady Hastings said, a smile curving her lips as they looked at each other across Daphne's lap, their gazes meeting in understanding. "It's truly best if you ignore her starts, but such a response is a struggle for him."

Daphne sat up indignantly. "I'm sitting right here!"

Christina couldn't help but laugh at the small smile still playing on Lady Hastings's lips. She'd thought the lady to be so quiet and meek she barely had a personality, but apparently she was hiding a wicked sense of humor. The lady's green eyes danced as she studiously tilted her head away from her sister-in-law, as if Daphne hadn't spoken.

"What *do* you want, Lady Stanhope?" Lady Hastings asked. While there was curiosity in her voice, it seemed as though she was mostly asking as a prompt, a question for Christina to answer for herself.

Turning her head to look at the bouquet again, Christina felt her lips twist. Not quite a smile, not quite a frown.

What *did* she want?

When she'd left town before Christmas, she'd been sure she wanted to move on from Benedict, to come back with her emotions firmly under her control, and enjoy the same kind of nonthreatening friendship she still had with Lords Haversham and Conyngham. But his surprise arrival at the Wutherings' ball had forced her to face him without preparation, and she'd been stunned by the strength of her feelings for him as they'd surged up at the sight and touch of him. Then, his shocking appearance in her bedchamber, his masterful wresting of control from her, had made her change her course. She'd begun to adjust her plans - spending the Season as his lover might be harder to recover from than the month they'd spent together previously, but she'd thought she could do so. She'd had some vague thought of traveling or spending some time away from London after this Season, giving her more time and space from him once the Season ended. By then, surely, he'd be willing to let her go.

Instead he'd made the insane offer of marriage. Marriage for love... a marriage based on the one thing she couldn't trust, couldn't countenance. When she'd occasionally considered remarrying - as a distant kind of idea, something which would happen years in the future if at all - it would be because she wanted children. She'd never thought about love as being a part of her future at all, other than as something to avoid.

Benedict said he loved her.

What did *she* want?

Some part of her, some deeply buried yearning in her heart, wanted to believe him.

But marriage?

If his feelings changed, if his love slowly slipped away, they would still be married. She'd be trapped again. Of course he wouldn't mean to, he was presently absolutely in earnest, but who could predict the future?

Certainly not her.

BENEDICT'S COMMANDS

ALTHOUGH BENEDICT WASN'T ENTIRELY surprised to be turned away from Christina's front door with the butler claiming the lady was out visiting friends, he was disappointed. A quick query did confirm his bouquet had been delivered and received before she left. The butler's stern lips had twitched very slightly, his brow arching just a touch, giving a general impression of amusement at Benedict's expense.

Yes, the bouquet had been a bit overmuch, but Benedict had wanted to ensure every one of his intentions and emotions were laid out bare to her in the message. There would be no retreat or pretense on his part; he was going to court her, convince her to marry him, and that was that.

Sighing, he walked down the street, slowly, keeping his eyes open for her returning carriage. Unfortunately, despite the busy traffic, there was no sign of her. Benedict couldn't help but wonder what she'd thought of the bouquet. The butler's opinion had been clear enough, but what was Christina's?

Had she already had plans to visit this friend of hers, or had it been a snap decision after she'd received his bouquet?

And, if the latter, was that a good sign or a bad sign?

Benedict always thought he had an exemplary understanding of women and their behavior, but Christina sometimes confounded him. Then again, that was part of what he enjoyed so much about her. While she was often entirely predictable, she occasionally astonished him by behaving in an unexpected manner he could have never anticipated.

Even now knowing how her past might affect her current behavior didn't entirely help him, although he supposed he had a bit more insight into the motivations behind her behavior. It didn't seem to help him predict it. He had thought she would be at home, hiding from him, and he'd seriously considering entering through her bedroom window again. But the butler had been telling the truth when he'd said Christina was out, Benedict could tell.

He wished he'd been able to discover who the friend she was

visiting was, but Christina had chosen well with her butler - the man had become positively frosty when Benedict tried to offer him a bribe for information.

Returning to Manchester House, rather than to the lonely house on Jermyn Street, Benedict went looking for his brother, but it quickly became clear Isaac was not at home either. He was wandering his way back to the front entrance - meandering more like - when he heard Lydia calling his name. Backtracking, he peered into the morning room and smiled at her.

"Where's Arabella?"

"Shopping with Gabrielle," Lydia said with a smile, setting down the book she'd been reading. "I meant to go with them, but I think I must have not slept as well as I ought, I'm a trifle fatigued." The smile curving her lips turned a little dreamy and her fingers drifted towards her stomach, making Benedict hide his own smile. Yes, he was completely confident his sister-in-law was increasing, even though she and Isaac hadn't announced it yet.

The day dress she was wearing was loose to conceal any changes to her figure, its sunny yellow color giving her honey-blonde hair a soft glow - or perhaps that was just the glow of impending motherhood.

"I take it your trip to visit Lady Stanhope was unsuccessful?" she asked, after ringing for some tea. "You returned much more quickly than anticipated."

"The lady was not at home," Benedict said with a sigh, not bothering to hide his disappointment, knowing his sister-in-law was good for sympathy. Something neither of his siblings would indulge in.

"How unfortunate," Lydia sympathized, reaching out and patting his hand in an encouraging way. He adored his sister-in-law. She was exactly the kind of soothing, sympathetic ear his bruised ego needed and his own siblings would never proffer. "Perhaps you will have better luck this afternoon?"

"If I return," he said with a slight frown, sitting back against the couch. One of the maids brought in the tea service, and Lydia busied herself with pouring both of them a cup while Benedict contemplated his next move. "Do you think I should go back again today?"

"Perhaps not today," Lydia conceded, with a rueful smile. "If her butler informs her of your morning visit, a second attempt might seem a bit importuning."

"Or desperate," Benedict muttered, picking up his own cup of tea. It wasn't considered particularly masculine to like the stuff, but Benedict secretly enjoyed drinking tea as much as any of the ladies did. Having a good cup was just another benefit of spending time with Lydia, as he could claim he was only doing so to be polite.

"Yes, perhaps a bit desperate too," Lydia said, teasing. It was as harsh as her teasing ever came, making her the gentlest member of the family. "You must introduce us to her as soon as possible so Arabella and I may befriend her. Then we can take you with us for visits at-home and invite her to our smaller gatherings."

"I don't suppose I could just introduce her to you, and not Arabella?" he asked, only half-joking. Lydia laughed.

"How unkind you are to your sister," she said, her eyes sparkling with mirth even though she attempted to sound reproving. "And here I believed you told your brother my influence had improved her behavior greatly."

"In public, certainly... here at home with me?" He made the question plaintive and whining, making her laugh again.

A knock on the door and clearing of the throat had them both looking up. Sulman stood in the doorway, a small smile on his face. Unlike his counterpart on the estate, Rigby, Sulman didn't allow being a butler to entirely erase his personality and it was clear he had a soft spot for the new Duchess.

"A note for you, my lord," he said to Benedict.

"Interesting," Benedict said, standing up as Sulman walked over to hold out the small tray he'd carried it on. It didn't surprise him that a note would be delivered to this house, rather than the one he often stayed in as he kept the address of that house mostly private, but he didn't receive notes often at all. Normally any notes sent to the house were for the family as a whole.

Swiftly opening it, his eyebrows felt like they were sliding into his hairline by the time he was done reading.

"Benedict?" Lydia was looking up at him, alight with curiosity. "What is it? Who is it from?"

"An ally," Benedict responded, a grin spreading across his face.

Lord Dearborne,

Please excuse my presumption if this note is unwelcome, but I thought you might be interested in knowing that Lady Christina Stanhope will be my guest at the Royal Theater tomorrow evening for A Midsummer Night's Dream.

Perhaps I will see you there?

Lady Daphne Parker

Countess of Marley

P.S. I also particularly *hope you will be able to attend my ball this Friday, your sister-in-law, the Duchess, will have received your invitation.*

CHAPTER 5

The theater was one of Christina's favorite pastimes, although she often longed for the power to silence others when in attendance. Too many of Society came to the theater to see and be seen, rather than enjoy the performance. Christina loved the spectacle, the show, and while she was perfectly happy to socialize during the intermissions, while watching the actual play she would prefer silence in the audience. As a result, she'd become rather adept at blocking out the sights and sounds of everyone else, so she could focus on the stage.

For the first time since her first Season, she was struggling to pay attention to the play rather than the audience, and it was all Benedict Windham's fault.

Even though he was just *sitting* there.

Right over there.

Sitting in the Manchester box, just across the theater and a bit closer to the stage than she was in her box. Sitting right where she could see him out of the corner of her eye, no matter how she tried to train her gaze on the stage.

Seated next to his sister in the chair closer to the balcony, behind the Duke and Duchess of Manchester, he cut an elegantly handsome figure. Despite the imposing presence of the Duke, Benedict's aura of authority held its own against his brother's, even in such a small space. She couldn't help but wonder if the Duchess and Lady Arabella felt crowded, being so confined with two such larger-than-life men.

Perhaps she might have been able to ignore his presence, his mahogany hair curling over the stiff white collar of his shirt, the way his broad shoulders filled out the dark superfine of his jacket, and the fitted, gleaming bronze of his waistcoat - which no doubt brought out his eyes - *if the blasted man would stop staring at her.*

He made no pretense of watching the play.

His eyes did not wander the audience.

He just watched her from across the room.

Which meant he saw every single time she looked back at him.

"Everyone is watching you two," Daphne whispered from behind her fan, leaning over slightly.

Unlike Christina, she sounded delighted by the situation.

The two of them were seated together, in front of Daphne's sister younger sister Hazel and Hazel's husband, the Earl of Jermyn, in the Marley box. The Earl of Marley was noticeably absent, but that was because he hated the theater and avoided it if he could. Fortunately, Daphne's brother-in-law adored the theater and was happy to escort them as it meant he didn't have to sit in his family's box, which was currently occupied by his parents, the Marquess and Marchesse of Bristol, and their guests. It would have been rather cramped if David and Hazel joined them there, rather than sitting with Daphne and Christina.

Nervously, Christina smoothed her hands over the indigo silk of her skirts, promising herself for the hundredth time that she was *not* going to look towards the Manchester box again. Instead, she turned and looked around the theater, as casually as she could, and nearly groaned aloud.

Everyone whose opera glasses weren't trained on the Manchester box were trained on her, and quite a few were moving back and forth between the two. Even before the play, upon arrival at the theater, she'd been questioned by more than one curious gossip about the

Marquess' apparent interest in her at the Wutherings' ball. Any efforts she'd put forth to laugh off the "mistaken impression" that the Marquess' was courting her were now being scuttled by his behavior.

Although, at least those who had approached her this evening assumed honorable intentions on his part; some others would undoubtedly be more malicious with their gossip.

"My bad luck he chose to come on the same night as me," Christina muttered. She was so focused on trying to ignore Benedict, she missed the guilty expression which flitted across her friend's face. By the time she glanced at Daphne, the Countess' expression was quite composed although unsympathetic.

"He hasn't looked away from you once," Daphne whispered, sounding elated. "He's utterly besotted."

Christina's betraying heart tumbled in her chest at her friend's declaration, thrilling to the idea she might be right.

Firming her jaw, she turned away from Daphne and back towards the stage - but as usual, Benedict's gaze made her eyes flit towards him for a brief moment on the way. The intensity of his look seared her, before she jerked her eyes back to the actors. She desperately wished herself at home, but with half the eyes in the audience on her there was no way she could leave in the middle of the performance without drawing attention.

Perhaps she could sneak out at intermission.

"SHE'S VERY BEAUTIFUL," Arabella murmured, leaning forward slightly to look around Benedict at Christina. "At least, from this distance. I assume she's beautiful upon closer examination as well."

"Both inside and out," Benedict murmured back, too distracted by Christina's presence and pretense at ignoring him to be drawn into his sister's attempts to needle him.

At least Arabella was mostly behaving. Last year, she wouldn't have hesitated to lean forward and stare, her comment would likely not have been made *sotto voce*, and it would not have been unsurprising to find her suddenly gone from his side and brazenly entering the Marley box to be introduced.

Arabella's previous season had been fraught with little moments where she skirted the line of scandal, pushing the patience of the *ton*, and using her position as a duke's sister to her advantage. Most young ladies would not have been able to get away with half of what she did. Being incredibly beautiful, sibling to one of the most powerful men in Society, and keeping just to the side of respectability, Arabella had earned a reputation as an Original rather than a young lady to completely avoid.

This Season, thanks to Lydia, even the highest-steppers seemed approving of her conduct, and she kept her more hoydenish starts confined to the privacy of Manchester House or murmured asides to her siblings. It was a relief not to have to divide his attention between keeping track of his sister and his own pursuits.

After a moment, he became aware of Arabella's weighted silence and he tore his eyes away from Christina for long enough to see what had quieted her. Turning his head, he met her gaze and found her hazel eyes staring at him, in just as intense a manner as he'd been staring at Christina. He frowned and raised his eyebrow at her in question.

"You really do love her," she said quietly in response.

"I do."

He turned his head back to where Christina's gaze was fixed on the stage. If he raised his opera glasses, he could see the swell of her creamy bosom over her blueish-purple gown, the long line of her neck, and the pink blush in her cheeks.

A blush which deepened every time she turned her head and met his gaze.

A blush which bolstered his spirits, no matter how determinedly she turned her head away from him each time their eyes met.

"Then I shall help."

It took five precious seconds to register what Arabella had just said. Three more seconds to turn his head and realize she was no longer sitting beside him. The little sneak was far too adept at moving quickly and quietly; Lydia and Isaac hadn't even looked to see where she'd gone because they hadn't noticed she'd left.

Stifling the urge to curse under his breath, Benedict also attempted to sneak away unnoticed, but as soon as he reached the curtain, Isaac's soft, deep voice had him turning.

"Where are you going?"

"Arabella needs a breath of fresh air," he lied, unwilling to admit their sister had slipped away without him noticing. He didn't even know how she'd done it in her voluminous skirts when he couldn't and he had much greater freedom of movement. "It's almost intermission anyway."

With a brief nod, Isaac turned his attention back to his wife. Thank goodness for Lydia; with her presence distracting Isaac, he didn't even appear to be suspicious.

Moving as quickly as he could, Benedict hurried after Arabella. With his ground-eating strides, he should have been able to catch up to her easily, but she had already reached her destination. Hazel eyes sparkling with glee, looking livelier than she had all Season now that she was up to some mischief, she was standing outside the curtain of the Earl of Marley's box. Head tilted slightly, she appeared to be listening intently.

He wanted to shout at her, but doing so would draw the attention of all the occupants of the other boxes. And she knew it.

Blasted chit.

Benedict couldn't wait until she was married and some other poor sod's problem.

That wasn't entirely true. He loved her dearly. Just perhaps not at this particular moment.

As applause suddenly rang out, Arabella grinned at him and darted between the curtains before Benedict could lunge and catch her.

"Damn."

Of course he'd intended to find Christina at intermission, but on *his* terms. Not his sister's.

Maybe they could find a nice Scottish Laird to marry Arabella, one which preferred to remain in Scotland for the majority of the year, he thought grimly. A sentiment which completely ignored how much he'd miss his sister and would actually be quite upset over such an arrangement. But in the moment, it didn't seem too unreasonable.

~

EVERYONE in the box jumped in surprise as a beautiful young woman in a misty blue gown burst through the curtain, interrupting their applause.

"Oh... my apologies," said the Lady Arabella. Christina recognized her immediately. The young lady's lips made a little 'o' of shock, her face a picture of innocent alarm. "I've mixed up my boxes." Benedict stepped through the curtains behind her, a slight frown on his face, contrasting sharply with Lady Arabella's overly innocent, wide smile. "I meant to speak with my friend, Lady Gertrude Withers. I must have gone one box too far."

"Please excuse my sister," Benedict said, giving the occupants of the box a short bow, although his gaze lingered on Christina. Heat and desire coiled within her, making her mouth dry, at his close proximity. "She's rather impetuous at times."

"I'm quite in sympathy with her," Hazel said, a wide smile on her face. "I've been known to be rather impetuous as well." She exchanged a glance with her husband, as though sharing a private joke.

"It can be quite confusing, all these curtains," Daphne said, also smiling widely at Arabella, giving a wave of her hand at the rich, velvet curtains which kept the box private. Turning slightly to Benedict, Daphne's smile widened. "Please, Lord Dearborn, introduce us?"

And that was how Christina met a member of Benedict's family for the first time.

She'd expected to be a bundle of nerves if she ever met any of his siblings, but Lady Arabella's sudden appearance hadn't given her anxieties any time to sprout. That the lady in question also seemed very pleased to meet her helped assuage some of her anxiety as it attempted to rise - although it also gave way to wondering exactly what Benedict had told his sister about Christina.

He'd certainly told her something.

While Lady Gertrude Withers was a lovely young lady, and probably had been introduced to the Lady Arabella, it was unlikely they were close friends. The Lady Gertrude was a complete flibbertigibbet and far too obsessed with rules and being the perfect picture of propriety to be friends with Lady Arabella, who was intelligent, capable, and entirely an Original when it came to her behavior. Beyond that, Lady Arabella's interested gaze returned to Christina far too often between introductions, making it clear where her true interest lay.

"...champagne?" Hazel asked, making Christina start as she realized she'd completely lost the thread of conversation.

"Absolutely, I'm parched," Daphne said, standing quickly in a rustle of fabric. "Lord Dearborn, Lady Stanhope was planning on staying in the box during intermission; since you are here, would you mind keeping her company so I might join my sister and her husband in having some refreshments?"

It was an effort not to kick her friend. "Oh, I don't mind-:

"Champagne sounds wonderful," Lady Arabella enthused, quite cutting off Christina's protest that she was perfectly happy to join them in the lobby for the intermission, since she'd told Daphne no such thing. "I'm sure my brother won't mind leaving me in your care."

Before Christina's second attempt at a protest could fully form on her lips, she found herself alone in the box with Benedict, who was looking at her like a cat which had finally cornered the mouse it had been chasing.

"Christina," he said, sitting down beside her and trapping her between him and the edge of the box. There was no way past him without practically sitting in his lap - and wouldn't that cause talk! While most of the audience had taken advantage of the intermission to mingle, there were quite a few people still in their boxes - or visiting their neighbors' boxes - and probably watching her and Benedict.

"Lord Dearborn," she said archly, turning up her nose at him.

"Now, love, don't be like that," he murmured, turning his body so he could slide his hand along her leg, making her gasp at both the sensation and his audacity. "You don't want me to remind you of our intimate connection and why you should use my given name right here and now, do you?"

He wouldn't...

He probably would.

Christina glared, trying to ignore the excitement pounding in her breast, the way her nipples tightened as his gaze slid over the creamy expanse of her breasts, and the coiling need between her thighs.

"Did you ask your sister to clear the box for you?" she asked abruptly, deciding a retreat was the better part of valor. Best to ignore his outrageous warning.

"No. I wasn't too pleased when she took it upon herself to gain an introduction to you, but I can't argue with the result." Disgruntlement flitted over his expression. "I might even have to thank her." The admission looked as though it pained him and Christina couldn't stop her lips from twitching.

He had told her that Lady Arabella could be a hoyden and far too headstrong for her own good.

Still, that he hadn't planned on introducing her to his family did not exactly raise her confidence in his purported desire to marry her.

"So you hadn't planned to introduce me to your family?"

"Oh, I most certainly do. Did." A rakish grin flashed across his face. "My sister-in-law, Lydia, is eager to befriend you, but she has far more manners than my sister. She'll wait until I'm able to secure an appropriate moment for an introduction."

Oh...

Her stomach fluttered. Nerves? Happiness?

"What do you think of the production?" he asked, nodding his head down towards the stage. She felt a moment of gratitude for the change in subject to a far less fraught one.

"Quite enjoyable," she said immediately, even though she hadn't been able to enjoy it as much as she ought. Her eyes narrowed slightly at him as he leaned back, the very image of an affable rake. "What do you think of it?"

Something glinted in his eye as he smiled widely. "I confess, it hasn't held my attention."

"Perhaps if you made an attempt to pay attention at all," she responded tartly.

∼

BENEDICT WAS MOSTLY ENJOYING HIMSELF, riling Christina's temper in full view of the *ton*.

It also helped distract him from his nearly painful level of arousal.

She was stunning, with her hair piled high, jewels winking about her throat, her breasts heaving in annoyance. He even imagined he could see the outlines of her dusky nipples, pressing at the front of her gown.

"I'd rather stare at you," he said baldly, enjoying the way she flushed and averted her gaze.

She liked to hear him say it, even if she pretended she didn't. Whipping out her fan, she began to flutter it, sending wafts of scented perfume his way. She smelled like violets, of course.

"What is taking them so long?" she murmured, her eyes flitting past him to the curtains.

"Would you like to go find them?" he asked, chivalrously.

"Yes, please."

Offering her his arm, he quite properly escorted her out of the box.

However, upon stepping into the empty hall, he immediately pushed her up against the wall, his mouth covering hers and swallowing her surprised cry. Lust pounded through him as her soft body was trapped between him and the wall, squirming slightly against him. Keeping his ears pricked for approaching interlopers, Benedict took the opportunity to kiss her deeply, thoroughly.

It only took her a few shocked seconds before she was kissing him back, her legs parting to allow him to thrust his aching cock against the softness of her body. Benedict groaned into her mouth, shuddering with the effort of not ravishing her against the wall of the theater... but it was far too risky. Even just this kiss could damage her reputation if they were seen. The *ton* expected discretion, even though widows and married couples were extended a great deal of leniency when it came to affairs.

As his future wife, her reputation was his to protect, not ruin.

So Benedict forced himself to pull back, his cockstand practically ready to burst from his breeches. Christina blinked up at him, dazed with lust, her lips swollen, cheeks flushed, and ready and willing to do whatever he pleased. She'd certainly be primed for the rest of the evening.

But if she was a naughty girl and touched herself, he'd make sure she paid for it.

"Come, love," he said, leaning down to brush a soft kiss across her lips. "We should join the others."

"But..." Christina wet her lips, her eyes begging him for more, before she blinked and looked around, remembering where they were. "Yes... yes of course."

"Just think," he whispered in her ear as he began to lead her down the hall, the noise of conversation growing louder as they moved. "If you were my wife, we could leave right now and no one would think a thing."

Christina glared at him.

Benedict smiled.

Then they reached the mass of Society, crowded together and gossiping as always. He heard the little dip and wave in conversations as he and Christina appeared. No one could guess that he'd just kissed her senseless in the hallway, but everyone wanted to know exactly what was happening between the two of them. Benedict acted like a courting gentleman, Christina behaved as a respectable young widow would with a friend, and all the observers were heartily confused.

After all, if Benedict was courting her, it would be sheer lunacy - from Society's point of view - for her to reject him.

To see her constantly ignoring his flirtations and attentions, and hear her explanations for his behavior (which were becoming less and less convincing) made no sense to anyone unless he truly wasn't courting her. But he was being so obvious in his attentions, no one could think of any other explanation for it. If he were trying to dally with her, he would be discreet.

The speculation was running rampant. Benedict even heard two gentlemen muttering about a bet in the book at White's as he and Christina passed by. It wouldn't surprise him. The bored noblemen of the *ton* would bet on just about anything, and this situation was more baffling than most.

Several acquaintances greeted both of them. Benedict cleaved to Christina's skirts, making it clear his attention was entirely on her. Christina pretended he was doing no such thing. It was a competition of sorts, and one which he was winning.

He was quite sure more than one person walked away from them smug with the knowledge that the Marquess of Dearborn was courting the Dowager-Marchesse of Stanhope... and she was playing hard-to-get but would acquiesce in the end. After all, she'd be mad not to.

Benedict wished he shared that assurance, but seeing as he was privy to her secret reasons for why she was so against marriage, he couldn't be quite so confident. Still, Society's expectations would hopefully help him fend off other parties from trying to take his place in her bed. More than one gentleman gave him a disgruntled or even hostile look when he refused to be budged from Christina's side.

Unfortunately, it was all too soon before the intermission was over, and he had to escort her back to the Marley box before returning to his brother's. Isaac and Lydia had barely had time to be introduced, but at least the deed had been done so now Lydia could call on Christina and - hopefully - help press his suit. They'd seemed to take to each other even though they'd barely had a full minute to converse before the bells signaling the end of intermission had begun to ring.

At the next intermission, Benedict had gone out to find Christina again, hoping to bring her back to the Manchester box for more private conversation with his family - and another signal of his intentions - but she and the Marley party had left the theater.

As tempted as he was to appear in her home again, he decided to stay away for now. After all, Lady Daphne's ball was only two days away, and Lydia and Arabella had quickly found and responded to the invitation once he'd told them why he wanted to attend.

Christina might be running, but it was the Season... she couldn't hide.

CHAPTER 6

The delicate wood of Christina's fan creaked in her hand, making her relax her grip lest she snap the thing in half. She felt sick with churning jealousy as she watched Benedict, politely smiling and nodding to an entire bevy of beautiful, young, virginal misses. The very kind of beautiful, young, virginal misses Society would expect him to choose from when he married.

"I heard the mamas have realized he means to marry and are hoping to tempt him to marry one of their darlings instead of you," Daphne said in her ear, having noticed Christina's distraction. "Too bad for them, he doesn't seem so inclined."

Did he not?

He didn't look at them with any kind of lust or passion... but many men didn't view their wives in such a manner. Something she knew all too well. They were everything a nobleman like him was supposed to marry - pure, virginal, and without a single blemish to their reputation. While she'd been discreet with her lovers, everyone still knew who her 'special acquaintances' had been. That was just the way of the *ton*. No one would look askance at Benedict marrying one of the young misses while keeping Christina as his lover. Not even many of the young misses.

Certainly none who were currently pursuing him. They had an eye on his title, with his youth and good looks making him a much more palatable choice than many other titled gentlemen on the prowl for a young, dewy-eyed wife.

A virginal bride and a widow lover would make sense to everyone.

Of course, she would never allow it. Benedict's involvement with another woman, in any way other than family or friendship, would end her relationship with him. Christina would not be put in such a position again. She had not understood it when she realized George had been unfaithful to her, and she would not countenance it now.

Especially not when her feelings for him already ran so deep. Her care for herself ran deeper.

"You should go rescue him, put him out of his misery," Daphne whispered.

Part of her wanted to but...

What if he decided a young, virginal miss suited him better as a bride? Shouldn't he at least have the option? And she would much rather know sooner than later if one of the young ladies appealed to him. No matter how bitter jealousy clawed at her insides while she was forced to watch.

She also had to admit, she did feel better seeing them all angling for an invitation to dance, while he stood stiffly and ignored the first notes of music lifting into the air.

"Pardon me, Lady Stanhope? Would you like to dance?"

Christina turned to see Mr. Chestertown, second son of the Earl of Rawling's cousin, addressing her. She'd met Mr. Chestertown last Season, before ending her affair with Haversham, and found him to be rather good company. Handsome, with a nose that was just a tad too big for his face, his sandy blonde hair just brushed the stiff, white collar of his shirt. As usual, his sartorial splendor was colorful; his dark rose waistcoat was quite pretty next to the plum jacket he was wearing and Christina made note of the color combination. Mr. Chestertown dressed as a dandy, but he had a reputation as a rake and he flirted the same way he breathed - without thinking.

They got along rather well as she appreciated his style as well as his warm occasional hints about furthering their relationship. He took no umbrage when she ignored those hints, nor did he take her disinterest in being seduced as a challenge. All in all, his company was often both flattering and fun.

"I would love to," Christina said, perhaps with more feeling than usual, which made the man blink and refocus on her, a glint of heightened interest in his eyes. As he led her to the dance floor, he was examining her out of the corner of his eye, as though appraising whether she was interested in more than a dance with him. Inwardly, she cursed, because she hadn't meant to give off that impression at all.

As they took their places for the dance, her head instinctively turned towards where Benedict was besieged by the young misses. She didn't know if he'd seen her heading towards the dance floor with Mr. Chestertown - or even if he'd care - but it was as though Benedict was a lodestone. Her gaze was drawn to him, regardless of all else.

However, he wasn't where she expected him to be, and her gaze skittered around the ballroom, seeking out his broad-shouldered figure. Fortunately, as he was quite tall, it did not take her long to locate him, moving towards the dance floor with his sister on his arm. The little coterie of young misses had already scattered, many of them having accepted an invitation to dance from another gentleman if they didn't already have a name on their dance card.

"Ah, I see the rumors are true," Mr. Chestertown said suddenly, amusement tinging his voice, and Christina looked up into his warm brown eyes, which flicked back and forth between her and Benedict. A hot blush suffused her cheeks.

Christina didn't bother to pretend she didn't know what he was referring to. "My apologies for my distraction, sir," she said, as the dance began.

The smile she received in return was filled with amusement and just a touch of mischief. "Quite alright, my dear, I'm happy to assist."

She gave him a repressive look, but his grin just widened.

"If you really want to make him jealous, you should smile adoringly at me," he teased, and Christina's eyes narrowed.

"That was not my aim," she said, although she suddenly wasn't entirely sure. Had part of her wanted to make Benedict feel a bit of what she had been feeling? It seemed rather petty of her but she couldn't deny the sense of satisfaction it gave her to watch Benedict dance with his sister rather than any of the young debutantes.

Three dances later, Benedict came seeking her hand for the waltz, deftly avoiding the young beauties and their mamas or chaperones who attempted to converge on him at the end of each set. So far, he hadn't danced with a single one of them, confining his attentions to his sister, his sister-in-law, and Daphne. That last gave Christina the most unease, because her friend had been speaking quite animatedly throughout the entirety of their dance, and the pair had constantly looked across the dance floor to where Christina was dancing with Lord Burlingstroke, a cheerful elderly gentleman who was a particular friend of her father's.

As Benedict pressed his hand against her back and began to move, his powerful stride leading her through the circles of the waltz, Christina's body responded with tingling awareness. He pulled her close - closer than was necessary and certainly closer than propriety allowed. Yet trying to step away was impossible with his strength set against hers, his body leading hers through the steps.

"Are you trying to drive me mad?" he asked softly.

Frowning, Christina looked up at him, distracted by the question, no longer noticing how closely their bodies brushed as they moved.

"Drive you mad?" she repeated, not understanding.

"By dancing every single dance with a different gentleman," he replied, his voice low.

"You've danced every dance," she retorted, tilting her head to the side as she realized perhaps she truly hadn't been the only one of them pricked by jealousy. While his expression was bland, now that she was paying attention she could feel the tension in his body, the possessiveness in the way he held her. It both surprised and pleased her... and yet she couldn't help but feel wary.

Seeing the covetous and disapproving looks sent their way by the marriage-minded mamas didn't reassure her.

"It's not the same," he said, a hint of a scowl threatening his brow. "The quality of my dance partners vastly differs from yours." His voice lowered further, his head tilting forward to speak so low only she could hear. "In fact, with every dance, my hand itches a little more. Believe me, I'm counting every dance you partake in."

Christina's bottom tingled at the implied threat, her heart suddenly racing as arousal and anxiety welled. Breathless, she couldn't even think of a response, because she was too taken aback by his brazenness. Taken aback, and yet completely taken in.

When the dance ended, Benedict remained by her side as Daphne and Hazel joined them, followed by a small crowd of gentlemen, many of whom eyed Benedict's presence at her side with competitive glances. Christina might have found it amusing if Benedict's presence hadn't also attracted the young ladies as well. It took a concerted effort by several parties, but after a few minutes he was no longer by her side, and now she was having to watch him deal politely with the importuning young women and their mamas from close quarters.

Their mamas were not very subtle in their biting remarks about the differences between their young, pure daughters against widows who ought to know their place. As much as Benedict sallied back, just as biting even as civility was maintained on both sides, it didn't deter any of them, and the constant malice was giving Christina a headache.

So when Mr. Shipley asked her to dance, she accepted, just to have a momentary break from the nasty glares and judgmental comments.

SEEING Christina being led to the dance floor by Shipley - who had no reputation as a rake but did have stars in his eyes whenever he looked at Christina - grated on Benedict's temper. Especially because she didn't even glance back at him as she walked away.

He'd been aware of her growing distress over the matrons' remarks and their daughters' presence, but Society's dictates were very specific about what a gentleman could and could not do. So far, he'd availed himself of hiding behind the skirts of women he trusted in order to avoid testing Christina's trust in him without causing offense.

Watching her with Shipley, hemmed in by the petticoat-line and their spiteful mothers, Benedict was rapidly losing his patience with both Society's strictures and the importuning women who were using them to their advantage. *He* was supposed to be the one using Society's rules, to catch Christina, not to be caught himself by some young miss he had no interest in.

"Oh, I do love this song. It is my favorite to dance to," said Miss Russell, her eyes wide and calculating. She tipped her head to the side, expecting him to do the gentlemanly thing and offer his services.

But Benedict's patience with being a gentleman had reached its limit. "It is a lovely song," he agreed, and turned away to address Lady Daphne's sister, the Lady Hazel, who was quite lovely as well as being someone who wouldn't rouse Christina's uncertainties. "Lady Hazel, would you do me the honor?"

Small gasps rose up around him and Mrs. Russell turned pale with horror. Out of the corner of his eye, he could see Miss Russell's lovely blue eyes fill with sudden tears as her lower lip trembled. Guilt suddenly assailed him. It wasn't the poor girl's fault that she'd angled for a dance just as he'd run out of patience. She certainly wasn't the first to drop a broad hint, but he'd been much kinder to the previous aspirants, excusing himself by saying he'd already promised the dance to another. By being so blatant in his refusal, he'd basically cut her when she hadn't been any more importuning than the other young ladies, and a good deal less than some.

Even Daphne and Hazel's expressions were reproachful. Such an action could actually do the young woman a great deal of harm when it came to making a match, as the gossip could be quick and vicious. Not only had he marked her out, but with his social standing against hers, others would be quick to follow suit.

Inwardly sighing, he looked at Daphne, a silent plea on his face. Rolling her eyes heavenward, she nodded as he led Lady Hazel away from the group.

A minute later, his brother Isaac was leading the starry-eyed Miss Russell onto the floor and shooting him a look which promised future retribution. Benedict was certainly in for a lecture, one which he rather deserved. His impulsive snappish behavior was more like Arabella than himself.

"That was not well done, but I believe you may have achieved your goal," Lady Hazel said. "Your harem is already dispersing. And your brother has ensured there is no lasting harm to Miss Russell." Her tone was still somewhat reproving.

"Believe me, I did not intend to sink Miss Russell's prospects," he said contritely. "I am merely at the end of my patience... and yet that's no excuse either. Still... I can't entirely regret it if what you say is true."

A little smile turned up the corners of Lady Hazel's lips. "Seeing as Lady Christina's patience is also already stretched thin as well and no real harm done, I can't bring myself to scold you." She glanced over to where Miss Russell was obviously in alt to have been singled out by the Duke of Manchester. It didn't matter that he was married, his attention would be noted and far more influential to her status among the debutantes than Benedict's cut. "And I don't believe Miss Russell will have any complaints in the end either."

Indeed. Although Benedict still felt a bit guilty - especially later in the evening when Miss Russell hastily swerved away from him, obviously changing her path to avoid him - he hadn't done her any lasting harm. Several gentlemen, intrigued by whatever had brought the Duke of Manchester out onto the dance floor with a debutante, had converged on the young woman immediately following her dance, including the second son of the Duke of Richmond (incidentally, Benedict's guilt in its entirety was assuaged when the pair's engagement was announced six weeks later and was, by all accounts, a love match).

Fortunately, neither Hazel nor Daphne informed Christina about why all but the most aggressive of the young ladies had disappeared from his side between dances. Despite her obvious unhappiness with the young ladies, she would not condone outright rudeness and possible harm to a young woman's reputation. By the end of the night, most of them seemed to have taken the message as well. No matter how they implored or hinted, he steadfastly danced and strolled only with ladies Christina personally knew and trusted or his family members, and Christina herself. The number of young ladies surrounding him slowly dwindled in the face of his steadfast sidestepping, much to his relief.

On the other hand, Christina continued to dance with whomever she wanted.

While watching her dancing with other men exercised his possessiveness, Benedict didn't miss where her attention fell - continually on him. Her eyes sought him out whenever he wasn't by her side, constantly flicking his way during the dances, and she only truly relaxed when he was beside her. Yes, he still had moments of jealousy, but the emotion didn't ride him the same way it did her. Considering her past, he supposed that was only natural.

He was determined to prove she could trust him. Therefore, he would do his best to avoid piquing her jealousy, even as she pricked his. Responding in kind would be the surest way to prove her fears about marrying him. Since her own behavior showed no other man to be a serious threat, he managed to ignore those who certainly wished they had a chance for her affections.

Since he found his way back to her side at the conclusion of each dance, he was able to see when she began to wilt and immediately suggested a stroll outdoors to breathe some fresh air. To his relief - and the disappointment of her coterie and those young ladies too stubborn to give up on Benedict yet - she immediately agreed and he offered her his arm.

Sadly, the terrace was not as sparsely populated as he might have liked, and neither were the gardens. Daphne's ball was such a crush that quite a few attendees had taken advantage of the fair weather to venture outside for a bit of fresh air and slightly more privacy.

Christina idly fanned herself with a lacy cream confection, which matched the trim on her jade ballgown, wafting her floral perfume towards him. No matter what color she chose to wear, she always smelled of violets.

"It's quite lovely out tonight, isn't it?" she remarked as they began to stroll about the terrace. The air was decidedly cooler than in the ballroom, but still warm enough both she and Benedict could appreciate her fan.

"Not as lovely as you are," he responded, moving his arm to draw her closer to him, rather than following the approved social script of discussing the weather. Christina made a shushing sound and thwacked her fan against his arm as she pulled away to put a respectable amount of space between them again, making him grin in the face of her reproving look. No matter how she tried to hide it, he could still see the pleasure she took in his comment.

"Behave," she hissed. "You've caused enough talk when it comes to me already."

Shrugging, Benedict sighed and complied. "The moon is very full."

He missed their time together before Christmas, when they hadn't been quite so hemmed in by social mores. When Christina hadn't had to be quite so stringent about the rules regarding their conduct in order to keep her reputation intact. When so many eyes hadn't been watching them.

Declaring his interest so blatantly had alerted the *ton* to his intentions, just as he'd wanted, but it had also roused Society's interest. People would be watching each step of their courtship, which meant following the rules so as not to cause Christina any hardship. Or himself, for that matter. Not that he truly cared about being admitted to the highest sticklers' houses or Almack's, but Christina certainly did - and it was an unfortunate truth that Society was much less forgiving to women than men.

Benedict would do nothing to harm her standing - all he had to do was be patient. Once they were married, or even engaged, they wouldn't have to be quite so circumspect. Until then, he had to remember to behave.

At least in public.

Exhausted, footsore, and strangely happy, Christina made her way out the front door of Daphne's house... and frowned. Her carriage was nowhere in sight, but Benedict was standing on the sidewalk beside his own conveyance. With the lights from the house still brightly lit, she could see the anticipatory expression on his face. Something about the way he was standing made her think of a small boy who'd just done something naughty but was sure he was going to get away with it.

Her eyes narrowed as she approached him, but her heart beat a little faster with excitement.

Even when she objected to his high-handed ways outside of the bedroom, her body often responded as if they were within. It was a dashed nuisance at times.

"Where is my carriage?" she asked, setting aside her manners since he was the only person within earshot other than a nearby footman, who perked up as he realized he was going to witness some contretemps firsthand.

"Apparently there was a mix-up in the mews and your carriage was sent home early by mistake," Benedict said smoothly, his face so blankly serious it fairly screamed his involvement in the 'mix-up'. "I happened to be nearby when Lady Marley was informed of the mistake and promptly offered my services to see you home."

Christina could feel her back teeth grinding together. Perhaps he truly was innocent and just taking advantage of the situation... but if he truly hadn't had a hand in the dismissal of her carriage, she would be willing to bet her house that Daphne had. She might confront her friend later, but she already knew Daphne would be full of excuses. The worst of it was she also knew Daphne truly was doing this in what she thought was Christina's favor.

Or perhaps that wasn't the worst of it... the worst of it was the feeling of happy satisfaction at this further proof of Benedict's affections and the lengths to which he was willing to go to prove them.

He held out his hand to help her step up. Out of the corner of her eye she saw the disappointed footman, whose gossip wasn't going to be as juicy as he'd hoped. Suppressing a resigned sigh, Christina grumpily took Benedict's hand and allowed him to assist her into the coach.

Her feet hurt too much to do otherwise and her only other option was to wait for another suitable party to leave the ball and hope they would be willing to take her home. Since she didn't doubt Benedict would stand out here with her through that, and perhaps even sabotage an attempt to secure a seat in another's carriage, it would be a pointless venture which would only garner more gossip.

Sitting back against the comfortably plush seat, Christina decided this wasn't her worst decision. While she was well situated financially, her carriage wasn't this comfortable, and it did feel nice to settle back. Especially with her senses singing on high, thanks to Benedict's presence... and yet, being alone with him allowed her to relax for what felt like the first time all night.

Settling in beside her, Benedict's thigh pressed against hers as the footman closed the carriage door. He rapped sharply on the ceiling, and the carriage lurched forward in response.

Eyeing the closed curtains, Christina frowned. "Would you mind open- ah!" She shrieked as Benedict hauled her over his lap with a suddenness that left her breathless even as her body pulsed in excited response. "BENEDICT!"

Ignoring her enraged cry, he flipped up her skirts, opening the slit in her drawers to bare her bottom, and suddenly Christina was quite grateful for the drawn curtains keeping them private. She gasped, wriggling to get away as he palmed her bottom, her fatigue and sore feet quite forgotten as excitement sizzled through her.

"Did you enjoy your evening?" he asked evenly, his fingers tapping against her bottom, close enough to her sex to make her lips swell in anticipation. "I certainly hope so. You danced fourteen dances with fourteen different gentleman who weren't me, and so you've earned fourteen swats on this pretty, little bottom."

"Benedict! Put me down!" she whispered in mortification. He

hadn't even bothered to lower his voice! "Don't you dare! Your coachman will hear!"

"Jacobs is paid very well to be discreet, don't worry about that," Benedict said, his fingers giving her one last playful caress before lifting away.

SMACK!

She pressed her hands over her mouth to muffle her shriek, which was more outraged embarrassment and shock that he was actually spanking her in a carriage than pain. Benedict rubbed his hand over the spot he'd just spanked, making her want to moan as a little shot of warmth spread through the area.

SMACK!

Rub.

SMACK!

Rub.

The swats were loud but not particularly painful, just enough to make her bottom tingle and sting, warming her flesh - especially when he rubbed the swatted spot immediately after. This was not a punishment spanking, this was a much more playful spanking, one meant to arouse... and it was working. Christina wriggled on his lap, doing her best to keep quiet as the heat level across her bottom and between her legs rose together.

There was something incredibly naughty, incredibly exciting, about being in a moving carriage, her bottom bared and turning pink under Benedict's firm hand. Could the coachman hear her? Did he know what was happening inside the carriage? Could anyone else passing by the carriage hear the crisp smacks of flesh impacting flesh? Would they possibly guess what the cause was? For some reason, all those questions just excited her more as Benedict spanked her squirming bottom.

SMACK!

Rub.

SMACK!

Rub.

SMACK!

Rub.

She moaned in disappointment when he suddenly stopped swatting her and began to rub his palm briskly over her tingling bottom, realizing he'd reached fourteen and the spanking was over. Heat fizzed along her skin, making her feel far too warm, like she wanted to strip everything off. A sudden image flashed in her head of herself, completely naked inside the carriage, a slave to Benedict's desires during a journey, and everything inside of her clenched as a wave of arousal swamped her. Such an idea was scandalously depraved and yet incredibly stimulating.

"Nice and pink," she heard him murmur, before she found her lower body sliding off his lap and into a kneeling position on the floor. Although her eyes had adjusted to the darkness, it was still so dark she could barely see as Benedict unlaced the front of his breeches, pulling out his cock. It was like they were wrapped in their own little sensual cocoon.

Knowing what he wanted, she leaned forward to lick the tip of his cock, feeling her way in the dark to the rigid, throbbing erection. Her hand wrapped around his root, helping her to angle its stiff length towards her lips. The musky, male scent of his body filled her nose as she began to swirl her tongue around the blunt head, her mouth watering in anticipation.

Benedict was the man who'd introduced her to giving oral pleasure, and she loved it. Loved feeling him hot and throbbing in her palm, loved tasting the salt of his flesh, loved hearing him groan as she pleasured him, loved the way his hands slid into her hair, urgently pulling her down on him. The more of his cock she took in her mouth, the more she ached between her thighs, her body hungering for him in every way.

The smooth flesh of his cock glided over her tongue as she took him between her lips, pins scattering on the floor as he buried his fingers in her hair, disassembling her coiffure. Her nipples brushed against the carriage seat as she leaned forward farther, the stimulation making her moan around his cock. Thrusting his hips upward,

Benedict filled her mouth, using his hands to press her down on his cock.

She released the base, allowing him to slide fully between her lips to the root, the blunt tip thrusting into her throat, feeling almost dizzy with the scandalous depravity of the act in such surrounds. No milk-and-water miss would do this for him, no young virgin could please him like this... Christina gloried in his soft groans and muttered curses as her head bobbed over him, pleasuring him, giving to him. She sucked hard, her throat working as the head of his cock pressed into it, almost frantic to swallow him completely.

"Bloody hell!"

Arching, Benedict's fingers dug into her scalp as he shuddered and thrust. His cock swelled, pressed deep into her throat, and then throbbed against her tongue as his cream spilled. She sucked and swallowed, greedily drinking him down, hazy with the satisfied glow which always came from pleasuring him even as her body whimpered for release.

His body relaxed back against the seat, the hold of his fingers gentling to a caress, and his cock began to shrink in her mouth. Christina's tongue licked over him, still needy, still wanting.

When the carriage came to a halt, her head popped up in surprise... she'd forgotten where they were, had become so accustomed to the rocking gait of the carriage that she'd been moving with it without thinking.

"We're here," Benedict said, his voice low, almost smug, as long fingers pressed under her chin and lifted her face away from his softened cock.

Christina nearly screamed with the sexual frustration winding about her body.

CHAPTER 7

Before the carriage door opened and Christina saw where they were, Benedict thought she might have been close to slapping him. She was practically quivering with need, her hot mouth had still been suckling his cock despite its deflating state. When she realized he'd brought her to *his* house on Jermyn Street - rather than her London home on Brooke - she'd practically gone limp with relief.

And then she'd blushed furiously when she took a surreptitious peek up at Jacobs, still in his perch at the front of the carriage. The good man remained stone faced as he shook the reins to get the horses moving again, headed towards the mews behind the house.

"Come, love," Benedict whispered in her ear, pulling her in close with one arm. "I believe you deserve a reward for taking your punishment so well, don't you?"

Of course, it hadn't been a true punishment, but they both enjoyed the game. Benedict might not like watching her dance with other men who obviously desired her, but he wasn't going to actually punish her for doing so either. She deserved to feel desirable, and she deserved to dance every dance. After tonight, however, he was seriously considering mustering the troops so she at least wasn't dancing *every* dance with a competitor; he'd much rather have her dancing with his friends and family. Gentlemen who were *safe*. Who wouldn't exercise his self-control so badly.

"I feel like I shouldn't reward you for whisking me away without my permission, and yet I think if you had actually brought me home, I might have exploded," she murmured, half to her herself as Benedict escorted her up the stairs and into the entryway.

He chuckled. It had been rather high handed of him, but Lady Daphne had provided the excuse to give them some privacy and he'd taken full advantage of it. She likely had just meant him to take Christina to Brooke Street, but Benedict was feeling far too primitive, too needful of staking his claim on Christina after an evening of not being able to rightfully call her his in any socially meaningful way. As soon as he'd realized Christina could be his for the evening, he'd sent a messenger to his house, ensuring the servants would ready the bedchamber and then play least-in-sight by the time they arrived.

"Perhaps you should just lay your trust in me and allow me to whisk you away whenever I want," he said, following her into the house. Grasping her hips, he pulled her against him, his front pressed to her back, his hot breath wafting over the sensitive nape of her neck. A fine tremble shivered through her body as she arched slightly, pressing her bottom against his groin where his cock was already beginning to swell again. "I promise to make it pleasurable."

"Absolutely not," she said, but her voice lacked conviction as he pressed his lips to her neck, his tongue licking against the sensitive skin. Considering how aroused she already was, it was no wonder she was distracted from their actual conversation.

"You could just marry me and then I wouldn't have to whisk you away," he murmured, tracing the delicate shell of her ear with his lips, his hands moving up to cup her breasts, squeezing the soft flesh and making her gasp with need. "Other than up to our bedroom every night."

"No." She shook her head even as her bottom pressed more fully against his groin, squirming against him, her hands covering the backs of his as he kneaded her breasts. The movements she made against him were rhythmic, her body responding as if he was already inside of her.

Pinching her nipples harshly as punishment for her rejection - which elicited a pained cry as she thrust her breasts forward, begging for more - Benedict quickly released her and spun her around as he bent his knees enough to get his shoulder level with her middle. With one swift movement, he hoisted her over his shoulder, bottom high in the air and began carrying her towards the steps as she burst into giggles.

"Benedict!"

THWAP!

His hand swatting her bottom through her skirts made a muffled sound and he was fairly certain she barely felt it, no matter how sensitive her ass already was from the spanking he'd given her in the carriage. Carrying her up the stairs, he headed for the bedroom, trying to ignore the way her hands were pulling up his coat so she could sensually caress his lower back, pulling his shirt from his breeches as she did so.

"I should whisk you away to Gretna Green," he grumbled, kicking open the door to the bedroom. As he'd instructed, the candelabra by his bedside was fully lit, so they weren't in total darkness. Benedict grinned. He had a few new items in his nightstand which he was eager to torment his lover with.

"Gretna Green or here, I still have to say *yes*," Christina reminded him, but her words were almost teasing.

"I could lock you up and spank you every day until you agree to say yes," he retorted, pulling her forward so she slid down his front to her feet, her breasts pressing against his chest, her flushed face only inches from his. Her eyes glittered with arousal and need, her tongue flicking out to lick her lower lip in anticipation.

"That wouldn't work, I would enjoy it too much," she whispered sultrily, a smile curving her lips before she went up on her toes to press her mouth to his.

Kissing her back, Benedict began working on her dress, undoing the row of buttons down the back, and pulling away just enough to let the fabric fall to the floor. She kissed him back hungrily, pressing her body against him, squirming as his hand cupped her bottom through her drawers. Moving his mouth down her neck, he undid the laces of her corset, leaving her clinging to him as he nipped and sucked at her soft flesh. Her soft moans and panting urged him onward, her body moving against his with urgency, rousing his own passions all over again, his cock slowly lifting in response to her ardent desire.

Stripping her down to just her stockings and garters, Benedict let his hands roam as he moved her back towards the bed, step by step. As they moved, she pushed his jacket from his shoulders, undid his waistcoat, and was working on his cravat by the time they reached the bed.

Ending the kiss, Benedict placed his hands over hers, taking the cravat from her grasp.

"Close your eyes, love," he said, lifting the cravat over them. A delighted smile curved her lips, her head tilting back as if for a kiss as he tied the cravat around her head. The disarray of her hair was adorably seductive, the soft curves of her naked body a constant temptation which he fought against.

DARKNESS BEHIND THE BLINDFOLD, as it had been in the carriage, was surprisingly sensual. Now that Benedict had use of his sight and she did not, it was even more so. She cried out with surprise as his lips suddenly closed over a turgid nipple, sending a hot flash of pleasure through her. Between her legs her need throbbed so powerfully, her knees buckled, and Benedict caught her, holding her up.

He moved his mouth back and forth, suckling each tender bud, driving her wild as she clung to his broad shoulders. The rough rasp of his tongue, the sharp nips of his teeth, somehow felt so much more intense, so much sharper, when she couldn't see... when she could only *feel*. His fingers dug into the soft, tender flesh of her bottom, bending her back so her breasts were thrust up towards him, leaving her panting with need as the growing hardness of his cock pressed against her mound. Between her legs she was wet, swollen, and wanton, the ache inside of her an ever-growing, gnawing hunger to be filled.

"Please..." she gasped out the word, rubbing herself against him, almost in a frenzy. "Please, Benedict... *more*..."

Suddenly lifted and tossed onto the bed, she let out a little shriek of fear just before she bounced onto the mattress. A swift tug on her ankle pulled her down the bed, her tender bottom rasping over the covers, and she fell back bonelessly, her breasts heaving, legs spread. Benedict's hand slid up her leg, from her ankle to her thigh, over the silk of her stockings to the soft, plump flesh just below the needy lips of her pussy.

"Arms above your head, love, wrists together."

Christina trembled, but did as he ordered. Pleasure would come faster if she didn't fight his commands. His hand on her thigh disappeared and she whimpered.

Soft cloth wrapped around her wrists as her arms were pulled upwards, tied in place above her head, leaving her helpless to his touch. Christina moaned as he returned his attention to her breasts, his hands roughly massaging the swollen mounds, plucking at her nipples, his hot mouth searing kisses across her skin.

"Benedict! *More!*" Half-order, half-plea. Christina was on fire from the inside out, her breasts heavy from being handled, her pussy aching to be. She arched, her legs spreading, inviting him to settle between her thighs.

His low chuckle was not reassuring.

"I have a surprise for you, love."

Movement, which she could hear but not immediately interpret. Then something hard closed around her nipple, pinched as tightly as his fingers ever did... and held. Tighter than any of the clips he'd used on her before. The pressure was intense, painful, and yet fed the ache of her arousal, the height of her pleasure. The process was repeated on the other nipple, making her gasp and writhe at the twin bites of pain, the exquisite agony that left her shuddering and wanting to beg for the pressure to be released. Something light but hard rested along the underside of each breast, attached to whatever was tormenting her nipples.

"What are they?" she asked, shuddering as Benedict's fingers glided over the tip of each trapped bud. The sensation was shockingly intense, startlingly pleasurable against the backdrop of sexual pain and excitement.

"Stop thinking," he said, rather than answering her question. Hands lifted her up and turned her over, settling her on her knees and forearms so that her breasts hung low beneath her. Whatever was on her nipples tugged as gravity pulled at them, like weights, sending another hot flash of pain and pleasure through her. "Just feel."

Fingers traced down her spine, into the cleft between her buttocks and over her tiny rosebud. Christina shuddered, the little hole automatically clenching as he teased it. The pad of his finger rubbed, sensation tingling outward from the small, sensitive star, her pussy pulsing beneath.

His finger moved away, hands pressing open her bottom cheeks, and he *licked her there*. She cried out in shock. It was a hot, sensual assault, a height of depravity she'd never dreamed of, and it felt so wickedly good. Her body jerked in response, making her breasts sway, her nipples tugging and sparking with pain at the movement.

Pressing her face against the mattress, she moaned, shuddering, losing herself in the perverted sensations as Benedict's tongue probed her forbidden hole, his hands kneading her bottom all the while. She desperately wanted his touch a few inches lower, and yet she didn't want him to stop what he was doing either.

When he did pull away, she mewled in disappointment, her bottom wagging as cool air drifted over the wet little hole. Was this it? Was he going to plunge his cock into that dark aperture, the way she knew he desperately wanted to?

A sharp pinch on the left lip of her pussy, shocking in its unexpectedness and the harsh bite, made her cry out with shock and pain. Immediately, a matching pinch followed on her right pussy lip. It hurt, but it felt good too as her pussy swelled in response. Fire lanced through her. More pinches followed and her body was caught somewhere between heaven and hell, so she didn't even know any more if she was experiencing pain or pleasure.

~

THE NEW SPRING-CLOTHESPINS were everything Benedict had hoped for and more. He'd first heard of their possible use in the bedroom from a friend, the Earl of Spencer who had a reputation as an utterly depraved rake. The man had reformed in some respects - his proclivities were now confined to his wife - but he was still quite open among his friends about new inventions which could be used in bedroom sport.

The springs allowed him to tightly clamp the rosy buds of her nipples without completely crushing them. The light wood, tightly gripping those darkening pink tips, looked sinful. Even more so, the darkening pink of her swelling pussy lips as he lined the outer lips with clamps, starting from the back of her pussy near her glossy anus and moving towards the front where her clit was poking through her damp curls.

He left a little space between each pin on her lips, allowing her darkening flesh to swell between them. With each one placed, he swore he could see her clit actually grow a little more. Between her folds, her cream was flowing freely, turning her pink petals glossy as the sweet scent of her musk wafted through the air.

Speech seemed to have deserted her as he tormented her succulent, sensitive flesh; the unholy noises she made were completely incoherent, soft ululations, whimpers, and sharper cries as he practiced his sadistic urges on her submissive form. Every sobbing sound wrung from her sent another surge of blood flowing to his cock, which was rampantly hard again, eager to plunge into her decorated pussy.

When he reached her clit, she finally used real words again as he positioned the clothespin on the little bud and very, very slowly began to let it clamp down.

"No! Oh god... Benedict... nooooo... please... I can't take it... I can't... I can't.... ooooAAAAHHH!"

Her shrill scream as the clothespin finally pinched closed around her sensitive organ was caught somewhere between ecstasy and anguish. She sobbed, she shuddered, and she was nearly insensate, caught right on the edge of orgasm but too wracked with the pain of having that tiny bundle of sensations so tightly gripped.

Benedict loved to draw out his sensual torture, to wind her tighter and tighter until she exploded. What he'd done in the carriage, while enjoyable, hadn't been quite enough for him. This was infinitely more satisfying. Reducing her to a quivering, submissive mass of need, completely vulnerable to him, completely under his control, satiated the dark need which had gripped him tonight as he'd watched her dance with man after man.

Tomorrow, no matter whom else she spoke with, whom she danced with, she would feel the after effects of tonight - the imprint of Benedict upon her body.

As she struggled with the sensations coursing through her, shivering and shuddering, tugging at her bound wrists, Benedict took the opportunity to swiftly divest himself of the rest of his clothing and take out the next box of surprises from his nightstand. A small vial of olive oil and a box of Dr. Young's Rectal Dilators were something he'd been holding onto for a while. While they were intended to be used medically, he knew he wasn't the only gentleman to have other designs for them.

After using her hairbrush to prod that tender orifice, and her amorous response to it, he'd decided it was time to move beyond his fingers to the dilators. The sturdy rubber bullets came in four different sizes, the largest of which was just as wide in girth as his cock, although it was an inch or so shorter. Picking up the smallest, which was about the size of her hairbrush handle, Benedict spread the oil over its hard surface, watching Christina as her shivers slowed, her whimpers quieting. She had adjusted to the grip of the clothespins, even that most devilish one, although her panting breath indicated she was by no means entirely sanguine about it.

When he pressed the cool, slick tip of the dilator to her anus, her body jerked, and she cried out as all the clothespins wobbled, tugging at her flesh.

"Hold still, love," he said, practically crooning the words, enjoying watching her struggling with all the sensations assaulting her. "The more you move, the more they'll pull."

She moaned, low and almost mournful as he pressed the dilator in a little before drawing it back, working the rubber bullet in a little deeper with each insertion. The tiny opening stretched, and she quivered with the effort not to pull away nor to move towards it. Watching the prod slowly disappearing into her virgin hole, Benedict's cock throbbed, imagining the slick tightness, the incredible heat.

Her pussy glistened wetly, the curls soaked, her lips nearly red now as the flesh bulged between the clothespins lining her slit. Benedict firmly pressed the dilator into her anus completely. The bullet curved in just before flaring out again at the base, keeping her body from swallowing the dilator whole, and the flange now rested between her slightly pinked cheeks, its black base a stark contrast to her creamy skin and juicy, reddened pussy.

Moving quickly, he began to open and remove the clothespins clinging to her lips. Starting from those nearest her anus, he tossed them to the floor, out of the bed and out of the way now they were no longer needed. The compressed flesh began to swell, the indents puffing out, and Christina let out another strangled cry as he neared the one on her clit. From his own experiments, Benedict knew the tingling sensation as blood returned to pinched areas could be quite intense... he could only imagine how it would feel on Christina's most sensitive areas.

SHE WAS LOST in a maelstrom of pain, so close to climax she could practically taste it on her tongue, and yet she hurt... oh god, she hurt. Her pussy was on fire - not immediately as each pinching thing was removed, but a few moments later every area she expected to feel relief started to tingle and sting and burn. It felt like stinging nettles, and yet she was so fraught with arousal some part of her gloried in the torment.

When he removed the pinch on her clit, the tiny bud seemed to tremble, and then utter agony ripped through her as it came to life. She screamed, sobbed, and then screamed again as Benedict's cock suddenly pierced her, stretching open her inner muscles, his body smacking against all the sensitive flesh he'd just tortured. The sensations were keen, sharp, and her nails dug into the sheets as she was pinned down on her knees, his hand pressing down on her lower back to hold her in place as he mounted her.

Her climax exploded without permission as he began to thrust, pain and pleasure melding together in a chaotic symphony, pounding through her with all the force of a freight train. Her entire world dwindled, focused, blackness clouding her mind - or was that still the blindfold, blocking her sight? She didn't even know whether her eyes were open or not, she was just lost...

Lost...

Sensation ruled.

Her senses roiled, Benedict's every movement creating havoc.

He was not gentle.

He rode her, fucked her, ravaged her.

She was so full of him she was choking on it.

The slight burn in her ass was nothing compared to that of her swollen, abused pussy, and yet the feeling of fullness - stuffed to the brim in both of her holes - held as much sway over her as the throbbing, burning, agonizingly pleasurable pulsing of her overly sensitive clit.

The thing in her ass moved, jostled, as her inner muscles squeezed. Every thrust Benedict made into her body smacked against the thing's base, pressing it into her.

As often as he'd dominated her, as often as she'd given up her control to him, she'd never felt so submissive to him... so completely overwhelmed by him, as she did in this moment. She was entirely his,

his to play with, his to conquer, his to claim. Her body throbbed, ached, and reacted to his manipulations, to his dictates, completely at his mercy.

When his hands slid beneath her to cup her breasts, knocking the clips from her tender nipples, she screamed again as another wave of orgasmic bliss rose within her, taking the pain and turning it into that secret, special ecstasy her body produced. She sobbed as he massaged her soft mounds, his hot palms searing her sensitive buds, which felt swollen to three times their size after having been so tightly crushed for so long.

Benedict withdrew and Christina started to slump... but he swiftly turned her over onto her back, her arms still over her head, her distended nipples pointing towards the sky. They burned as her breasts jiggled.

"Oh no...." She cried out as Benedict's cock slid home again, his body pressing firmly against her, his crinkled chest hair abraded her nipples even as the stiff curls round his cock did the same to the poor, abused bud of her clit. Christina writhed, her pussy clamping around him in spasmodic response, her body arching beneath him. "Benedict... oh please... it's too much... I can't... I can't..."

"Hush love, you haven't a choice," he said, groaning as he began to move again - more gently than he had been, but still with firm, sure strokes into her battered pussy. She let out a strangled cry as his mouth pressed against her neck, his teeth nipping at the delicate skin. The tide of her orgasm was already rising again, her body answering his assertion with ecstatic abandon rather than outrage. "Keep that dilator in your pretty ass, or I'll have to put in the next size up."

With his threat delivered, he began to ride her again.

She clenched down, tears sliding from the corners of her eyes at the utterly overwhelmingly intense passion running through her and the sensitivity of her body as he moved his cock powerfully within her. Trying to keep the thing - the dilator - inside her now that his every thrust no longer pressed it in forced her to keep herself tight, her muscles taut... and doing so heightened the sensations of his cock splitting her open, the hot friction of his thrusting, the quivering of her channel around him.

"Oh please..." she begged, writhing, tightening, desperately trying to keep the thing inside her. She could feel Benedict's cock hardening, a steel spike impaling her, his body pressing against her tortured, sensitive parts. It was excruciating. "Oh please, oh please... Benedict *please!*"

He thrust. Pressed. His body rubbed against hers. Abraded her pussy. The pressure on her clit was immense. His hips circled. Ground against her. And white lights sparkled across her vision as her body was wracked with an all-consuming euphoria.

THE INCREDIBLE TIGHTNESS of Christina's pussy, made even tighter by the dilator filling her ass, was an assault on Benedict's self-control. If he hadn't already availed himself of her mouth, the intense sensations of her muscles rippling around him, holding him so snugly, might have had him spilling his seed like a callow youth.

She was a sensual goddess, an irresistible houri, writhing and sobbing with sexual ecstasy. With her red nipples and pussy lips, and the swollen red tip of her clit peeking through her folds against her creamy skin and dark curls, she was a sight to behold... the kind of sight which compelled a man to drop to his knees and worship.

And she was his. All his.

She wouldn't allow him to inflict this manner of pain and pleasure on her bound body unless she truly trusted him.

Completely.

As Christina screamed out her orgasm, her body shuddering beneath him, pussy pulsing around him, Benedict barely had the willpower to pull himself from the hot, shuddering clasp of her willing cunt and wrap his fingers around his cock. Frothy white cum shot from his cock in long ropes, spraying her stomach and breasts, decorating her front with his cream. The sight stirred something primal in him, no matter that he desperately wanted to release inside of her. Seeing her covered in his seed...

A smile curved his lips as he also saw the black dilator, standing out starkly against the sheets between Christina's legs. At some point, during the vigorous pounding, she'd allowed it to slide from her anus. Studying her limp form, her slowly heaving breasts with their red tips, the glisten of sweat making her skin appear pearly, Benedict decided he could probably wring one more orgasm from her this evening.

Picking up the dilator, he didn't say anything, just stood up from the bed and went to where the box was resting on the nightstand. Christina's head turned, following the sound of his movements even though she couldn't see him. A dreamy smile wreathed her lips. She probably thought he was getting up to fetch a cloth to clean her with... which he would - eventually. But he rather liked the idea of taking her to the heights of ecstasy with a dilator in her ass and his cum still on her body.

A new level of depravity for them to explore.

Quickly spreading oil over the dilator the next size up, Benedict returned to the bed, between her legs. A little frown wrinkled her brow, her lips turning down, as Christina blindly turned her head towards him, her elbows bending as she pulled at the cravat tied round her wrists and to the headboard.

"Benedict?" she asked, her voice uncertain.

Between her creamy thighs, her abused pussy was vermilion, still swollen, her clit still erect and brightly colored from its torture. Benedict grinned.

"I told you to keep the dilator in your ass, love," he said, his stern tone at odds with the expression on his face - since she couldn't see him, he needn't worry about hiding the physical signs of his enjoyment.

"But - oh! Oh no..." She groaned, her hips lifting slightly as the dilator pressed to her ass and began to push in. "Oh... Benedict! It feels bigger!"

"It is bigger love," he said wickedly, pushing it in deeper. Since she was already stretched by the previous dilator, he needn't be quite as gentle. Her body accepted the invader, although not comfortably. He could hear the strain in her whimpers, her tired confusion.

Very slowly, he began to fuck her ass with the dilator, inserting and withdrawing nearly the full length of the thing with every stroke. Christina moaned and arched, squirming as the artificial act of sodomy began to stimulate her. When he began to lick at her creamy pussy and she realized his full intent, she begged him to stop, swearing she couldn't possibly climax again.

Fifteen minutes later she was begging him *not* to stop as he used the dilator to ream her, thrusting mercilessly, his tongue laving her swollen clit, as he proved her wrong.

CHAPTER 8

"Oh..." Christina whimpered as she lowered herself into her bath.

She was so tired of whimpering, but she couldn't seem to stop.

Every muscle in her body hurt. Muscles she hadn't known she *had* hurt. The carriage ride home had been acutely uncomfortable, even after Benedict had hauled her onto his lap and set about soothing her... and she'd only been half-awake at the time. Unfortunately, he hadn't been able to accompany her inside - if any of her neighbors saw him dropping her at home at dawn there would have been far too much talk. As it was, no one could be sure she hadn't just stayed out very late at Daphne's.

Christina had dropped immediately into her bed, still completely exhausted, and slept until noon. Such a late hour wasn't unusual for a *tonnish* lady, especially not after a major ball, but she rarely rose so late in the day. Today she had slept like the dead until her household finally took it upon themselves to rouse her. She was grateful, as she hated to spend the entire day abed.

Although today she almost wished she had.

She was so tender. She couldn't move without remembering the previous night.

GOLDEN ANGEL

The sensual pain.

The perverse pleasure.

Her violent climaxes.

When Benedict had used the dilator to abuse her rear channel, suckling at her clit all the while, she'd thought she might actually die from the overload of sensations. Indeed, she eventually had - *le petite mort*, as the French called an orgasm. Christina had practically fainted after he'd driven her to her third orgasm of the evening.

She'd been insensible when he'd finally wiped down her trembling stomach and breasts with a warm, damp cloth. Although she did remember whimpering when he'd run the cloth over her nipples and pussy, which were still sore and a much darker color pink than they usually were.

She'd never be able to look at a laundry line again without blushing.

The things Benedict had done with those clothespins... pure wickedness. It exercised her imagination... what she must have looked like! But then her inner muscles would tremble, rather than clench, and she'd find herself whimpering again.

Although the hot bathwater felt lovely on her sore muscles, she found it rather stung her more sensitive bits. Which aroused her all over again, even more than her memories. Sighing, she slid further into the water, leaning back against the sloped curve of the tub, and allowed herself to just relax.

Lady Carmichael's musicale was this afternoon and Lady Winslow's ball was this evening but neither were major events. Christina could reasonably cry off, claiming a headache.

Even if that was the one part of her body which *didn't* ache.

DEPARTING the house before they could be dragooned into going to an afternoon of debutantes demonstrating their musical talents in a bid to catch a husband - although, this early in the Season it was more practice for later, more well-attended events - Benedict and Isaac

BENEDICT'S COMMANDS

hied off to White's, congratulating each other on their escape. Last year they'd been obliged to take turns escorting Arabella to such events, to ensure she made the right kind of connections - their great-aunt had tried, but she had not made a forceful enough chaperone for such a wily and spirited young woman. This year they were able to leave such outings to Lydia, but she had the unfortunate view that they should still be her and Arabella's escort to at least some of the events.

It was well enough for Isaac, who was no longer a matrimonial prospect and could hide behind his wife's skirts when the bored ladies of the *ton* approached to see if he might be interested in non-matrimonial prospects, but for Benedict such gatherings were near torture. Not only was he besieged by both the marriage-minded and those interested in clandestine liaisons, but either could easily queer his pitch when it came to Christina. And on top of all that was the deadly dull nature of musicales and afternoon teas themselves.

Arabella thought they were deadly dull too, but she went because Lydia said they must. Gentlemen on the hunt for a bride often indicated their earnest intent by their attendance to such events, which other gentlemen assiduously avoided.

Benedict was grateful his own intended bride was no debutante and thus he was spared that particular torment. Having an actual appreciation for music only made musicales more tedious, as very few debutantes had any real acumen, and even less possessed true talent.

On the way to White's, he and Isaac caught up chatting about business, Isaac's current interest in railways and Benedict's investments in the Funds. When Isaac slyly asked how Benedict's courtship was proceeding, he made a face.

Despite Christina's response to him last night and her utter trust in him, he had no idea whether or not he was making any headway into changing her mind on the subject of marriage. Trusting him with her body was one thing, trusting him with her future was another.

"There's always Gretna Green," Isaac said, chuckling at his brother's misery. Much as Benedict had chuckled at Isaac when he'd been trapped into marriage by Lydia. Obviously, if Lydia had been a social-climbing, gold-digging harridan, it wouldn't have been funny, but since she'd been quite clearly *not*, both Benedict and Arabella had enjoyed the entire situation immensely.

"As she reminded me, she would still have to utter the requisite vows," Benedict said with an exasperated sigh. "Something she's currently still unwilling to do."

"You didn't actually bring up Gretna Green to her?" Isaac asked, now outright laughing at him. Benedict shot him a darkling look as they entered White's, the soothing dark paneled wood and masculine furnishings soothing at least some of his nerves. There was certainly something to be said for a purely masculine retreat, especially when a gentleman was feeling in need of bolstering. The majordomo bowed them in, his keen gaze flicking over their attire with approval.

In the corner of the main room, Thomas Hood, eldest son of Viscount Hood, waved his hand in greeting, causing the men he was sitting with to turn and look. His youngest brother Felix was with him as well as the Earl of Spencer. Felix made a beckoning motion, which Isaac and Benedict were more than happy to respond to. The whole group of them had become rather close last year; Felix had married Arabella's best friend Gabrielle, but not before the two ladies had led all of them on a merry dance. Gabrielle's guardian had requested help from several of his friends, including Spencer, when it came to curbing Gabrielle's wilder starts, and the men had combined forces with Benedict and Isaac after the two young ladies had befriended each other.

The gentlemen had still felt outnumbered at times.

Now the men were all fast friends, and Benedict and Isaac knew they could still rely on the Hoods' assistance when it came to Arabella. After all, the connection was even more solid, as Gabrielle had married Felix.

Gathered en masse in the corner of White's, they were a gathering which would cause any group of women to fan themselves and possibly even swoon – and not just because of their social positions. Like Benedict and Isaac, Felix and Thomas greatly resembled each other with their black hair and eyes, although Felix had a less serious mien and a more ready smile - a smile which had supported his rakish ways before his marriage. Thomas tended to be more severe, both in personality and looks, especially his fashion, which was practically minimalist, from the gleaming Hessian boots he preferred to his highly-starched, simply-tied cravat.

In contrast to their well-turned out dark looks, Spencer appeared even more roguish than he normally did. His sun-streaked brown hair, which was held back in a queue as it was too long to be fashionable, and rumpled clothes made him appear almost piratical. That dangerous air had made him one of the *ton's* foremost rakes before his marriage to the ravishing Lady Cynthia - now he spent his time keeping his wild wife under his control. Altogether, they made for a rather disparate group, with Isaac falling out as the largest and most forceful among a group of rather dominant men, and Benedict landing somewhere in the middle of all the extremes, yet they all got along very well.

Once the requisite greetings were completed, and Benedict and Isaac had each ordered a drink from a passing waiter, Felix immediately took charge of the conversation.

"Not that we aren't always glad for your company, but I must admit, Thomas and I have an ulterior motive today," he said with a sidelong glance at his brother, whose expression didn't change one iota. "Wesley has already agreed to assist us." The Earl of Spencer made a face but nodded.

Benedict's curiosity was roused. There weren't too many duties Spencer would consider onerous. He'd rather enjoyed helping thwart Arabella and Gabrielle last Season - his wife had immediately found a kindred spirit in the two of them and enjoyed their friendship as well.

"What is Mrs. Hood up to now?" he asked Felix, teasing him, and surprising a laugh out of Thomas.

"It's not Gabrielle, it's my mother, Lady Hood who has requested our assistance," Thomas said, his face falling back into its serious lines. He'd be a more handsome man if he smiled more. "She's sponsoring our cousin, Miss Mary Wilson, for her first Season and is determined to launch her in a spectacular manner. We've been called upon to lend our assistance, including rounding up our friends to fill out her dance card."

"And if those specially chosen friends included such lofty personages as a Duke, a Marquess, and an Earl, all the better," Felix said, his voice taking on a slightly plummy tone in imitation of his mother's directives. He chuckled and his voice returned to normal.

The reason for Spencer's lack of enthusiasm was quite clear - doing the pretty for a debutante was not an exciting favor.

"Is she an antidote?" Benedict asked, grunting as Isaac kicked him. It might not be a polite question, but he was curious.

True to the older brother / younger brother dynamic, Thomas frowned at him while Felix laughed. Although, Spencer laughed too and he was the eldest of three brothers... but then, he was an original. It didn't make Isaac and Thomas any less stuffy though.

"She's pleasant enough. Takes after our uncle rather than our aunt, reddish hair and greenish eyes, although she does have our mother's nose. Quite pretty really, as long as she stays away from pink," Felix said. Thomas' stern look didn't faze him at all.

"Being unused to town she's a bit shy," Thomas said. "That's not necessarily a bad attribute however; she's quite sweet."

"You just like her because she's quiet and does whatever she's told," Felix said baldly. He rolled his eyes. "She's a bit boring, to be honest, but the comparison might not be entirely fair since next to Gabrielle just about any debutante would have been boring."

"Other than my wife, which is why she was never allowed to become one," Spencer murmured, causing Benedict to choke on his drink. The Earl grinned and winked at him.

Gads. Lady Cynthia as a debutante... the mind boggled. She was barely passable as the Countess of Spencer, in large part due to the Dowager-Countess' power within the *ton*, the Earl's reputation as an Original anyway, and the cache which came from being able to ensnare the ton's foremost rake and keep him ensnared. If she'd ever had a Season she would have set the *ton* on its head and very likely been ruined within a week. Although, with her beauty and dowry, some poor sod would have offered for her anyway, and probably spent the rest of his life wondering just where he'd gone wrong. While she was perfect for Spencer, any other gentleman would have probably been at a loss with how to deal with her.

"Of course we'll help," Isaac said, addressing Thomas and ignoring the other three. He also ignored Benedict's slight kick to his ankle for volunteering him. Benedict wouldn't have said no, but he might have held out just to torture Thomas for a bit. Felix would have appreciated the effort. "When's her come-out ball?"

"You should receive the invitation sometime later this week," Thomas said, as deadly serious about his cousin's debut ball as he was about everything. "But we'll be at the Richmond's ball on Friday of course."

"Then we shall make our bows there," Isaac said instantly, and this time Benedict really did feel like kicking his brother, and not just on the ankle. The Richmonds' ball was the opening event to the height of the Season; everyone would be there and the large house with a crush in attendance was the perfect venue to disappear in for some intimacies. He had plans for the Richmonds' ball and they'd all involved Christina but... inwardly he sighed. They did owe Thomas and Felix for their help with watching over Arabella last Season. Perhaps he could claim one of the earliest dances and then hunt down Christina. "I'm sure Lydia and Arabella will be thrilled to meet her."

The corner of Thomas' mouth tugged down at the mention of Arabella, as it always did. Although he very obviously cared for his sister-in-law, he was of the opinion her friendship with Arabella did neither of them any good. After all, Gabrielle couldn't have gotten away with half her mischief if it hadn't been for Arabella - and the other way round.

"She could use a little livening up, honestly," Felix said. "I think Gabrielle and Arabella's company could be good for her."

"Or perhaps she might rub off on them," Thomas murmured repressively. He shrugged off his brother's dark look. "Gabrielle has been much better behaved since you married her, I'll admit. But I still don't trust they won't get into trouble." He glanced at Spencer. "Especially with Lady Cynthia added into the mix."

Spencer smiled. "I can dance with your chit or I can hover over my wife and ensure her good behavior, but I can't do both at once."

"You dance with the boring cousin, *I'll* hover over your wife," Benedict said with a leer. Snorting with laughter and completely unthreatened, Spencer balled up a napkin and threw it at him.

"Boys," Isaac said in pretend warning, but with a real stern glance. Some ribaldry was expected at White's, but it was possible to be removed from the premises if they became too rowdy.

"She's not boring," Thomas muttered, glaring at his brother, obviously blaming Felix for the moniker. "She's not a troublemaker and that's a *good thing*."

"How many points on your list does she fulfill?" Benedict asked, curious.

Thomas, as first son of a viscount, had been eyeing the herd of marriage-minded misses for over a year now, without managing to settle on a single young lady upon which to bestow his favor. He did, however, have a list of requirements that he wished the paragon who would become his wife must meet.

"Quite a few of them," Thomas said, with more seriousness than the teasing question truly deserved. "She doesn't like to ride though, and seems to prefer Gothic romances over any literary works of substance." A faint look of confused disgust passed over his countenance, amusing Benedict even further. He wondered if it occurred to Thomas that most ladies either said they preferred Gothic romances or else they tended to be labeled blue-stockings. Arabella rather enjoyed adventure novels, although she knew better than to admit so in polite Society; such works were usually considered unseemly for young ladies.

"I don't know how you can say she fits your requirements when we barely know the chit," Felix said, shaking his head. "She barely speaks enough for one *to* know her."

"Yes, she's very restful."

Boring. Felix mouthed the word at Benedict with a roll of his eyes.

Benedict could only agree. While he was glad Christina didn't have the same wild starts as his sister, she certainly didn't sit quietly without speaking her opinion or offering up her views either. As much as he loved and worshiped her body, without enjoying her company he'd never have considered marrying her.

As it was, half his thoughts about their future involved scenes of discussions over the breakfast table, enjoying each other's company at plays and the opera, and aspects of the daily life he wanted to lead with her. The other half of his thoughts were much more lascivious and involved expounding upon memories he already had. Like the previous night.

He had enjoyed debauching her so thoroughly, although returning her home had been a wrench. One day soon, he was determined he would not need to do so. Instead he'd be able to keep her in his bed and tend to all her aches and tenderness the next day. At least he knew she'd be thinking about him all day today, just as he was her.

A question from Spencer recalled him to the conversation, which had moved on to a particularly fine piece of horseflesh the Earl had seen at Tattersall's, and Benedict pushed thoughts of Christina aside for now. He'd stop by to check on her later.

LOOKING in the mirror at herself, Christina bit her lower lip.

She was incredibly nervous. After her evening with Benedict, she'd avoided him completely. The man unnerved her. He'd stopped by the afternoon following, but she'd already told her butler that she was not at home to anyone. The next day she'd made herself go out, so as to truly not be at home. He'd left his calling card each day, so she knew he'd still come by.

Christina had been out busy making the most thorough rounds of her life; visiting all sorts of households where she usually did no more than leave her card. She was constantly on the move, suffering through some visits, surprisingly delighted by others, all to avoid being in one place for too long or adhering to her customary routine.

Daphne knew her usual rounds far too well and had already proven she couldn't be trusted.

In the evenings she did much of the same, successfully avoiding both Daphne and Benedict by accepting invitations last minute and appearing at multiple venues. More than once an acquaintance remarked that the Marquess of Dearborn was said to be asking after her. It felt like a game of cat and mouse, except she derived no excitement from it, only a worried feeling of anxiety...

She wasn't trying to hide from Benedict, not truly. If anything, she was trying to hide from herself. From her desires. After what they'd shared the other night... she didn't know if she could see him without throwing herself at him. She wasn't sure she could maintain the proper distance, the proper control over herself.

If he'd held out an offer of marriage again...

There was every possibility she wouldn't be able to resist. Time had been needed to think. Time away from him.

And knowing he'd been searching for her, among the many events, bolstered her trust in him. Perhaps it was unkind to make him chase her, but she truly hadn't been ready to see him yet, and it did feel nice to know he'd pursued her despite the obstacles and her retreat.

Tonight she could no longer hide. It was the Duchess of Richmond's ball and there were no other major social events within high society - not making an appearance was unacceptable. Tonight signaled the beginning of the Season in earnest, with all of the *ton* who were in London, kicking off the frenzied series of larger events.

She'd dressed to impress.

The amethyst gown with its silver lace netting overlay made the most out of her figure, the corset pushing her breasts up like pillowy offerings. Her shoulders were completely bare, her sleeves nothing more than little puffs of chiffon with an inch of skin between them and her long white gloves. She wore matching jewelry of amethysts set in silver, wrapping around her throat and wrists, dangling from her ears, and winking from the elaborate creation of curls and feathers atop her head.

BENEDICT'S COMMANDS

It was an outfit meant to draw attention, to flaunt. Certainly the neckline was the most daring she'd ever warn, drawing a deep breath felt positively perilous.

A knock at her door nearly made her jump.

"My lady?" Mrs. Jones, her housekeeper opened the door. "Lord Marley's carriage has arrived."

"Thank you, Mrs. Jones," Christina said, and smiled as Esther immediately came forward with her silver lace shawl, draping it over Christina's shoulders as a finishing touch to the dress.

"You look lovely, my lady," Esther said, dimpling as she bobbed a little curtsy. "If I do say so myself."

"Thanks to your efforts," Christina said with a smile, her hand drifting up to pat her hair. "Take the rest of the evening off, I can tend to myself when I return, or I may spend the night at Daphne's afterwards."

"Thank you, my lady!" The maid fairly glowed with excitement.

The truth was, Christina was hoping Benedict might sweep her away again or even return here with her, and she didn't want Esther's sensibilities taxed. But the maid deserved a night off anyway, she'd been running herself ragged all afternoon and she truly had done amazing work on Christina's hair with the hot iron.

Taking her reticule from the eager maid, Christina swept downstairs and out the door to the waiting carriage where Anthony and Daphne eagerly greeted her. Anthony was handsomely turned out, his black suit and bronze waistcoat, his impeccably starched cravat tied in a perfect *Trone d'Amour* knot. Wearing a green dress with bronze trim, emeralds set in gold shimmering around her neck and bringing out the green of her eyes, Daphne was just as splendid. Her neckline appeared even lower than Christina's, as if the slightest movement might make the fabric slip and reveal a pink nipple. From the way Anthony kept eyeing his wife, it was clear he appreciated the view. Christina knew he wouldn't mind other men looking either - he seemed to find it very satisfying that they could look while he was quite secure they would never touch.

They chatted quite companionably, Daphne and Christina

catching up as they had barely seen each other the past few days. Daphne slyly dropped a few hints about Benedict's search of her, which Christina pretended to ignore. There was a reason she hadn't spent much time with her friend - she was quite sure Daphne couldn't be trusted when it came to matchmaking attempts. After all, it had been Daphne who had "accidentally" sent Christina's carriage home from her ball without its mistress.

She couldn't prove Daphne's intent, but she strongly suspected it.

Still, considering how matters had fallen out, she couldn't be angry either. It was nice to catch up with her friend though, especially since once they arrived at the ball they certainly wouldn't be able to speak privately. Anthony stayed mostly silent, listening with amusement to their blathering, although he occasionally dropped in an observation.

The line of carriages at Richmond house was quite long, and by the time they were announced and entered the ballroom, the dancing had already started. Thus, Christina's first sight of Benedict in days was him leading a young, unknown miss out onto the dance floor. It felt as if all the air in her lungs suddenly seized, her chest aching, and for a moment she thought she might actually faint.

CHAPTER 9

*W*aiting for Christina to arrive had Benedict on pins and needles. Lady Daphne, whom he'd become a rather regular correspondent with over the past few days, had informed him Christina would be arriving to the Richmond's ball with her and her husband.

As a close connection to Isaac, Benedict and the rest of the family had been invited to the dinner preceding the ball, which meant they were on hand from the beginning and had far too much time to wait. The Hood family had arrived quite early, nearly on time, and introductions to Miss Mary Wilson had immediately been made. Viscount Hood had taken her out for her first dance, once the music had begun.

Knowing what time Daphne planned to arrive, Benedict had hoped to secure Miss Wilson's hand for either the second or third dance - more likely the third, behind Thomas - so he would be completely unencumbered by duties by the time Christina arrived, but unfortunately Spencer was faster on the draw. Benedict claimed Miss Wilson's fourth dance - although he quickly asked Lady Cynthia to stand up with him for the third, the one Spencer would be dancing with Miss Wilson.

Actually quite fetching in appearance, Miss Wilson was as meek and shy as Felix had claimed, although she did begin to blossom a bit under the combined attentions of the ladies. She was very much a country miss, despite the highly fashionable dress the Viscountess had picked out for her, and seemed a bit overwhelmed by all the gentlemen surrounding her. Benedict felt rather sorry for her, as she was obviously much more comfortable with the other young women and completely at a loss when it came to interacting with high born, rakish gentlemen. Even Spencer's charm seemed to intimidate her more than set her at ease.

Almost as one, the gentlemen managed to step back and set themselves slightly apart from the group, creating a separate circle of conversation which still hovered around the ladies. While she was slightly more relaxed with her cousins, and certainly with her uncle the Viscount, Miss Wilson seemed to practically sigh with relief at the tiny amount of space.

One eye on the top of the staircase where newcomers were being announced, Benedict kept up with the conversation as best he could, mostly news about absent friends. Hyde and his wife had decided to stay in the country for the Season with his parents as Lady Hyde was increasing again and having a particularly bad time of it - Benedict interpreted Spencer's oblique remarks to mean she was having trouble keeping down most of what she ate. She wasn't the only one increasing, although Lady Cordelia and Dunbury were in town for the Season as she wasn't showing yet. The only reason Benedict knew was because Gabrielle had told Arabella. Lady Brooke had finally provided Lord Brooke with an heir last year but they'd just had a second child, a daughter, a few months ago, so it was unlikely either of them would come up for the Season. Petersham and his wife were traveling on the continent; although they'd certainly be back before the end of Season, after their first extended trip away from their daughter it was doubtful they'd be coming to London.

Which left Benedict, Isaac, the Hood brothers, Spencer, and Dunbury to watch over the ladies. Although Arabella and Miss Wilson were the only ones unwed, rakes still eyed the married ladies, hoping their husbands may have lost interest in them over the last year, making them more amenable to a dalliance. Spencer, in particular, sent the more dangerous blades some savage looks when they dared circle closer - Lady Cynthia was a particularly attractive young woman, and with Spencer's previous reputation not everyone believed in his reformation. It didn't help that Lady Cynthia obviously enjoyed provoking her husband's possessiveness either - much as he would when approached by ladies interested in testing his reformation. More than once last Season, the Spencers had disappeared during a ball or rout to express their possessiveness and commitment to each other.

When it came time for Benedict's dance with Miss Wilson, Christina and the Marleys still hadn't arrived which made him rather anxious. Still, he made an elegant bow to Miss Wilson before offering his arm as she gave him a tremulous smile. It was as he was escorting her to the dance floor that the Earl and Countess of Marley, accompanied by the Marchesse of Stanhope, were finally announced.

Immediately his head swiveled around to see Christina, drinking in the sight of her in a stunning gown of purple and silver which clung to her curves and dipped very low over her breasts. He was so taken by the sight of her glowing pale skin that he nearly tripped over Miss Wilson's skirts, and only then could he tear his eyes away.

"My apologies, Miss Wilson," he said, trying to focus on her instead of looking back to the staircase where Christina was descending. She was finally *here*, a few more minutes to actually speak to her was not long to wait, and he should give the poor, shy debutante the attention she deserved. "A friend of mine, whom I'm eager to see, has arrived and I became distracted."

"The Earl of Marley?" Her question was so soft he almost thought he'd imagined it.

"He is more of an acquaintance actually. The Marchesse of Stanhope is a... ah, good friend of mine."

Miss Wilson finally managed to raise her gaze to meet his as they positioned themselves on the dance floor, his hand in hers, greenish hazel eyes curious. She opened her lips and then closed them again, apparently unable to actually voice whatever question she had on her mind.

Trying to set her at ease, Benedict explained. "I hope to make her my bride, actually."

"Oh!" Miss Wilson's eyes grew even larger as the dance started and then, to his surprise, he felt her relax slightly. Sending her a curious look as they began the steps, he wasn't entirely surprised to see her blush, although her next whispered words did give him a bit of a jolt. "My aunt made a particular point of informing me you weren't married."

He blinked, startled, and then chuckled. He supposed he shouldn't be shocked that Lady Hood had an eye on him as a possible connection; after all, he had become good friends with her sons, was still single, and an attractive marriage prospect. Felix had told him she was thrilled with Gabrielle as daughter-in-law, but she was even more elated to have a young lady to fire off herself. No doubt she would be the most terrifying of matchmaking-guardians this Season.

"Well, I'm sorry to disappoint your aunt, but I'm quite intent I'm afraid," he said, giving Miss Wilson his most charming smile, so she understood she was not being rejected for herself.

She smiled back at him, just a tiny curve of her lips, still shy but apparently a touch less so. They finished out the dance without much more conversation, as answering questions seemed to tax her, and she wasn't quite able to dare any of her own. He could understand now why the Viscountess had tasked her sons with engaging their friends to help launch the poor girl; she was so shy it was almost crippling, and apparently the smaller events preceding the Richmond ball hadn't helped bolster her confidence. More worrying - perhaps they had and he was experiencing a more polished version of Miss Wilson. No wonder Felix found her boring; he much preferred a lady who would make conversation with him. He and his wife bickered and teased as much as they talked, and that was just how he liked it.

Escorting a relieved Miss Wilson back to her chaperone, Benedict looked around the ballroom, trying to locate Christina again. When his eyes finally found the purple feathers waving from her auburn hair, a thunderous scowl descended over his features.

What the devil was she doing talking with that rogue Hartford? Not just smiling, but smiling up at him flirtatiously?! How did he even get in here? Benedict knew he hadn't been announced; the resulting stir would have stopped the *ton* in its tracks. Gritting his teeth, Benedict picked up the pace a little, he needed to return Miss Wilson to the Viscountess, post haste, so he could focus on his own affairs.

"STOP BEING DRAMATIC," Daphne hissed in Christina's ear. "Just because he is dancing with a debutante, that does *not* mean he's thrown you over. It does *not* indicate anything about his marital goals. And it certainly does *not* mean you should make completely unfounded and illogical assumptions!"

A small voice inside of Christina agreed with everything Daphne said, but Christina had listened to that voice before. It was the same voice that had insisted her husband's late-night absences were just due to carousing with friends. The same voice had said it was completely natural for a couple to stop being so much in each other's pockets after a few months of marriage. The same voice which had always had some kind of rational, reasonable explanation for everything George had done. It was a voice that encouraged blind trust, and she already knew how that story ended.

She'd somehow managed to get a grip on herself and make the awful descent down the staircase while Benedict danced with the young debutante. He'd seen her come in, she knew he had, but he hadn't glanced at her again since that moment.

The little voice inside her head said good manners - and the movements of the dance - necessitated his focus.

The little voice could go drown itself in the duck pond as far as she was concerned.

"Good evening, Lady Daphne." The voice was deep and unfamiliar, a lazy drawl that hooked Christina's attention out of her unhappy ruminations. A very handsome, very large man was bowing over Daphne's hand, although his eyes were on Christina. His very unusually colored eyes; they were so amber they were nearly golden, half-lidded. With his tawny blonde hair and those exceptional eyes, he looked almost leonine, especially when he smiled wickedly at her. Despite her upset over Benedict, she felt a blush rising in her cheeks.

"Rex, what are you doing here?" Daphne asked, obviously befuddled. "You never come to these events."

Which begged the question of which events he did attend - very likely those of the demimonde, Christina realized. There were quite a few rakes and rogues who preferred the wilder events where polite society (and debutantes) never ventured. There were also some whose preferences didn't matter, as they were barred from polite society. Obviously, this Rex was either not so scandalous as to be barred - or he was of high enough birth to overcome whatever reputation he had. Since Christina didn't recognize his face or his impertinent nickname, she had no idea which.

"Amusing myself," he said, glancing at Daphne before returning to his perusal of Christina. "Introduce me to your dazzling friend."

Christina rather expected Daphne to give him a set down - her friend was not one for being dictated to by anyone but her husband - but Daphne shocked her. She was obviously reluctant to perform the demanded introduction, but she did it anyway.

"Rex, this is Lady Christina Rowan, Marchesse of Stanhope. Christina, this is Lord Michael Seymour, the Marquess of Hartford."

Christina's jaw dropped open in shock as the Marquess bowed over her hand, his eyes sparkling with mirth. The Marquess of Hartford was one of the most notorious members of Society - possibly *the* most - and the least visible. Rumors about him abounded. He'd supposedly been involved in at least twelve duels over other men's wives, emerging completely unscathed from each one. He was supposedly as rich as Croesus, as handsome as Adonis, and as charming as Lucifer. Right now, Christina could certainly confirm the latter two.

In the same way as Benedict and Lord Marley, Hartford had a very confident, authoritarian air about him, which was well deserved. Many said he had more power than a Duke when he chose to wield it, as he was a particular friend of Prinny's and had vouchers for debts from any number of influential figures.

From behind his shoulder, Daphne widened her eyes at Christina and shook her head. A warning. One which Christina shouldn't treat lightly, as Daphne knew him well enough to call him by a nickname. Or was it a kind of title? Rex did mean King after all, and she knew Anthony and Daphne sometimes moved in *very* different circles than most - very secretive, very scandalous circles. If Hartford reigned as king there...

Even if all her thoughts were incorrect, he was still scandal personified. And Christina was already feeling a little reckless. That tiny voice in the back of her mind reminded her that Benedict had arrived, and he would *not* be pleased at the company she was keeping. Another voice answered back - that was *his* problem, if he had it, the great bloody hypocrite.

"Lady Christina." Her name was a purr in Hartford's mouth, his fingers holding hers firmly as he bowed over them. "It is my utmost pleasure. If I'd known such a stunning gem decorated the *ton*'s ballrooms, I would have returned to them much sooner."

Cocking her head to the side, Christina looked brazenly back at him. She was not shocked by his forwardness - after all, she was a widow - or even by his focused attentions. She could not deny some part of her felt drawn to him. If she wasn't already quite so involved with Benedict, she would certainly be willing to flirt back with him.

As it was, she didn't currently know where she stood with Benedict, and it was that uncertainty which had her hesitating. If Benedict truly was about to show himself to be false, if he had now reconsidered his proposal and protestations to Christina, then this man might very well be the kind of distraction which could ease her broken heart. Like Benedict, he seemed like the kind of man who would be demanding in the bedchamber, as well as vigorous, no matter how lazy and lion-like he endeavored to appear.

She did not like to think of herself as the kind of woman who would keep a man on a string but… if Benedict was about to break her heart, then some comforting and distraction and reaffirmation of her attractiveness would be most welcome. That was something she had learned after she'd been made aware of George's betrayal.

"Thank you, my lord," Christina said finally, keeping her voice appreciative but not sultry. She forced herself to meet his eyes, ignoring the urge to drop her gaze when faced with a predator. "Considering your usual nonattendance, that is quite the compliment."

Daphne frowned furiously, her fan starting to silently tap against the skirts of her dress in consternation as the marquess began to chuckle. His grip on Christina's fingers tightened.

"I do believe I hear the violins readying," he said. "Come, dance with me."

It wasn't until Christina had her hand on his arm that she realized he hadn't asked - he'd ordered. And she'd obeyed. Daphne looked near to having an apoplexy, but didn't speak. Her eyes had darted across the room though, and she paled. Christina turned her head to follow Daphne's gaze and saw Benedict making his way through the crowd towards them.

Flashing a brilliant smile at the Marquess, Christina felt more than a little smug. After all, what was sauce for the gander was sauce for the goose.

THERE WAS nothing to do but watch as Hartford led Christina out onto the dance floor, creating a stir as they passed and the *ton* realized its most notorious and powerful Marquess was in attendance - without being properly announced. And that he was escorting the Marchesse of Stanhope to the floor - the same Marchesse whom Dearborn had been honorably and openly pursuing. Immediately all eyes turned to him, but then looked away again when they met nothing but a bored expression.

Thankfully, having two intelligent and observant siblings had blessed Benedict with acting skills he might not have otherwise had.

All three of them were masters at pretending to be unaffected by each other's antics, something which had served them in good stead when it came to those outside the family as well.

Feeling a hot angry gaze on his neck, Benedict turned to see Lady Daphne glaring furiously at him. Hmm. Perhaps there was something he could do.

Although, when he approached the lady in question he swiftly regretted it.

"OW!" Who knew a delicate wooden fan could hurt so much, even if it was wielded with all the force of a mace?

"This is your fault," Lady Daphne hissed at him, glaring malevolently. Her gaze cut to the dance floor where Christina was smiling up at Hartford while he looked down at her like she was particularly tempting crumpet he wanted to taste. "Do something about it! She has no idea what she's getting herself into!"

"You introduced them!"

"I couldn't *not* once he'd made his wishes known! I wouldn't have had to if you had been over here where you were supposed to be and not dancing with some debutante!"

"She's my friend's cousin, I was doing him a favor!"

"Well done, good job, now go *fix this.*"

Another stinging slap of the fan against his arm had him moving quickly away from the countess, as if her sharp tongue hadn't been enough. She reminded him rather strongly of Arabella; but at least now he knew why Christina was dancing with Hartford and not with him -

Christina still didn't trust him.

Which hurt, but he supposed he shouldn't be overly surprised. After all, they hadn't actually been able to speak for several days, and she didn't know about his promise to Thomas. If she hadn't been avoiding him, he would have told her, of course, and spared them both this pain. She was definitely going to receive a spanking for avoiding him, *and not a fun one*, he thought grimly as he tried to maneuver towards the dance floor.

Unfortunately, apparently having danced with Miss Wilson had given the other debutantes and their mamas the idea that he was no longer singularly pursuing Christina, and he found himself blocked at every turn by pale skirts and eager young faces. Tamping down on his temper, Benedict did his best to extricate himself from each encounter politely, but it did mean he didn't make it to the edge of the dance floor by the time the music ended. The couples dispersed, and it took him several more minutes to glimpse Christina again.

As a matter of fact, he saw the tall, broad form of Hartford first. At least the man's size made him stand out - much like Isaac. For just a moment, Benedict amused himself with the idea of standing the two men beside each other to judge which was the taller and broader. His amusement ended when he realized the blaggard was leading Christina out onto the balcony.

There wouldn't be privacy out there, but there wouldn't be as many eyes on them either, and it would be quite easy to take her to even more private surrounds.

Surely Christina wouldn't do that to him, though? Unless she truly thought he was done with her...

As sympathetic as he was to her insecurities, this had to end, Benedict thought grimly. The granite expression on his face must have given away some of his mood, for Lady Dunstead and her daughter halted their approach towards him and didn't attempt to gain his attention; thankfully, because he wasn't sure he could be held responsible for his actions right now.

The surge of possessiveness and nagging uncertainty over Christina's intentions with Hartford were riding him like a demon crouched on his shoulder. One way or another, he was going to make his intentions and his sincerity quite clear to Christina before tonight was over. Isaac's words about Gretna Green kept tumbling through his thoughts.

After all, hadn't he seen how a couple could make the best of things and come out happily on the other side within his own family? Hellfire, not just within his family, but within his group of friends. Felix had married Gabrielle to save her from ruin at the hands of a cad, and they were now utterly devoted to each other. Lord and Lady

Hyde's marriage had been arranged before the lady had even had a full Season as a debutante (she'd barely had a coming out before they'd been hastily wed, although it had quickly become clear there had been no familial need spurring the wedding). Gabrielle had told Arabella that Lady Cordelia had married Dunbury for security after she'd been widowed. And most recently, of course, Isaac had been trapped into a compromising situation by Lydia, which should have gone tits up for both of them but instead they were blissfully happy with each other (granted, not without some struggle along the way, but it all ended well enough).

Perhaps he really was going about this all wrong, trying to convince Christina to trust him so she would marry him. He'd been trying to be patient and undemanding, which really wasn't like him at all. Even when he'd been originally pursuing her he hadn't been undemanding, and while he'd been somewhat patient during that time, he certainly hadn't let her lead him around on a string the way he had been now. She'd been leading him on a delicate little dance, and he'd let her. He hadn't just appeared in her bedroom again, mindful both of the proprieties and her sensibilities... but things certainly went more his way when he ignored the proprieties and pushed the bounds of her sensibilities. Perhaps with Christina things would be easier if marriage came first, so she had no choice but to give him a chance - to try and trust him.

If they were already married, she wouldn't have been able to avoid him for the past few days. She would already know about Miss Wilson and would have herself been recruited to help launch the shy debutante. And she wouldn't be out on the balcony right now with bloody Hartford!

Scowling, Benedict kept pushing through the crush of people, moving as quickly as he could without being completely boorish. Unfortunately, that wasn't very quickly at all.

COMING out onto the balcony had been a mistake. If anything, she felt more melancholy, not less, once Benedict was out of her sight. She'd seen him making his way towards her and wanted to run... so she'd immediately agreed when Hartford made the suggestion they get some fresh air. She wanted Benedict to come bursting out of the French doors and carry her away, discipline her for her avoidance of him. Now she couldn't see him and didn't know whether or not he was actually following, she was terrified he wouldn't.

Hartford certainly seemed intent on seducing her. If Benedict didn't come after her, she very might well let him. Which would likely result in feeling lower than she already did, because it would be her own fault for pushing Benedict too far, but some consolation was better than none, wasn't it?

Strong fingers splayed across her lower back, directing her forward. "Come, my dear, over here."

Christina followed unthinkingly, distracted and anxious, she was even more easily led than usual. Hartford really was very authoritative; even if she'd been paying more attention, she likely would have had difficulty resisting his direction. No wonder Daphne had bowed so quickly to his demands. There was something about him which urged others to do his bidding, an instinctive air of command which everyone followed.

"You seem a bit distracted, sweetheart," he said, coming to a halt near a large potted plant and pivoting to look down at her. "I'm not used to being so unsure of a lady's attention."

"My apologies, my lord," she said, smiling up at him ruefully and suppressing the urge to look at the doors back into the ballroom. Even if Benedict came after her, he'd been more than half a ballroom away from the doors. He'd hardly come bursting through at any moment. "I don't mean to offend you."

"No offense taken, sweet," he said, lifting his hand to brush a tendril of hair away from her temple. Christina shivered, feeling a little bit like a mouse caught by a cat. The Marquess was all predator, stirring arousal in her physically with the intensity of his gaze and the gentle brush of his hand. Her heart might not be in this encounter, but the Marquess obviously knew how to seduce a woman... and his dominant personality was exactly the type she was most attracted to. "It just makes me wonder what I need to do to secure your attention."

His gaze focused on her lips and Christina sucked in a quick breath. Goodness the Marquess was potent... if it weren't for her feelings for Benedict, she'd be very much in danger of being seduced post haste. As it was, if Benedict were through with her, she very well might seek the Marquess out after tonight. Once she was sure. But she shouldn't lead the Marquess on now, when she wasn't truly free to do so.

"I must confess, my lord, my distraction comes from -"

"Lady Christina! How delightful to see you again!" The friendly but firm interruption made Christina jump as Benedict's sister Arabella suddenly materialized at her side. The young woman hooked her arm through Christina's, pulling Christina's hand away from where the Marquess had been holding it. "Who is your friend?"

Oh dear... one thing Christina was sure of was that Arabella should absolutely *not* be introduced to the Marquess. It was one thing for a widow, even one trying to remain respectable, and another thing entirely for a debutante. Just being seen talking to him would probably cause whispers - and the way the Marquess was now sizing Arabella up, his interest obviously engaged by the brazen young woman with her stubbornly tilted chin as she stared back at him, was not good at all.

As if sensing Christina's line of thought, and not wanting his prey to get away, the Marquess bowed deeply. "Michael Seymour, Marquess of Hartford at your service... Miss...?"

"*Lady* Arabella Windham," Arabella said with a sniff, while Christina moaned inwardly, too frozen to stop what was happening right in front of her. What on earth was Benedict's sister doing out here on the terrace by herself? How was Christina supposed to save the young woman and her reputation without insulting the Marquess?

Where was Benedict when she needed him?!

"Lady Arabella." The Marquess held out his hand and - well

trained, Arabella immediately lifted hers. Christina made a strangled noise as he kissed it, his golden gaze studying Arabella's lithe form. "It is a delight to meet your acquaintance."

The young woman flushed pink under the Marquess' close scrutiny, which seemed rather at odds with her usual brash demeanor, but there was something about the Marquess which was really quite unnerving. Apparently, he had that effect on all the ladies.

"Well, ah... that is, the pleasure is mine, I'm sure," Arabella stammered, looking a little stunned as she tried to bob a curtsy, forgetting her arm was still attached to Christina's. The Marquess didn't chuckle as they nearly tumbled, he just took a tighter grip on Arabella's hand to help keep her upright, his head tilting to the side and studying the pair of them. For some reason, Christina got the distinct impression he liked what he saw - which was not entirely reassuring.

"I was just about to speak to Lady Christina about a... gathering I thought might interest her," the Marquess said, speaking to Arabella, who was having a little more trouble meeting his eyes now. "Normally, a young lady such as yourself wouldn't be -"

"Arabella!"

Oh, thank God, another interruption, because Christina hadn't known how to stop whatever the Marquess was going to say, even if she'd managed to find her tongue.

But when she turned and saw who was standing there, she couldn't help almost wishing the interruption hadn't been made at all. The eldest Mr. Hood was glaring at Arabella, looking nearly as foreboding as her eldest brother might have. Christina was not well acquainted with him, but she certainly felt herself shrinking a bit under his censorious gaze, knowing she must surely bear part of the blame for Arabella's current company.

It was his companion who caused her to wish him away, however. Wide eyed, even more beautiful up close, the pocket Venus clinging to his elbow was none other than the young debutante Benedict had been dancing with when Christina had arrived at the ball. Her features were delicate, her face a perfect oval, and she was lushly curved, yet exuded innocence from every pore.

The Marquess barely glanced at her, focusing instead on Mr. Hood, whom he grinned at, completely unrepentant.

"Your brother is looking for you," Mr. Hood said, glaring at Arabella and ignoring the Marquess completely.

"I bet I'm not the only one he's looking for," Arabella mumbled, so quietly only Christina could hear her.

She wanted to sink right into the stones beneath her feet. It hadn't occurred to her that any of Benedict's family members might come chasing after her in his place! Had Arabella actually come out onto the balcony *for her*? To ensure Christina didn't go off with Hartford before Benedict could reach her?

In that case, it really was her fault Arabella had just been introduced to Hartford, no matter how unintentionally.

"What was that?" Mr. Hood asked, managing to loom without taking a step.

"Nothing," Arabella said sulkily, pressing a little closer to Christina as if for comfort. Christina gave the young woman's arm a little squeeze, feeling heartily sorry for her part in putting Arabella in this position.

"You know, Hood, I was just about to discuss my club with the ladies," the Marquess said convivially. "I wouldn't have thought it, but you seem like a gentleman who might fit in well there."

Mr. Hood gave the Marquess an icy look. "I don't think so. Don't you have somewhere else to be?"

With a rakish grin and an even more rakish bow to her and Lady Arabella, followed by a lecherous look down both their persons which left Mr. Hood fuming and all three ladies blushing, the Marquess sauntered away. He'd barely left earshot when Mr. Hood turned on Arabella again, his dark eyes furious.

"What were you doing speaking with him?! Do you have any idea who that was?!" Mr. Hood's voice was low but thick with emotion, his body tense as though he were holding onto control of his temper by inches.

"Michael Seymour, Marquess of Hartford," Arabella said saucily, glaring back at Mr. Hood, completely defiant in the face of his disapproval.

Christina felt suddenly very awkward, as if she were intruding on a private conversation between the two... and she wasn't alone. The pretty debutante was chewing on her lower lip, looking as though she'd rather be anywhere but on Mr. Hood's arm right at this moment. The air between Arabella and Mr. Hood was charged and strangely intimate, despite the obvious animosity between the pair. If Christina didn't know better, she'd think they had an understanding.

HARTFORD STROLLED BACK into the ballroom just before Benedict reached the French doors, and for a moment he almost went after the man... but Christina wasn't with him and finding out where she'd gone was more important. He'd been waylaid by his hostess as he'd passed through the crowd, delaying him even further, although he'd shaken her off as politely and quickly as he could.

Practically bursting onto the terrace, he swung his head around frantically, searching for Christina.

The scene which met his eyes was completely unexpected.

Arabella, her arm hooked through Christina's, was glaring up at Thomas, who was escorting Miss Wilson on his arm. Both Christina and Miss Wilson looked distinctly uncomfortable, unsurprising as they were attached to two people who appeared to be squaring off for combat.

He didn't know how his sister and Thomas had become involved - although he could guess that Arabella saw Christina with Hartford and decided to intervene. Following that line of thought, it wouldn't be surprising if Thomas had spotted Arabella and decided it was *his* duty to intervene on her behalf.

His footsteps slowed as he approached, no longer feeling the need to rush, taking the opportunity to regain control over his emotions (and his breathing). Seeing him coming, Christina's eyes widened and he felt his lips spread in a grim smile. She *should* look wary. Benedict was not feeling particularly patient nor pleased, and he was more than happy to work out his frustrations on her upturned arse. In fact, that'd be his preferred method.

When she started to move away from Arabella it broke the staring contest between his sister and Thomas; the latter looked at him with relief.

"Dearborn! Thank God, come and corral your sister. She was speaking with Hartford!"

"Was she?" Benedict asked, giving his sister a quelling look, which went completely ignored because she was back to glaring at Thomas. He held out his hand to Christina, who hesitantly took it. Their gloves blocked actual skin-to-skin contact, but he still felt immeasurably better the moment he held her hand in his. Not that he was completely soothed, but he no longer felt quite like he was about to reach a tipping point. She was here, with him, where she belonged... and now he had hold of her, he wasn't going to let her go without a fight. "I wonder how she gained an introduction."

Christina's hand trembled in his, her body tensing as he pulled her away from his sister's side and against his, placing her hand on his arm, but Arabella just switched the focus of her glare. "Don't blame Lady Christina." Arabella sniffed. "The Marquess was perfectly polite. Lord Thomas is just being a unnecessary prig."

Predictably, Thomas bristled, glowering at Arabella, and causing Miss Wilson to look around for rescue. Unfortunately, her gaze landed on him - understandably, as he and Christina were the only options to play rescuer and she'd only been introduced to him - and caused Christina to bristle. Deciding he could at least fix one problem, Benedict ignored his sister and friend, and performed introductions.

"Lady Christina Rowan, this is Miss Wilson, Lord Thomas' cousin. Miss Wilson, I would make you known to Lady Christina Rowan, Marchesse of Stanhope. Miss Wilson is embarking on her first Season, sponsored by Viscountess Hood."

As Miss Wilson bobbed a curtsy, blushing furiously for some reason (her shyness really was astonishing), two things happened simultaneously - Christina immediately relaxed at the easy explanation for why Benedict had been dancing with Miss Wilson previously, and Thomas realized he was being rude. The conversation was still stilted, and Benedict was relieved when Thomas suggested they return to the ballroom. The sooner he could pass his sister off to his brother, the better... he had his future wife to handle.

CHAPTER 10

*B*ack in the ballroom, this time on Benedict's arm, Christina didn't know how to behave.

She felt incredibly foolish once she'd realized Lord Thomas had, quite reasonably, called upon his friends to help him launch his cousin into Society. The poor thing, although quite beautiful, was so shy it was nearly crippling. Although the large, dominant males surrounding her certainly didn't help. Nor did the more confident, garrulous young ladies; no matter how they tried to draw her out, it was still obvious an effort was being made on all sides.

Christina included herself in that effort after Benedict planted her in a circle of conversation between his sister and Viscountess Hood with the whispered order, "Stay put."

If she didn't feel so guilty over what was an obvious overreaction on her part to his dance with Miss Wilson, she might have been incensed. As it was, she couldn't exactly blame him for his short temper or his command. Especially since she'd been avoiding him for so long.

Only half paying attention to the conversation, she watched Benedict move across the ballroom and intercept Daphne. They had a very quick conversation, during which Daphne turned to peer at Christina almost curiously before turning away. Then she said something to Benedict, who nodded and began making his way towards his brother, although he constantly glanced over to ensure Christina was where he'd left her. Despite being stopped several times for conversation and introductions to young ladies, his focus never wavered.

She really had been a ninny.

Guilt welled up, tinged with shame, and also a bit of annoyance at herself for getting so worked up into a needless frother. She'd also hurt Benedict by her actions, which she certainly hadn't meant to do. She'd been so convinced he was done with her, that she hadn't thought she could hurt him.

And look where that had gotten her.

So now she was behaving herself and staying right where she'd been put, just as he'd commanded; waiting for him to come back and trusting he would.

The Duke of Manchester was escorting his Duchess from the dance floor when Benedict reached him. The three of them spoke quickly and quietly before the Duke lifted his head looked heavenward, as though appealing to a deity. They were very likely talking about Hartford and his introduction to Arabella, Christina realized, biting her lip.

"Don't blame yourself," Arabella said in a low voice, making Christina jump. She hadn't even realized the young woman had been watching Christina watch her siblings. "Don't let Benedict blame you either." Arabella snorted. "As if a mere introduction to a Marquess, when you were right beside me, could be improper. They're a bunch of stuffy old prigs." That last was said with a glare directed at Lord Thomas, who responded with a dark look, his eyes lingering on Arabella even after she'd sniffed and turned away from him.

"For a debutante, a conversation with Hartford is always improper, no matter who else is present," Christina murmured, distressed. She didn't think Arabella properly appreciated exactly how scandalous the Marquess' reputation was.

Then again, as sister of a powerful Duke, Arabella was much more indulged than the usual run of young lady. As quite a few people had been out on the balcony and Arabella had been within full view the entire time the gossip could only go so far anyway, but there would still be whispers and she'd be closely watched to see if he ever approached her again. Christina certainly would be as well.

She couldn't help but wonder about the club he'd made reference to, although she was certain it must have something to do with the salacious activities Daphne had made reference to in regard to herself and her husband. There were quite a few scandalous clubs, of course, the Hellfire Club being the most notorious. Daphne never said much specifically about the one she and the Earl belonged to, but Christina knew it existed and that it was quite outrageous in its activities – a few of which Daphne had outlined in very general terms. Enough to know her friend was quite an exhibitionist.

Benedict was now making his way back to Christina, an almost grimly determined expression on his face. Behind him, the Duke and Duchess were following a little more slowly but they were coming as well, and anxiety welled up in Christina's breast. Their introduction at the opera had been brief, although they'd seemed pleased to meet her at the time, she couldn't help but think they'd be less pleased with her now.

But if she ran, "displeased" would scarcely begin to describe how Benedict would feel.

Lady Hood saw Benedict's approach and immediately moved over, allowing him to slide into the circle next to Christina, giving them both an approving smile. Christina wasn't entirely sure what the Viscountess approved of, since Christina had been nearly as quiet as Miss Wilson during the conversation. She'd barely managed to keep up with the social patter while keeping an eye on Benedict and controlling her rising anxiety.

Despite taking her hand and securing it on his arm, Benedict didn't speak to Christina; his first words were for his sister, spoken low enough she doubted anyone else could hear them. "Isaac and Lydia are coming to look after you. Stay out of trouble."

"I don't need looking after," Arabella said irritably, not bothering to lower her voice, her tone haughty. "I am not a child and I wasn't in trouble."

"But you could have been."

The withering look Arabella gave him was prize worthy, and Christina wished she had mastered such an expression. It even seemed to affect Benedict a little, as he seemed rather sour about having to admit she hadn't really been in trouble... just skirting on the edge of it.

Benedict made their excuses to the Viscountess, who was happy to wave them away as the Duke and Duchess of Manchester joined their circle. Miss Wilson appeared ready to faint dead away as the large Duke asked her a question while the Duchess smiled at her encouragingly.

"Poor Isaac, she's scared to death of him and he hasn't a clue how to make her more comfortable," Benedict said, his voice tinged with humor as he led Christina away. "I've never met such a mouse before."

"Where are we going?" she asked him, confused as he seemed to be directing them *away* from the dance floor. She'd thought he meant to dance when he'd excused them from the conversation. She also didn't particularly want to talk about Miss Wilson, she felt silly enough about her jealous assumptions without having her nose rubbed in how uninterested Benedict truly was in the debutante.

"Away from here."

THERE WAS no way he could tell Christina the full truth right now. It would be far too easy for her to escape.

In the past twenty minutes, his plan had taken shape and solidified. He'd informed Daphne, and then Isaac and Lydia of his intentions. While he'd certainly never intended to ever elope or be married to a less than willing bride, he'd never realized exactly how deeply devoted Christina would be to mistrust either. She kept testing him, testing his own devotion to her, and making the worst possible assumptions about him.

Perhaps he could have written her a letter about Miss Wilson, informing her of Thomas' request, but he honestly hadn't realized it might be necessary. He'd thought she'd at least believe him that he wanted to marry her, that she'd have some trust in his word.

It hurt rather deeply to know she didn't.

To his relief, she didn't argue as they took their leave from their hosts and exited the ballroom rather early. There would be some gossip over such an early departure, but Christina probably thought it would blow over easily. If only she knew.

He handed her up into his carriage before having a quiet word with John Coachman, who looked surprised, but willing - especially when Benedict told him he'd be amply compensated for the trip they were about to undertake. Climbing into the carriage, Benedict sat across from Christina and rapped his knuckles on the ceiling. Immediately, the carriage began to move forward. Benedict wasn't sure if it was his own imagination, but the momentum felt more brisk than usual.

Sitting across from him, Christina had her hands folded in her lap, head slightly bowed, the very picture of a contrite repentant. As soon as the carriage was moving, she looked up at him, a remorseful expression on her face.

"I believe I owe you an apology, Benedict."

"Do you?" he asked, his voice incredibly mild, entirely at odds with how he was truly feeling. Christina actually winced, her teeth dragging across her lower lip in consternation before she straightened up again, like a soldier bravely facing the battlefield.

"I do," she said firmly, looking him directly in the eye so he could easily gauge her sincerity. "When I arrived this evening, I made an erroneous assumption when I saw you dancing with Miss Wilson, based on nothing more than my own insecurities and jealousy. The assumption was rather insulting to your character, and my subsequent behavior was not very kind, and I am very sorry."

Leaning back against the carriage seat, Benedict cocked his head, studying her as a soft blush began to rise in her cheeks, a testament to her emotions and her discomfort with his silence.

"Are you sorry for avoiding me the past few days?" he asked, just as mildly as before.

"Avoiding you?" The prevarication made her flush even deeper as her gaze averted.

"Are you going to claim you weren't?"

"I-... um, no, I..." Now her cheeks were bright red, her hands smoothing down her skirts over her thighs as she shifted uncomfortably, looking very much like a naughty little girl. Which, to his mind, was exactly what she currently was. "I suppose I was, a bit. I just needed some time to think."

"Yes," said Benedict seriously. "I have always found constant social engagements to be quite conducive to contemplation."

"I misspoke, I didn't mean time, I needed *space*," Christina snapped back at him. Her hands' movements became more aggressive as her agitation increased, still brushing at her skirts and making soft shushing noises as the fabric rustled.

"I think you wanted to test me," he said calmly, although he felt anything but; his own frustration and anger rising as he spoke. "I think you wanted to see how I would react. And when you saw me this evening with Miss Wilson, you thought I had failed your test, and you responded by trying to punish me by inflaming my jealousy. Congratulations. It worked."

To his surprise, Christina looked rather upset by his assertions. "That's not... I didn't... that's not precisely what... I didn't mean to do that. I really did want some space to think... and I didn't mean to inflame your jealousy exactly, at the time I was convinced you would not actually be jealous. I might have been testing you, but I didn't *mean* to, not really."

Surprisingly, Benedict believed her. His poor love was a bit of a mess emotionally, he was coming to realize. With her parents abroad, her in-laws estranged, she seemed to have no one to guide her and no close friends to advise her other than Daphne - and Daphne had begun working with him. Which was not against Christina's interests, but it did explain why Christina had been avoiding her friend as well.

"Did you come to any conclusions after taking some time and space?" Benedict asked, legitimately curious.

CHRISTINA FELT LIKE A NAUGHTY CHILD, given an assignment by her governess which she'd failed to complete and now had to account for; except none of her governesses had been as intimidating or as strict as Benedict. She'd written lines for them or had privileges taken away, but with Benedict she knew a spanking was very likely imminent and not a pleasurable one.

She hoped it wouldn't take much longer to get to that point.

Waiting was almost a worst punishment for her than the actual spanking. Disciplinary spankings hurt, but right now she felt so guilty for hurting Benedict, shamed at her own behavior, and thoroughly regretted jumping to conclusions about his intentions towards Miss Wilson, a spanking would feel cathartic.

A way to pay for her transgressions.

To make up for them.

To be forgiven.

She truly preferred not to spend a large amount of time wallowing in guilt.

"Nothing definite," she said, finally answering Benedict's question. It was the truth, and yet she felt it an entirely unsatisfactory answer. A sentiment he obviously agreed with as he frowned at her. "I... I don't know. I'm very confused."

To her surprise, Benedict didn't seem upset or unhappy with her lame explanation; he nodded in understanding, straightening up. "Well, then I'm happy to help clear a few things up for you."

When he held out his hand, she took it, not at all surprised when she found herself over his knee a few seconds later, the skirts of her ballgown flipped up at the waist. Christina pressed her face against the soft velvet of the seat cushion, squirming slightly against Benedict's hard lap as his hand stroked the bare skin of her bottom. Even knowing a punishment was coming, she couldn't help but feel amorous as his fingers skimmed over her curves.

The dark interior of the carriage had turned into their own little world, shutting everyone and everything else out. Here it was just him and her, with no need for insecurities or jealousy. She wanted him to spank her, to claim her, to make her feel secure and wanted, to claim her as his own.

Perhaps she had been testing him, more than she realized, by her avoidance. Despite specifically acting to evade him, a small, secret part of her had been disappointed when he hadn't caught up to her anyway - or appeared in her bedroom again. Maybe, deep down, she'd been hoping he'd appear again, like a possessive fury, the way he finally had tonight. It was certainly something George would never have done. He hadn't given a fig what she did or whom she spoke with once he'd lost interest in her.

Benedict's hand lifted and her buttocks clenched for a moment before relaxing again, knowing his hand would never fall while her muscles were tightened.

SMACK!
SMACK!
SMACK!
SMACK!

She let out a muffled cry as his hard palm impacted against her flesh, with absolutely no intention of warming her up before he moved into a harder spanking - this *was* the harder spanking. The stinging blows didn't just smart, they burned, and he barely gave her a moment to catch her breath before the next was already biting into the opposite cheek.

SMACK!
SMACK!
SMACK!

Benedict alternated between each cheek, back and forth, peppering the sharp blows all over her upturned mounds, turning them hot, throbbing, and red. It wasn't long before Christina was gasping, tears running down her cheeks as she bucked against the hand pressing down on the small of her back. No matter how she tried to stifle her cries, she couldn't manage to stay completely silent. The tender skin felt seared and swollen, but emotionally she was beginning to feel a bit better, as though she'd atoned.

Unfortunately, despite her growing conviction she'd been thoroughly punished, Benedict didn't seem to feel the same and showed no sign of stopping.

"Please!!!! I won't do it again!!!" She writhed, shrieking as the next two swats landed on her sensitive sit spots with an explosion of painful heat. "OW! Please!!!!"

SMACK!

"No, you won't," Benedict said, his voice deep and harsh, easily heard even over her sobbing gasps for air as his paddle-like hand continued to rain down punishment on her already chastened nates. "No more avoiding me."

SMACK!

"No more assumptions about my sincerity."

SMACK!

"And definitely no more flirting with other men."

Christina shrieked as his hand smacked down the center of her bottom, spanking the tender crease between her already burning nates. The white-hot pain as his fingers snapped against the sensitive crinkled hole of her anus was shocking in its intensity - and in her reaction as her pussy clenched despite both her embarrassment and shock.

He'd never spanked down the center of her bottom before and she hadn't realized how much more sensitive that area was, especially when his hand laid down vertically rather than going across it where her cheeks could provide some cushion. Christina cried out as he did it again - once, twice, three times more.

Her whole bottom felt hot and swollen and she really did feel very, thoroughly sorry. Not just because it hurt - the pain aroused her even if her arousal only shielded her somewhat from the blazing torment - but because she knew from Benedict's words and how hard he'd spanked her that she'd hurt him as well. Hurt him, disappointed him, and made him feel all the things she *didn't* want to feel. She welcomed the pain from the spanking, because she felt she deserved it for how she'd behaved. She didn't know why he was putting up with everything.

She knew she wouldn't have tolerated her behavior if the situation had been reversed. She'd certainly never tolerate him avoiding her and then running off to flirt with other women because he'd seen her having a perfectly innocent encounter! Somehow, she'd become the worst kind of hypocrite.

"There love, it's over now." Benedict couldn't help but worry as he gathered Christina up onto his lap. She was crying quite a bit harder than he'd thought she would - while he knew how sensitive a woman's bottom crease could be, he hadn't quite expected this reaction.

"I'm sorry, I'm so sorry," she said as he cradled her against his shoulder, her small hands clinging to the front of his jacket as if she was trying to pull herself deeper into his embrace, snuggle closer than they already were. "I don't know why I was so awful."

"No, love, you weren't awful," he murmured, holding her tighter, his hand moving down to squeeze her bottom, making her gasp and squirm on his lap. "You have some insecurities we need to work through, and I would like you to trust me more, but I understand why you were out of sorts. We just need to change how you react sometimes; especially when it comes to avoiding me."

"It's because I'm a horrible, hypocritical harridan!"

If she wasn't sobbing like her heart was broken, Benedict would have been amused at her alliteration. As it was, he was starting to worry she was working her way towards hysteria. While he appreciated her remorse, he certainly hadn't meant to make her hysterical.

Although, he wasn't entirely sure it was anything he had done either.

She'd definitely endured harsher punishments from him. This seemed to have more to do with her own miseries than anything else.

Protectiveness rushed through him, urging him to help her, to bring her back to an even keel. Usually a spanking did that, but today it didn't seem to have done enough.

Perhaps the activities which usually followed a spanking would achieve a happier effect. Benedict did the first thing which came to mind, given their positions; he started kissing her neck.

Christina hiccupped, seeming to be slightly shocked out of her sobbing, although she was certainly still crying.

"Benedict? What are you doing?"

"If you have to ask, I must not be doing it correctly," he murmured, palming her bottom through her skirt, kneading the already tenderized flesh hard enough to make her squeak as he continued to move his lips over her sensitive skin. She hiccupped again, but her tears were definitely slowing, encouraging him as his cock came back to attention.

He'd been hard while he'd been spanking her - he was always hard when her skirts and bottom were up - but his arousal had ebbed when she'd started pitiably sobbing. Now it came roaring back in full force as she squirmed on his lap, her body obviously responding to him.

"How can you still want me?" she asked in wonderment, sniffling. "I'm a mess... I treated you horribly... I'm a terrible hypocrite..."

"You're an adorable mess," he said, his hand sliding away from her bottom to massage her thigh, tipping her back slightly so he could start to inch her skirts up her legs as his fingers moved. "I wasn't pleased that you avoided me or went off with Hartford, but you've been punished and you're forgiven. I suppose it's only natural you feel inclined to test me, to test us, now that I've made my intentions clear, but whenever you do I will have this same response - I will spank you and keep you."

She was fully tipped back now, leaning against the carriage as his lips brushed down her collarbone towards her breasts. Her soft pants were from arousal rather than tears, and she let out a little moan as he pulled her skirts all the way up, whimpering as he slid away from underneath her and her sore bottom landed against the seat cushion.

When he kissed her, she kissed him back almost frantically, her mouth pressing against his, lips opening, tongue sliding into his mouth to dance with his. The small space of the carriage made him fumble with his breeches, and he felt more like a novice than a rake as his hands searched for her body through volumes of skirts.

His hands finally found her pussy, wet and hot, and she moaned against his mouth as his thumb slid over her clit, making her jerk.

A bump in the road jolted them both and Benedict nearly fell off from atop her. Growling as she giggled, he pulled them away from his side of the coach, landing so he was sitting on the opposite seat with her atop him, straddling him. His cock out and stiff as steel, ready to delve between her thighs.

"Ride me, love," he said hoarsely, using his hands to lift her skirts up and away.

They were both mostly fully clothed, but it didn't matter as she sank down onto his waiting cock, her skirts spilling over his arms, his hands cupping the hot cheeks of her ass. He groaned as her wet heat slid around his cock, quivering and squeezing the length of his rod. Christina whimpered as his fingers dug into the seared skin of her bottom, her body arching, hands on his shoulders to help keep her balance.

The rocking of the carriage only intensified their pleasure as she rode him, her pace almost frantic, as if she was racing headlong to her climax. Benedict didn't even attempt to slow her, he was feeling as needy as she was, as desperate for the closeness and intimacy which their pleasure brought.

She cried out, grinding herself down atop him, her pussy spasming around his cock. Shouting his own cry, Benedict squeezed her chastened bottom hard, his hips surging upwards as his cock pulsed... throbbed... and exploded inside of her for the first time. Her orgasmic shudders milked him, giving him the most intense orgasm of his life... the pleasure went on far after he'd been emptied of his seed as her movements slowed, her body beginning to slump on his lap.

Taking deep, shuddering breaths, Benedict wrapped his arms around her, helping her to resettle on his lap in a comfortable position with her head on his shoulder. Her sleepy murmurs indicated she'd been completely drained of energy - a condition he felt as well.

Holding her tightly, he leaned back against the seat and closed his eyes. John would alert him when they arrived at a suitable inn.

For now, he would just enjoy holding his soft, warm woman in his arms. He had little doubt she'd stop being so peaceable once she awoke and thought about the significance of the culmination of their coupling... and noticed they were no longer in London.

CHAPTER 11

The bed was unfamiliar.

Harder than her bed. The sheets not quite as soft. And it smelled wrong.

The only thing which felt right was the hard male body pressed up against hers from behind. Christina frowned, wrinkling her brow as she opened her eyes, blinking. She vaguely remembered being carried out of the carriage last night, but she'd been mostly asleep and hadn't bothered to look where Benedict had taken her. In the back of her mind she'd assumed they were at her house or, more likely, the house on Jermyn Street.

Instead it looked like they were at an inn.

Frowning, Christina sat up, looking around the unfamiliar surrounds, wincing slightly as her weight rested fully on her bottom, which was still a bit sore from last night's spanking. It certainly looked like a room at an inn. Sounds from below stairs drifted up, muffled but... there were definitely other people down there.

A clatter of horseshoes in the courtyard confirmed it.

The arm across her lap tightened, pulling her into Benedict's hard, warm, naked chest as he rolled onto his side, smiling up at her.

"Good morning," he said, looking adorably mussed with his hair completely rumpled, his dark eyes half lidded. His eyes dropped down to her breasts, which she realized were completely bare as well. With a slight hiss, she grabbed the sheets and pulled them up to cover herself. Not because she minded him seeing her nakedness, but because she was feeling completely off balance and vulnerable, and being naked on top of that was just too much for her to bear.

"*Where are we?!*" Her voice came out as a hiss, nearly a whisper. She didn't know whether to panic, or be furious, or.... or...

"About two hours outside London on the Great North Road, in a small but comfortable inn called The Purple Rose. I took its name to be a sign."

Benedict grinned.

Christina stared.

He reached for her.

She scooted away with such haste she nearly tumbled off the bed.

Dragging the sheets with her, draping them around her, she managed to stand, her head swinging around wildly as if the room might suddenly dissolve, like a dream.

But the room went nowhere. Benedict sat up on the bed, naked as the day he was born and his expression was one of determination tinged with regret. The floor was solid beneath her feet, the furniture all hard, unfamiliar lines, and the whole room stood out with stark clarity and no fuzzy edges.

This was real.

"Why are we here?" she whispered, her voice a mere husk.

The thought bubbling up in the back of her mind couldn't possibly be correct. It was too insane. Too infuriating. Too unbelievable.

"It's our first stop on the way to Gretna Green," Benedict said, finally getting to his feet on the other side of the bed, his voice flat. While his cock was partially hardened, he made no move to come towards her, just watched her from across the bed, waiting to see what she would do.

Christina's knees almost buckled.

He *was* insane.

But hard on the heels of that thought, the strangest bubble of happiness rose in her chest, filling her almost to bursting. Then fear slid in, reminding her of past mistakes and quelling any excitement she felt about his admission... followed by furious indignation.

He'd *kidnapped* her! Actually kidnapped her!

"You kidnapped me!"

Benedict grimaced as he came around the bed, heading for the chair where his clothing was neatly folded. Christina's ball gown hung from a nearby screen, next to a small wash pan of water, and her underthings were neatly folded and piled on another chair next to the screen. Turning, watching him, Christina just stared as he began to pull on his breeches.

"You didn't bring a change of clothing?"

"I didn't exactly plan this out," he admitted, almost ruefully, turning on the boyish charm he occasionally employed. "Perhaps the innkeeper's wife can help, or we can find a store with some ready-made pieces on the way."

She narrowed her eyes at him. "That won't be necessary."

"Traveling that distance in a ball gown is going to be dashed uncomfortable."

"I'm sure it would be," she said icily. "But we're only a few hours away from London and that's where *I'm* going."

DESPITE THE HEAT from Christina's glare, Benedict was actually feeling rather cheerful. They were back in the carriage, sitting across from each other, physically much more comfortably than they might have been if they hadn't been quite lucky in Benedict's choice of inn. The innkeeper's wife had actually had a small selection of clothes he'd been able to choose from, left by previous travelers, and he'd paid her for two dresses for Christina and pants and a shirt for himself. His evening jacket looked ludicrously formal atop his new outfit, but he was much more comfortable, and so was Christina.

Even if she was infuriated.

Benedict had locked her in the room while he'd gone to ask Mrs.

Mastaery about clothing. He'd returned to a pacing Christina, who had tried to tell him his plan was ludicrous, predicted they'd both be miserably unhappy if he followed through with it, and called him a bloody idiot.

What she hadn't done was give him a firm refusal.

She hadn't fought when he'd dressed her in the pale green day dress he'd purchased from Mrs. Mastaery.

She hadn't called out for help when he'd escorted her downstairs.

She hadn't tried to run when they reached the courtyard.

She hadn't resisted getting into the carriage.

In fact, other than glaring at him and insisting they return to London rather than continue on to Gretna Green - a completely verbal insistence - she didn't make any move to change her situation whatsoever.

As far as Benedict was concerned, he was doing very well indeed.

Four hours later they stopped to change the horses and have a quick luncheon at the Turtle and Dove. Christina hadn't stopped glaring at him, and she wasn't exactly speaking to him either. Every time he attempted to start a conversation, he received the same response -

"I have no interest in attempting to speak with someone who belongs in Bedlam." She would state firmly, and follow her declaration with a sniff as she turned up her nose.

He'd been tempted to put her over his knee again, but he decided his time was better spent sitting back and letting her come to grips with their upcoming nuptials.

Descending from the carriage, Christina looked around. The courtyard was swept clean, the bushes tidy, and the building a rather attractive place with pretty blue shutters on the windows and a brightly painted sign. Benedict had stopped at the inn before and knew their food to be excellent.

"This seems like a good place to eat before we turn back for London," she said in her haughtiest voice, her nose still up in the air.

Chuckling, Benedict escorted her to the front door of the inn. "My

GOLDEN ANGEL

love, at some point you'll need to resign yourself to returning to London as the Marchesse of Dearborn, not Stanhope."

"I still live in hope you'll regain your sanity before this farce reaches that point," Christina said, a little darkly.

Despite the plainness of the dress she was wearing and her simply done hair, it was impossible not to recognize her aristocratic bearing, and the innkeeper came hurrying forward as soon as they stepped through the door. Mr. Turner was quite pleased to welcome them to his inn, happy to assist them with whatever they might desire. Benedict requested a private room for them to dine while they waited for the horses to be changed out, and they were immediately whisked into a small room off to the side, prettily decorated in blue and white with painted porcelain figurines on a shelf above the unlit fireplace.

Wandering around the room, Christina examined the small figures, obviously taking the opportunity to stretch and look at something other than the passing countryside.

"Is there anything in particular you'd like to eat?" he asked, casually leaning against the door frame.

"Nothing too heavy," she said, almost absent-mindedly, picking up the figure of a goose girl, complete with a fat, happy goose standing beside her. "A collation and some bread perhaps."

"Very well," he said. "I'll return momentarily."

The startled expression on her face as her head came up in surprise made him grin, which he hid by quickly turning away and exiting the room. Waving Mr. Turner over, he requested a light repast for the lady, as well as some wine, and a bowl of warm water to refresh themselves. The innkeeper was happy to do as asked, hurrying away immediately to see it done.

Ambling along, Benedict made use of the privy, checked on the horses being harnessed to his carriage, and asked some of the men in the courtyard about road conditions ahead.

He wanted to give Christina ample time to try and escape or secure some help if that was her desire. By the time they reached Gretna Green, he wanted there to be no question that she could have been rid of him along the way if that's what she truly wanted. A tiny quiver of doubt niggled at him, but... that was the risk he had to take.

While he might technically be kidnapping her, he had no wish for an unwilling bride. His Christina might be submissive, but she was also a firebrand. It was likely she'd give him a bit more of a fight, but as long she didn't run, didn't try to escape, they'd be married by tomorrow evening. And if she did, then he'd follow along behind her and find some other way to prove to her that he wasn't going to change his mind about marrying her.

WHEN BENEDICT LEFT her in the small, private dining room, Christina immediately rushed to the door and pressed her ear against it. The sound of his footsteps moving away was clear enough, but it made her frown.

He was just going to leave her here? With the door unlocked?

Nibbling on a fingernail, she moved away from the door and over to the window overlooking the courtyard. There were quite a few people coming into the inn's yard and even more passing by on the road. Quite respectable people too; merchants, traveling families, a coach. People who would certainly help her if she were to raise a hue and cry.

But then what would happen to Benedict?

What would happen to *them*?

Perhaps it made little sense to worry about her relationship with a man who had just kidnapped her, but just because she was unsure about marrying him didn't mean she wanted their affair *now* – she'd already decided she wanted to see out the Season with him. Returning to London, running from him... surely he would spurn her if she flew back to the capital without him. But he refused to listen to reason and return *with* her.

Part of her was thrilled. Relieved even. She wanted him to take her to Gretna Green, to marry her... to force the issue. Another part of her was furious he would be so high-handed. Yet, here they were in the inn and he'd just removed his watch on her.

She could leave at any time.

As if to punctuate that point, there was a knock at the door and she'd barely responded before a young woman was pushing her way through the door, balancing a tray between her hands.

"Pardon, my lady, the lord ordered a luncheon for ye both," the maid said, bobbing a quick curtsy before making her way to the table.

There was a large plate of fruit, fresh baked bread and butter, some cold chicken, and a tureen of soup. Perfect traveler's fare. A pitcher of wine and two glasses finished off the tray.

"Thank you," Christina said as the young woman began to lay out the meal and silverware, barely glancing at Christina. She certainly didn't look as though she'd been sent to check on Christina or watch her. As soon as she was finished, the young woman smiled, bobbed another curtsy, and hurried back out the door. She closed it behind her, but it remained unlocked.

Sighing, Christina made her way over to sit down, her stomach grumbling with hunger. It had been a while since breakfast.

Why hadn't she asked the young woman for help?

Why was she sitting here eating instead of going to the courtyard and finding a conveyance back to London?

Was she really going to marry Benedict?

The questions, the uncertainties, whirled around her head. Firming her lips, she buttered her bread. She could decide what she was going to do after she ate. Maybe even later today. After all, turning back to London was irrevocable. She didn't *have* to make any decisions until they actually reached Scotland.

As she tried not to think about how flimsy an excuse that was, the door opened and Benedict came striding in. The smile which spread across his face when he saw her sitting there made her feel a little smug. Perhaps he wasn't quite as sure of himself as he seemed.

His gaze dropped down to the table, noting the meal they'd been provided.

"Is everything to your liking?" he asked, taking the seat beside her. "Or is there anything I can fetch for you?"

"The food is wonderful," she said, keeping her voice cool. After all, she didn't want him to think she was happy or even indifferent to being kidnapped. So she didn't thank him either.

But she did want to slap him when a smug little smirk appeared on his lips.

In order to keep her hands busy - because she wouldn't put it past him to turn her over his knee right here and now - she picked up her spoon for the soup. She also wished she hadn't thought about being turned over his knee. While her bottom was mostly healed, it was still tender enough to remind her she'd been spanked last night, and just thinking about being over his knee again today aroused her.

Last night she'd been practically hysterical at how awful she'd been; today she was more coolly collected, which also meant she was feeling more amorous. And he did look rather appealing in the more casual attire he'd acquired this morning. Without all the usual gentlemanly accoutrements, it would be quite easy to strip him down to the nude.

As she was without her usual ladies' garments, the same could be said for her.

Avoiding his gaze, Christina leaned forward to sup on the soup, wishing she could push away her traitorous thoughts. After all, it wasn't as if they were on holiday!

BY THE TIME they reached the inn they'd be staying at for the evening, Christina was quite visibly exhausted. Even though his carriage was well sprung and the road was in quite good condition, a full day of traveling was wearing. Fortunately, they'd reach Gretna Green tomorrow... and then have to turn back around.

Although Benedict would certainly be amenable to taking their time returning home. He'd informed his brother of his intentions after all, as well as Daphne. Besides, he needed to give them time to move his household.

Christina's home in Mayfair was from her family, rather than her late husband's. Tomorrow, once he and Christina were wed, he would send a messenger back to London to begin the process. Isaac would oversee the closing of his house on Jermyn Street and Daphne would oversee his move to Brooke Street. At some point he would have to buy himself and Christina a home in London, so as not to rely on their relations, but the arrangement would work well enough for the remainder of the Season.

Or perhaps sooner, if Arabella would finally settle on a suitor.

As much as Benedict wanted to take Christina on a romantic honeymoon, watching over his sister during the perils of the Season took precedence - something he knew Christina would understand. Besides, he could take more time to plan if they waited. They should certainly stop in Brussels during their travels, so she could see her family and he could become acquainted with his new in-laws.

The thought made him smile as he signed the register. Anticipating the event a little, he identified Christina as his wife; while giving her time and opportunity to "escape" was well and good, he had no intention of sleeping alone. Even if she was too weary to engage in bed play.

There would be time enough for that tomorrow - after they were wed.

"Did you come here of your own free will and accord?" The blacksmith looked rather bored as he asked the question.

This was not how Christina imagined a wedding - certainly not her wedding, when she'd thought about having another wedding again. The forge was a plain forge, with nothing to differentiate it from any other forge in either Scotland or England. The blacksmith was typical of his kind; a very large, muscular man in well-worn clothes and a heavy apron for protection against the heat and sparks of his fires, although he had put aside his gloves for the wedding.

"Yes," Benedict said firmly, smiling widely over their hands, which were wound about with a ribbon.

He and the blacksmith both looked at Christina, who felt as though she were in a daze. Everything was hazy, almost dream-like. This *was* a dream, wasn't it? Surely she couldn't actually be here, hand in Benedict's, actually marrying him over the anvil at Gretna Green.

"Yes?" The answer sounded more like a question than an actual affirmative, but the blacksmith barely seemed to notice.

Standing across from her, Benedict's dark eyes seemed to glow as his fingers tightened around hers.

Christina felt a bit faint. Part of her was crowing with triumph. Part of her was screaming in despair. It was like her mind was torn asunder, creating two completely different women rather than one whole one. She stared back at Benedict, hoping against hope that she wasn't making the most terrible mistake of her life.

"Do you take this woman to be your lawful wedded wife, forsaking all others, kept to her as long as you both shall live?"

"I will," Benedict said fiercely, the intentness in his gaze taking her already shallow breath away.

Out of the corner of her eye, Christina could see the blacksmith turn his head towards her, but she couldn't bring herself to take her eyes away from Benedict. His expression seemed to urge her on, drawing the words out of her, appealing to the hopeful woman still inside of her, so that when the blacksmith repeated the question, she answered -

"I will."

Her voice was a whisper, but it was enough.

The blacksmith produced the rings Benedict had bought them upon arrival, and two minutes later the rings were on each of their fingers. Christina's felt far heavier than it truly was, as though it were a great weight trying to drag her down. Trapping her. Confining her.

"Foreasmuch as this man and this woman have consented to go together by giving and receiving a ring, I therefore declare them to be a man and wife before God and these witnesses in the name of the Father, Son, and Holy Ghost. Amen."

It was done.

The blacksmith's daughter and son-in-law signed the marriage certificate as witnesses, and then Benedict and Christina signed their names upon it as well.

Married. She was married again.

She felt joy, she did, so much joy… but she also felt fear. So much fear that her joy would not last.

THE FROZEN EXPRESSION on Christina's face worried Benedict. She was smiling, but it was not a natural smile, and her dark eyes were so large in her pale face that she looked quite pallid. Almost ethereal.

Keeping their bound hands together - as Mr. Sawyer had warned them removing the handfasting ribbon before consummating the marriage was ill luck - Benedict pulled her towards the small inn they were staying at. For such a popular marriage site, the accommodations left a bit to be desired, but Benedict was perfectly happy to make do with their small room and bare necessities.

She'd said yes.

He honestly hadn't been sure, up until the last moment, whether or not she'd really say yes. And he'd rather gotten the impression she hadn't been either. But she'd said yes.

Now she was his.

His wife.

Lady Christina Windham. No longer the Marchesse of Stanhope. No longer bearing another man's name.

Benedict circled her body with their connected hands and scooped her up into his arms, enjoying her squeak and the way her frozen countenance jolted back to life.

"Benedict?"

Instead of answering, he picked up the pace, practically rushing towards the inn.

They were wedded, now he was going to bed her and make it official. There would be no question as to the validity of this marriage, not in either of their minds.

She giggled, hiding her face against his shoulder as a grinning man held the door open for them and Benedict carried her into the taproom. The locals and travelers at tables nearest the door, eating dinner or having a pint, began to cheer and toast them, drawing the attention of tables farther away. By the time Benedict had reached the stairs, the entire room was cheering him on and calling out ribald suggestions.

"Och! Happy to the newlyweds!"

"Bed her good, laddie! A wee one in the belly makes the ladies happy!"

"'e's in a rush! - Don fergit 'er pleasure too, boy-o!"

Giggling helplessly, Christina curled in to make herself smaller so Benedict would have an easier time navigating the narrow staircase, the sounds from the taproom fading behind them. Thank heavens she wasn't a virgin, he thought with a grin, they could get right to the fun part of the evening without any missishness or misunderstandings.

"We're married, love," he whispered in her ear, shouldering his way into their room and kicking the door shut behind him. "You said yes. You're all mine now."

Possessiveness grabbed hold of him as Christina tilted her head up at him. Her eyes still showed her surprise at finding herself in this situation, but she wasn't protesting. A mix of emotions crossed her face as she looked at him - happiness, wariness, excitement, anxiety. He'd known exchanging vows would not soothe all her insecurities - how could it when her first husband had so easily broken those vows? - but he hoped it had soothed some.

After all, despite her evasiveness, despite all she'd done to put him off, despite her protests, she'd married him anyway. And time would prove to her that he'd meant every one of the vows he made.

Lowering his mouth to hers, he began kissing her earnestly, letting her lower body slowly slide down to the floor. As he began to work on her clothing, he realized the handfasting ribbon wound around their wrists was going to make things extremely interesting... especially since they wouldn't be able to disrobe completely. He felt sorry for the poor sods with a virgin bride who had to try and attempt to endeavor.

He supposed there were some who would feel sorry for him, for his bride's lack of virginity, but more fool they. Christina had had lovers, but he completely trusted she would remain true to her vows. From what he'd seen, being a virgin on her wedding night certainly did not predict a woman's faithfulness throughout marriage; it entirely depended on a woman's character and the strength of the relationship with her husband.

Benedict was determined his and Christina's relationship would be among the strongest.

Moving them towards the bed, he continued kissing her, amused as she made her own frustrated noises when she realized how the handfasting ribbon confined their movements. After all, she couldn't move without moving his hand as well.

By the time they tumbled onto the bed, only partially unclothed, Christina was giggling madly and even Benedict was having difficulty suppressing his laughter. Although he'd imagined their wedding night as being more serious, he couldn't be upset when amusement had chased all anxiety from Christina's eyes. She giggled as he climbed atop her, her skirts rucked up about her hips, showing off her long legs, and the front of her bodice gaping open to give him access to her breasts.

Pressing the palm of his hand bound by the ribbon against hers, Benedict wove their fingers together, pinning her hand down to the mattress as he leaned down to kiss her again. A little smile still on her lips, Christina tilted her head up to meet his, her free hand sliding up the front of his shirt to caress his bare chest, and then back down to continue working on unlacing the placket of his pants. Since she was using her left hand, which was not her dominant hand, and his cock was pressing insistently at the front of the cloth, straining the laces, it was not an easy task.

Benedict took advantage of her struggles to torment her breasts.

Palming one mound, he moved his mouth to the other, enjoying the way her giggles turned to breathy moans as he kneaded her soft flesh with his hand, his tongue laving over her hard nipple and teasing the little bud to ruche even tighter. Spreading his fingers over the mound of her breast, he trapped her other nipple between his forefinger and thumb, rolling it between his fingers even as he massaged her swollen flesh.

No longer giggling at all, Christina writhed, her hand on his pants becoming almost frantic as her fingers scrabbled at the laces.

"Oh!" She let out a little cry as he bit down on her nipple, her fingers tightening around his as her back arched, thrusting her breasts upwards. Benedict moaned as his cock finally sprang free of his pants, landing hot and heavy in the palm of her hand, and her long fingers curled around its length.

～

Hot need coursed through Christina as she pulled Benedict towards her, guiding him to her pussy. Not that he needed the direction, but she was feeling quite desperate.

She needed to feel him inside her, to feel his skin against hers, to affirm the vows they just made.

Because she so badly wanted to believe them. To believe she hadn't made a mistake. She wanted to wipe away the memories of her first marriage. To slip free from the invisible bonds George had placed around her... she was no longer defined by him. No longer his wife, no longer his widow, and no longer bearing his name or title.

She was all Benedict's.

The blunt head of his cock pressed against her pussy and she moaned, squeezing the rigid flesh as she pulled him forward. Benedict's mouth lifted from her nipple, his hand sliding from her breast to prop up beside her, pushing himself up so he was hovering over her, looking down at her. She blinked up at him, gaze hazy with lust, with desire, and that was when he entered her.

Christina moaned as her muscles stretched, his cock sliding into her soaked sheathe, filling her the way her body craved. As he moved deeper, her hand fell away, clearing the way for him to thrust fully into her. She pressed her palm against his chest, running her fingers through his hair as he pulled his hips back and then thrust forward again, brown eyes glowing with an inner fire as he watched her writhing on his staff.

"Mine," he said, his voice both tender and possessive as he leaned forward. Christina gazed up at him, but her heart felt the words... repeated them. *Mine. He's mine too.* "My wife."

The word made her quail, but it didn't cause the instant revulsion and fear she'd once felt.

Which was good, because it was too late. For better or for worse, she was Benedict's wife. She'd given him her future, and now she had to trust him to keep the coming days bright.

"Make love to me," she whispered. What she truly wanted to say was *love me*. But then, he'd already claimed he did.

"Your wish is my command."

He began to move, his free hand finding hers, twining their fingers together the same way their bound hands were. Christina moaned, arching, as he pushed their hands up by her head so she was pinned down on either side. Wrapping her legs around his waist, she canted her hips upwards, meeting him thrust for thrust.

Their lips came together in a desperate kiss, as if they could drink each other in, sink into each other far deeper than mere physical bodies would allow.

Pleasure was swirling through her, building within her. She could feel Benedict's hard groin as he rubbed against her swollen lips and clit with every thrust, his hips circling, grinding, stimulating every millimeter of her aching core.

Looking up at him, his hands pressing down into hers, their bodies connected so passionately, was incredibly intimate. Christina felt so vulnerable as he moved atop her, not physically but emotionally. He was watching every small movement, every change of expression in her face, every quiver, every sigh; he was seeing her. The way no other man ever had.

She arched as ecstasy crested, bubbling up inside her as her legs pulled him closer.

The soft, hoarse pants of breath as his thrusts became wilder heated her skin as he bent down towards her, his groans becoming animalistic as he pumped harder, faster. Christina screamed out her ecstasy as the angle pressed his body against her swollen clit, sending fireworks shooting through her veins. Their joined hands squeezed as her pussy spasmed around him, massaging, sucking at his cock.

He swelled inside of her, his thrusts relentlessly pounding her into the mattress, and then she felt the hot burst of his seed spurting into her grasping channel. The sensation of wet heat sent her spiraling, setting off the hazy memory of him spilling inside of her in the carriage as well.

Sobbing out her climax, Christina quivered and writhed beneath him, her muscles spasming as if trying to milk him of every last drop of cum, her body thirsty for his fluid. Feeling him finally releasing inside of her, when she was entirely cognizant of the fact, gave her a strange sense of completeness. Not that their encounters had ever been unsatisfactory, but this just felt *right*.

CHAPTER 12

The ride back to London from Gretna Green was much more pleasant than the ride away from London to the anvil. For one, Christina was speaking to him again, without any unhappy rebukes about his sanity. For another, they were moving at a much slower pace, which made the actual ride much more pleasant. Both of them were still dressed comfortably, although the clothing was certainly becoming more travel worn. Benedict was looking forward to having access to his wardrobe again.

Although he'd sent all the necessary messages, he was sure his valet would have quite a few harsh words when he saw Benedict's current attire. Lewis did take pride in his work, and a sloppily dressed employer did not reflect well on him - or so Benedict had been told. Truthfully, usually Benedict was quite in line with Lewis' thinking, but right now he found his appearance had dropped drastically in his priorities.

Christina took the news of his move to her house rather well, he thought. She huffed a bit at his high-handed maneuvers, but agreed she'd rather they have more privacy than they would if they were to join Isaac, Lydia, and Arabella in Manchester House. Obviously the house on Jermyn Street was out of the question; only bachelors lived on the street, and while it was well enough for a lover to visit, it would be scandalous for a married couple to be in residence. Not to mention, uncomfortable for the neighbors, who wanted their lovers and mistresses to be able to visit with ease.

As they approached the city, however, Christina began to behave more nervously again. Her foot tapped against the carriage floor, her fingers moving restlessly over her skirts, up to her hair, and back to her skirts, and she seemed incapable of sitting still.

Reaching over, Benedict took her hand in his, and she froze immediately, as if she'd just realized how fidgety she was when he'd stopped her movement.

"What's wrong, love?" he asked. He'd enjoyed the past three days of slow travel, with plenty of time for meals and to stretch their legs. She seemed to have enjoyed herself as well. The countryside made for lovely viewing when it wasn't flying by. The time alone in the carriage had given them the opportunity to make plans for the future. Christina was perfectly happy to spend the majority of their time in the capital while Benedict tended to Isaac's affairs there, and they'd visit the countryside occasionally as well. She'd also been thrilled at his suggestion that they spend their honeymoon at the end of the Season traveling, including a visit to her family. They'd made love every night and, despite not having his usual array of implements to torment her with, they hadn't felt the lack.

However, now she was obviously agitated and growing unhappy.

She sighed heavily. "I am not looking forward to facing the *ton*, to be perfectly frank. Not knowing how they will react to our marriage... I just... I do not like unknowns."

Quite understandable, especially considering how her first marriage ended and what must have been a constant fear over gossip discovering the circumstances, but in this case she was causing herself unnecessary distress. Chuckling, Benedict brought her hand up to his lips, giving her fingers a reassuring kiss.

"If it will set your mind at ease, I can tell you exactly what will happen upon our return."

Looking a bit piqued at his cavalier reaction, Christina raised one eyebrow at him. "You can?"

"Oh yes." He lowered their hands, keeping his fingers entwined with hers. "As soon as we arrive home, either Lady Daphne, my siblings, or both will descend upon your house. Whoever arrives first will be filled with news, gossip, and will be eager to tell us exactly how we'll be received in Society. Isaac will have already posted the announcement in the paper. He, Lydia, and Lady Daphne will already have led the charge in establishing us creditably. Isaac will chuckle and sigh over my jealous, romantic nature which impelled me to sweep you off and marry you as soon as possible, shaking his head over my lack of patience for a special license.

"He and Lydia will have already informed my friends what tale to spread, which they will delight in doing. Granted, not everyone is currently in the capital, but I can guarantee the Spencers are doing the rounds, along with the Hoods. Lady Daphne will be making her own visits to the gossips, gushing over the incredible romance of it all and how she played a role in ensuring our wedded happiness."

"What about your sister?" Christina asked, that little wrinkle in her brow still refusing to smooth out.

Benedict laughed. "I pity anyone who even hints at displeasure about our marriage in front of Arabella. Set Arabella up against the stuffiest, most righteous, most powerful old dragon in Society, and I would still place my bet on Arabella... in fact, I wouldn't be surprised if Isaac sent my sister to prime Lady Jersey and Lady Cowper before they heard the news officially. They disapprove of her in a general way, but they also dote on her horribly, they can't seem to help themselves."

"Goodness..." Christina blinked in surprise. Those two ladies were among the most stern of those who guarded the doors at Almacks. They were two of the foremost hostesses among the *ton* and led many others in both attitude and action, and everyone was compelled to follow. Christina had made their acquaintance, and then done what everyone else did - her best to stay out of their way.

The picture Benedict was painting was very different from the one she'd been conjuring in her own mind. His family had been warm enough to her during their brief meetings, so she hadn't worried about their reaction as much, but she'd started to become anxious wondering about how the *ton* at large would respond.

Elopements were considered a bit scandalous, and certainly widows didn't usually elope. They shouldn't need to.

Following her sudden departure from the ball where she'd been talking to the most scandalous man in Society, only to return to London nearly a week later married to another man, a man who had already caused a stir in his pursuit of her... well she just couldn't fathom what people might be saying, what gossip might be stirring. She'd spent so much time afraid Society might discover the truth about her first marriage, waiting for the derision and disdain when they did... it was like a track she couldn't move her mind away from. Except now she knew they would be talking; there was no way to hide her and Benedict's elopement. It would be the *on dit* of the week, unless something truly shocking had happened while they were away.

She'd been alone for so long, with only Daphne as her main ally, too afraid to allow any others close for fear they'd turn on her if the truth were ever known, she hadn't even thought how *Benedict's* friends and family might rally. How they might pave the way for her as Benedict's wife.

Still chuckling, Benedict pulled her onto his lap so she straddled him, his eyes alight.

"Benedict!" She slapped her palm against his shoulder. It was broad daylight and the curtains were open on either side of them! They were only a few hours from London and the closer they drew towards the city, the more they encountered other travelers.

"Not to worry, love, I won't strip you down right here, much as I might like to, but I will give you something to think about other than your worries."

By the time they finally reached their destination, Christina was practically melting with need. Fortunately, Benedict was the same. He insisted on carrying her over the threshold of her - their - home, and he carried her directly up the stairs to her bedroom from there, much to the horror of her straight-laced butler, Mr. Jones.

There, Benedict stripped her down and set her on her hands and knees on the bed, mounting her from behind all the while his hand beat down a rapid tattoo on her bottom, turning the creamy cheeks pink while she cried out from the combined effects of pain and pleasure. They spent the next two hours lounging in her sheets, shutting out the world as they caressed, cuddled, and loved on each other, and Christina reveled in it.

Benedict had been entirely correct in his suppositions about how they'd be received however; after two hours had passed Mr. Jones had knocked on the bedroom door and, in a rather strained sounding voice, inquired if they were at home.

The Duke and Duchess of Manchester had come to call, accompanied by the Lady Arabella, Mr. and Mrs. Hood, and their arrival had been immediately followed by the Earl and Countess of Marley.

"My apologies, my lord and lady," Jones said through the door. "But they are becoming rather insistent."

"Put them in the drawing room please, Jones, and we'll be there momentarily," Christina called out, trying to stifle her giggles.

As she had always kept her more scandalous activities away from her own household, she could only imagine how her staff was reacting. While they knew she'd married Lord Benedict Winchester, it would take some time to adjust to serving newlyweds rather than a somewhat reclusive widow.

"Yes, my lady, thank you," said Jones, sounding relieved. Christina covered her mouth with her hand. She'd never heard her butler use quite that tone of voice before.

Of course, he'd never been faced with possibly needing to turn away a duke before either.

Beside her, Benedict groaned, trying to pull her back down to him and the soft, warm sheets. "Must we?"

"We must," she said, leaning over to give him a kiss, as reluctant as he was to leave the little haven of love they'd created for themselves in the bedroom. However, unlike him, she was also rather anxious to make a good impression on his family and she wasn't entirely certain how circumspect Daphne would remain if she were kept waiting. "Poor Jones might faint if I told him to turn away a Duke. So truthfully, it is your own fault for belonging to such a lofty family."

With a groan, Benedict pushed himself into a sitting position. "Well, for Jones' sake then."

Laughing again, Christina rose to dress. She found herself smiling when she entered her closet and found it full to bursting - a state it had never quite achieved before - with Benedict's wardrobe added to her own. There was something quite satisfying about seeing their clothing arrayed together in one place.

EVERYTHING HAPPENED JUST as Benedict had said it would, at least in regards to his family and Society's reactions. What he hadn't counted on was Christina.

The first night in London as man and wife went swimmingly. His household was already well on its way to integrating into hers, although some of his had returned to Isaac's house as they would have been extraneous in Christina's. His wife had practically glowed as her new family welcomed her, Lady Daphne and her husband looking on approvingly. Marley, Isaac, and Felix had all immediately gotten on well, to the delight of their wives and Benedict.

Arabella had been in alt to welcome her newest sister to the family, and Lydia looked much relieved - probably hoping to have a second steadying influence on the young woman.

Christina's staff had rallied and prepared a splendid dinner on short notice, after which Benedict had been happy to see the backs of everyone so he could take his wife back to their room and ravish her all over again. The next morning they'd spent their time going through the sea of cards and invitations which had been left at the house, Christina's eyes going wide at the personal notes written on the majority, extending the host's hopes of an acceptance. There might be some gossip, but scandalous or to be avoided they obviously were not.

When Christina decided to be at-home that afternoon it was a mob scene - one which Benedict was tempted to flee, but which he endured so as not to leave Christina to the vultures. After all, they'd all come hoping to see the couple together, not the wife on her own, and it was no hardship to dance attendance on Christina.

It was also when he detected the first sign of trouble.

His wife was possessive.

Extremely possessive.

Which was not a problem in and of itself. Benedict considered himself a rather possessive man after all, although many of his own anxieties had been soothed by legally binding Christina to him. However, it was becoming obvious Christina's insecurities had not benefited from the same effect - if anything she'd been more possessive and on edge than ever, verging on almost manic as she began to look with suspicion and ire at any lady conversing with him.

Understanding why, Benedict did his best to dampen her jealousy by being on his best behavior and not engaging in conversation with any one lady for more than a few minutes before ensuring Christina was also included. Slowly, his love began to relax as Benedict remained by her side, openly admiring of her, and only civil to the visiting ladies.

That night, he took his time with her, pleasuring her into a blissful heap of limbs before finally reaching his own culmination.

His wife's trust and security would take time, he reminded himself as he stroked her hair, her head nestled on his shoulder. Staring up into the darkness, he counseled himself to patience. After all, he had married her so she would be forced to give him the opportunity to show her she could trust him, not because he thought it would solve every one of her doubts immediately.

And he'd always been better at patience than either of his siblings.

The very next night, Christina seemed determined to test his patience.

The rout at Lady Waverly's was well attended, and it seemed many ladies of the *ton* were curious over his and Christina's marriage. Not just the ladies, but the gentlemen as well. At one point, Benedict was sure he even saw Hartford in the crush, speaking with someone who looked very much like Walter Hood, but they were too far away to be sure of either man's identity.

"Lady Shaftesbury is looking rather lovely this evening," Christina murmured, low enough only Benedict could hear her. She was looking across the room at the lady in question, who had very pretty auburn hair not too dissimilar to Christina's, but didn't have the abundant curves Benedict preferred. Of course, his preference hadn't kept him from indulging with Lady Shaftesbury for about a month a few years ago; the lady in question had been quite insistent and, at the time, he'd been both unattached and happy to find an amorous companion. It hadn't taken him long to discover that, while she was adventurous in the bedroom, the lady was a bit of a shrew and they parted ways.

Christina had been keeping up a running commentary on the amount of beautiful ladies present this evening, and an uncomfortable number of them had - at one time or another - graced Benedict's bed. He wasn't entirely sure she knew whom his past lovers had been, but she certainly seemed to have a fairly good general idea.

"Yes," he replied, his voice bland. "If only she weren't so bitter and peevish; she quite ruins her looks with her demeanor."

Startled, probably because this was the first time he'd said something so rude about one of the ladies she'd commented on, Christina looked up at him with wide eyes. Benedict raised his eyebrow at her. Yes, he knew what she was doing by constantly asking him about the other ladies.

Blushing, Christina looked away, obviously trying not to squirm with both anxiety and embarrassment.

Bending down, Benedict whispered in her ear. "It doesn't matter how many lovely ladies you bring my attention to, love, not one of them will compare with you. Ever."

It was true. She was looking particularly splendid tonight in a shade of purple that was almost scandalously close to being royal, her creamy breasts pressing against a delightfully low neckline which had Benedict's own possessive nature rumbling, and amethysts in silver practically dripping into her décolletage. Just looking at her amounted to foreplay as his cock swelled against his breeches.

She looked up at him again, her expression tinged with remorse. "I'm sorry, Benedict. I know I'm being a trial. I just can't seem to help myself."

"I'd rather you spoke your worries aloud than keep them bottled up, love," he said, reaching over to place his hand atop hers on his arm, where it had been resting the whole evening unless they were on the dance floor. They'd only danced a few; Benedict with Arabella, Gabrielle, Lady Spencer, and Miss Wilson, and Christina with Isaac, Felix, Thomas, and Spencer. He was quite sure anyone else would tax Christina's nerves too much.

Her low, unhappy laugh made his heart clench a little, his arousal subsiding at the sound. "If I did not bottle them up, I'm afraid I would never stop speaking. My imagination quite gets the better of me at times."

"Then we will just have to ensure reality keeps your imagination at bay," he said, giving her fingers a squeeze.

For just a moment, he felt her lean into him, as if using him to prop her up, taking her strength from his. Unfortunately, they still had several hours to go before they could leave the ball and return home, where he could show her exactly the attention he wanted to.

IT WAS an unfortunate truth that a woman's bladder could only hold so much liquid. Even less liquid while she was wearing a corset, Christina had found, hurrying towards the ladies' retiring room. She had tried, she truly had, but after several glasses of champagne to calm her nerves, a dedicated effort not to think about how full her bladder felt, and realizing there was at least another hour before they could gracefully depart Lady Waverly's ball, she had finally admitted defeat.

Of course there was no *real* reason for her to feel so anxious over leaving Benedict in the ballroom. He wouldn't be entirely alone. She was sure he would still be there, standing right where she'd left him, when she returned. After all, he was surrounded by his family and friends and - when he wasn't reassuring her irrational jealousies - watching over Arabella.

While the young woman could be quite outspoken in private with the family, she was very well behaved once the company was less select, so Christina didn't entirely understand the worry. Benedict had told her about some of the contretemps his sister had gotten into during her first Season, but obviously she had matured since then. The way Isaac and Benedict hovered over her, glaring at any gentlemen with the tiniest spot on his reputation, one would think she was only inches away from total ruin.

Then again, she did also find their protectiveness rather endearing. She couldn't help but think about how Benedict might behave if they had a daughter.

Which just brought up another one of her fears.

Christina *wanted* children. She'd wanted them with George. Somehow, she wanted them even more with Benedict. But she was afraid to broach the topic. Obviously he'd realized she'd been married and never produced a child, but she still couldn't help worrying her inability to do so with him might ultimately result in disappointment on his part.

Of course, rationally, logically, Christina knew there was no reason to fret over Benedict's faithfulness. He'd hardly stray so early in their marriage with his family, especially his younger sister, watching them. There was no reason to worry about her child-bearing abilities - as she had no control over it – either. But she didn't feel particularly rational or logical. No matter how she tried to remain cold emotionally, to reassure herself with facts and sensibility, her mind wouldn't listen and neither would her heart.

Every time Benedict's gaze passed around the ballroom, her chest clenched, wondering if he was admiring a particular woman, a woman he might later find himself interested in. If he spoke to a woman, some part of her mind insisted the woman was flirting with him, trying to take him away from her. Even when he was solicitous of Christina, obviously sensing her jealousy, some part of her felt it must all be for show.

She was constantly waiting for the penny to drop, for the curtain to fall, for the illusion of love and security to vanish into ether.

Which wasn't at all fair to Benedict, and it was a terrible way to live, but she didn't know how to stop herself.

And, despite Benedict's reassurances, she absolutely could not tell him every manic thought which darted through her head. There were so many and they were so nonsensical, she wouldn't blame him for throwing her in Bedlam if she admitted everything her overactive mind conjured up.

Several ladies were in the retiring room when Christina entered, and she managed to accept their congratulations and well wishes with considerable aplomb, covering her anxieties, before tending to her own needs. She was somewhat reassured by the reactions of the *ton*, which were just as Benedict predicted. No one seemed surprised or scandalized by their elopement; indeed, the description she heard most often was "romantic;" while they'd created a stir, it was in a positive manner.

Which was all one could really hope for.

Thankfully other ladies had left the retiring room by the time Christina had completed her toilette. She patted her hands dry, checked her dress in the mirror, and exited the room, nearly bumping into another woman on the other side of the door.

"Oh, ex-ex-excuse..." Her apology stuttered and trailed off as she saw exactly who she'd just run into.

Several inches shorter than Christina, the perfect, porcelain features of Baroness Mathilde Alvenley rearranged into an expression of contempt. Ethereally beautiful, the Baroness' mass of blonde curls were swept up into a complicated coiffure which looked as though it might tumble free at any moment, with two curly tendrils hanging down to frame her oval face. The stunning blue of her dress matched her incredible eyes exactly, the rose trim bringing out the natural blush of her cheeks and lips. She was a stunning vision to behold, a vision any man would be caught by.

George apparently had been.

"What are you doing here?" Christina asked with a little gasp, feeling suddenly, utterly sick inside. She hadn't realized the Baroness was even in London. Daphne hadn't told her... Daphne must not have known.

One blonde brow rose in derision. "Accompanying my husband as he carries out his duties of course," the Baroness said in a musical voice. "As a good wife should."

Christina flinched at the barb, hating herself for feeling gawky, too large, and too dark in front of the Baroness' angelic, petite presence; hating herself for letting anything the Baroness said needle her.

Clenching her jaw, she started to swing around the other woman, but the Baroness was not through with her and her next words stopped Christina in her tracks.

"I hear you've remarried."

"I have," Christina said coldly, with all the dignity she could muster. She turned to regard the other woman, her heart stuttering along in her chest as best it could while she faced the source of her greatest humiliation and heartbreak. Although it hadn't been all the Baroness' fault, but she was the only person still living whom Christina could blame.

A smile spread the Baroness' lips, but it was not a pleasant one. "A love match, again, I heard. How very foolish of you not to have learned your lesson the first time."

"Stay away from my husband," Christina hissed, taking a step towards the other woman, her hand clenching into a fist.

The other woman's smile widened, her eyes sparking with malevolent satisfaction, and Christina froze. The Baroness knew she'd scored a point.

"How will you even know whether or not I do?" the Baroness

asked, tilting her head to the side, making her look like an evil doll. "After all, you had no idea the first time."

It felt like a cold sweat broke out on Christina's body as the other woman tinkled a laugh.

"Why?" Christina asked, her voice almost a croak as the Baroness started to turn away. "Why can't you just leave me alone?"

"My dear, if you wanted me to do that, you should have never poached Haversham." With a sniff, the Baroness tossed her head and went into the retiring room, leaving Christina alone and shaken in the hall.

Yes, her interest in Haversham had stemmed from seeing the Baroness flirt with him... she couldn't deny it. At the time, she'd only been thinking of how she wanted to show she was just as desirable to men. She hadn't truly thought she had a chance, compared to the lovely Baroness. But Haversham had turned his attentions to her, and apparently the Baroness was bitter about it rather than realizing how it had truly been tit for tat. After all, the Baroness had committed the first offense.

She was an abominable person, Christina realized, no matter how angelic she looked. Obviously she had no care for anyone else's feelings.

Overcome with an urge to flee the woman's noxious presence, even if a door did currently separate them, and to stake her claim on Benedict, Christina quickly fled the scene.

CHAPTER 13

"What is wrong with you?" Benedict asked, trying not to sound too antagonistic, but he was rapidly beginning to lose patience.

He thought he'd done a fine job of reassuring Christina, but when she'd returned to him from the retiring room, her jealousy seemed to have reached new heights for no reason he could see. She'd been short with Lord and Lady Pendleton, acerbic with Mrs. Wentworth, and downright hostile to Lady Capell, who had just come out of mourning and was quite beautiful but not at all flirtatious - at least not to him. There was no reason for Christina's foul mood and contrary attitude as far as Benedict could see, and if she did not curb her behavior, it was very likely people would soon begin to talk.

Christina's head snapped around, her eyes full of ire as she glared at him. Her voice started as a whisper but began rising as she spoke. "My apologies, my lord, did I interrupt your *tête'á'tête*? Did you wish to continue speaking with her? Is a raven-haired widow more to your liking than your own wife?"

That did it.

Something had happened and Christina was no longer able to behave rationally or even civilly. They needed to depart, immediately, and as soon as they returned home he was going to spank the dickens out of her. It was one thing to feel unsure and anxious, quite another to actually be rude to other members of Society without provocation.

And he was definitely not going to tolerate being accused of preferring other women when everything he said and did displayed his complete infatuation with her, his wife.

"Hush," he said, quietly, leaning in to ensure he wouldn't be overheard. "Not one more word other than to take our farewells."

Her mouth opened and then snapped shut as she took in his serious expression. There was a slight tightening of her fingers on his arm and then she turned her face away from him, but not before he saw a telling look in her eyes - that of a woman whom had just received a reprieve. But a reprieve from what?

He almost thought she'd been hoping to be taken in hand, although he couldn't imagine why the need had sprung up during a simple fifteen minute visit to the ladies' retiring room. She obviously realized he was upset, and yet, as he took her to say good night to their family and friends, then take their leave of Lady Waverly, she relaxed with every passing minute.

When they reached the carriage and he handed her in, he swore he heard her sigh with relief.

It was only when he was in the carriage, sitting across from her with a stormy expression on his face, she began to look nervous again.

"Ah... Benedict..." She faltered, looking down at her hands, which were clenched atop her purple skirts.

"Not one more word," he said, clenching his jaw against his anger and frustration. Whatever had happened, he did not wish to begin their discussion during a carriage ride while he was still trying to temper his own hurt and displeasure. "Whatever it is, we will discuss it once we've returned home. I need the ride to calm myself."

Because he couldn't - wouldn't - spank her while he was angry. Discipline should never be done in haste or while ruled by emotion.

And Christina was absolutely going to be disciplined tonight.

He was happy to cater to her possessiveness, to soothe her insecurities, and allow leniency for her jealousy, but she had been rude, disrespectful, and bordering on making a scene. None of which was acceptable, and he doubted she'd be very pleased with her behavior once she'd calmed.

From the very little Isaac had said about his and Lydia's relationship, Lydia occasionally required some form of discipline in order to keep her own anxieties from overwhelming her. It provided a release of a sort. Pondering that thought, Benedict wondered if such a tactic might work well for his own wife.

~

As relieved as Christina had been to leave Waverly House, she was even more relieved when they reached their own home and the silent, uncomfortable carriage ride was finally over.

Sitting in the darkness, she had been unable to stop thinking about the last time they'd left a ball like this. The spanking... the elopement... was Benedict regretting his hasty actions? She wouldn't blame him if he was. He seemed much more upset with her now than he had been that evening.

Without conversation, her mind focused on what had prompted his ire - her disgraceful behavior.

Now that she was away from the ballroom, away from the Baroness, away from the multitudes of other *ton* beauties, all Christina could think of was how she'd overreacted. How rude she'd been to poor Lady Capell, who had requested the introduction to Christina - not to Benedict. Likely she'd wanted to speak with another young widow, and Christina had been both short and cold.

The young woman hadn't deserved such a response in the least. Christina would certainly have to go and make amends.

Shame and guilt had swamped her during the entire journey home, especially when she thought about how she'd implicitly maligned Benedict. Of course, he hadn't been looking for a new lover, or flirting with other women, or preparing to begin an affair. No wonder he was both hurt and upset by her overzealous jealousy and especially her final accusation about Lady Capell.

Seeing the Baroness had made her overwrought and already more on edge than she had been before, but that was no true excuse.

Christina didn't know why she'd let her emotions run away with her so badly, she just wished she hadn't.

As they ascended the front stairs into the house, she felt her bottom start tingling in anticipation of her punishment. Not that she was looking forward to it, exactly... except, some part of her was. She felt almost itchy with the need for it.

"Thank you, Mr. Jones," Benedict said as the butler opened the door the moment they reached it. Despite their early arrival home. Christina wondered if he'd been watching at the window on the off chance they would return early or if he just possessed some innate sense which warned him of his employers' presence. Then she wondered why her mind chose to focus on such a ridiculous fancy. "Please inform Esther that my wife will not need her assistance this evening."

Because Benedict would help Christina out of her ballgown himself.

She both quailed and exulted at the thought as Mr. Jones nodded, murmuring his understanding, and closed the door behind them before moving away down the hall.

Firm fingers pressed against Christina's lower back, gently but purposefully.

"Upstairs," Benedict said, his voice soft, controlled. No longer angry, but she knew he still felt the emotion - he just had taken the time in the carriage to manage it. She wished she had done so at the ball. "I will meet you in our bedroom."

She opened her mouth to ask why he was meeting her there, instead of escorting her, and then snapped her lips shut when he raised his eyebrows at her. No, this was not the time to be curious. If he'd wanted her to know, he would have told her.

The dread spreading through her, the worry over what awful implement he might be fetching which wasn't already available in their shared room was probably part of her punishment. Trying to both dawdle and hurry along simultaneously, Christina made her way to their bedroom, chewing on her lower lip the whole way.

Once there, she began to take down her hair, pulling the pins from the heavy mass so the curls tumbled down around her shoulders and back. The activity gave her hands something to do; otherwise she probably would have just paced or fidgeted, waiting for her husband to return.

Her husband.

Hers.

Which she would do well to remember. He was not George. He would not hurt her as George had. She believed it, she did... even if she didn't always behave as though she believed. Her emotions had overcome her reason this evening, and she was already regretting her lack of control.

She had just begun trying to undo the small buttons securing the back of her dress when the door opened behind her.

Jumping, because she hadn't heard his approaching footsteps, Christina turned to see what her husband was holding. To her surprise, there was no huge, threatening implement in his hand. Just a small bowl with something in it, although she couldn't clearly see what.

His expression was mostly blank, but she thought it might have softened just a touch when he looked at her and saw her unbound hair.

"Undressing?" he asked, moving towards their bed and putting the bowl down on the nightstand.

"Yes."

"Good girl," he said, turning back to her with a smile. Christina felt her insides warm at the accolade, happiness trickling through her. While she might have hurt him, even angered him, with her behavior this evening, he would forgive her. Perhaps he already had, although she knew that would not stop him from punishing her.

She was glad. Because she needed it.

∼

His wife - and how he enjoyed thinking of her in that term during moments like this - shifted nervously as he moved towards her.

"Turn around," he said. "I'll help you with your dress."

Biting her lower lip, she did as he ordered, some of the tension leaving her when he dropped a kiss to her bare shoulder before brushing the thick strands of her hair over it, moving the silky mass away from her buttons. Benedict loved her hair. He also loved her in this dress. He wished they were ending the evening in a more enjoyable manner; he would have liked to undo her hair himself and slowly strip her dress from her body, while covering her newly bared skin with kisses.

A fantasy for another time, he supposed.

This was more important. He wanted to know what had set his wife off, why she had suddenly turned into a shrew so late in the evening. Benedict realized something must have happened; what he didn't understand was why she hadn't come and told him. Why had she left him in the dark?

Despite his lingering hurt, his cock still hardened as piece after piece of clothing was stripped from Christina's body. Her creamy, pale skin, rosy tipped nipples, and the dark thatch of curls at the juncture of her thighs was a sight which never failed to arouse him. Especially when he thought about what was going to come next.

Discipline for her could still be quite enjoyable for him, at least in a physical, erotic sense. He was rather curious to see how she would react to his plan for tonight.

"Come," he said, holding out his hand, which she took, looking almost shy. He picked up the hairbrush she'd left beside her hairpins, taking it with them towards the bed, enjoying the way she eyed it nervously.

He had deliberately left himself completely clothed while stripping her down. After remembering how he'd used her hairbrush when prompting her to speak candidly to him, he decided a similar tactic might be in order for tonight. A small smile curved his lips as she glanced curiously at the bowl he'd brought in, and wondered if she recognized the object it held.

"Over my lap, love."

Her hair spilled down as she laid herself where he directed, and he heard a little whimper as he tilted her forward more, lifting her bottom higher in the air. The creamy mounds were practically begging for some color... but not yet. He palmed her upturned cheeks, squeezing them gently for his own enjoyment while she squirmed slightly, anxious and waiting. The hard ridge of his cock was trapped between their bodies, pressing into her side as she wriggled.

"I am disappointed, Christina." Immediately, he felt her slump, obviously feeling her guilt. His fingers curved over the buttock closest to him, the tips seeking out the little rosebud nestled there. She stiffened slightly and then relaxed again as he began to massage the crinkled star. "I do not mind your possessiveness, and I hope I can help assuage your uncertainties about marriage in general over time, but I cannot countenance outright rudeness on your part - and I do not think you would want me to."

"I don't," she said softly, her body becoming even more pliable, which caused her bottom hole to press against his fingers. "I'm so sorry... I don't know what came over me. It will not happen again."

Smiling - she couldn't see his expression anyway, so she didn't need to know the loving, warm look he was bestowing on her - Benedict pulled away from her tight little hole and reached for the small finger of ginger he'd peeled and carved. It was not overly large, but it would certainly get her attention even more than her hairbrush had.

"I'm gladdened to hear that," he said, pressing the tip of the ginger to her star and beginning to slowly push in. A little gasp left her lips as her opening was stretched, without any lubricant. The ginger itself was soft and its entry would not hurt her, but it would feel quite strange. Once it began to burn, she wouldn't be as focused on her words; he wanted to hear the truth, unvarnished, without her being able to think overly much about her responses. "However, I would still like to discuss exactly what came over you. You were behaving perfectly normally, you went to the retiring room, and when you returned you had transformed. What happened in the retiring room, love?"

∽

SHE WAS TRYING to pay attention to Benedict's words, but it was difficult when whatever it was he'd just inserted into her rear entry was beginning to hurt much more than it should!

"Ow... Benedict... something's wrong... whatever you just did, it's starting to burn!"

"I know, love," his voice was soothing as his hand began to rub her lower back, but the soft caresses did nothing to slow the tingling, growing heat stinging the inside of her bottom. "That's what the ginger is supposed to do. Now, what happened in the retiring room?"

"Oh!" Christina had clenched, her body trying to expel the intruder, but the movement had only increased the burn! She gasped, her fingers scrabbling along the floor, as if finding purchase there would somehow help the increasingly uncomfortable heat spreading through her lower body. Even more disconcertingly, as her mound pressed against Benedict's thigh, she was overwhelmed by the need to press harder, to rub herself against him. Her nipples were puckered, aching to be touched, to burn like the rest of her, and she was beginning to feel almost frantic.

"Christina, what happened in the retiring room?" To punctuate the question, Benedict pumped the ginger, rasping it over her raw nerves, making her squeal as the burn increased with movement.

"Th-the Baroness!" She practically shouted her answer, quivering with the effort not to squeeze her bottom cheeks together again. "Baroness Alvenley! She was there!"

"What did she do?"

Her body was awash with sensation, completely overloaded, completely focused on the burn in her bottom, the ache between her thighs. It felt like every pulse of flames from the ginger spurred a responding pulse in her pussy, making her writhe on Benedict's lap like a cat in heat.

"She-she said she's going after you... she's angry about Haversham... she wants you... as if taking George from me hadn't been bad enough!" Christina's anger fought with her arousal, as a surge of indignation and hateful fury rose inside of her. She still couldn't believe the selfishness, the casual cruelty of the woman.

"Well she won't have me," Benedict said, his voice almost soothing as he squeezed her bottom cheek, making her moan. "I'm sorry love, if I'd known she was present I would have protected you better."

"N-not your fault," Christina protested, shaking her head, trying to turn to look up at him and then gasping as the attempt made her bottom automatically clench again. She moaned, panting for breath at the erotically charged pain which was sizzling through her. "D-d-d-didn't hear her announced."

"I also feel as though I should apologize for having to return to the capital in the first place," Benedict said ruefully, his hands gentle as he continued to caress her - which of course, only increased the sensual need curling through her. "Ideally, we would have been able to spend more time together without so many distractions and social events, to give you time to feel more secure in our marriage. Unfortunately, I am as obligated to my sister as I am to you, so we shall have to work to find a way for me to accommodate both of you."

Christina shook her head. "I'm fine, I promise, I just..."

"However," Benedict said, raising his voice slightly and continuing as if she hadn't spoken at all. "That does not excuse your behavior. If you had told me about the Baroness' presence, I would have been happy to cling even closer to your skirts and to soothe your worries. You certainly shouldn't have taken out your understandable apprehension on everyone else. So, I am going to spank you with the hairbrush now, and next time you will come to me and we will face your anxieties together, as man and wife."

SMACK!

SMACK!

The two swift blows cracked against her cheeks, making Christina howl as she clenched around the ginger in response, increasing the burning level of discomfort twofold. Even so, she found herself rubbing her mound even harder against Benedict's thigh, her pussy juices beginning to drip down her legs as her arousal soared.

SMACK!
SMACK!

The scent of ginger and woman filled Benedict's nose, seductively intoxicating. Christina's tears were already falling, even as she desperately moved against his leg, obviously highly aroused.

SMACK!
SMACK!

The crisp swats of wood against her flesh fell fast and furious, although not as painfully as they could have since he hadn't warmed her up with his hand first. Hard enough she had to work to keep her bottom from clenching around the ginger, but not so hard she would clench instinctively.

SMACK!

His cock ached as she cried out, squirming against him, her pink cheeks quivering around the tan end of the ginger finger. The little hole it was invading looked quite pink as well, although not nearly as pink as her swollen, glossy pussy lips.

SMACK!

Benedict had decided not to punish her too harshly. After all, he could understand why she'd become so overwrought and reacted so badly. If she were to do so again, he'd certainly employ harsher measures, but for tonight his sweetheart needed coddling as much as she needed punishment.

A sore bottom, inside and out, tomorrow should be enough to remind her to behave. The marks and ache needn't linger further than that. Not this time.

SMACK!

Christina's legs began to kick as she cried and writhed, rubbing herself against him even as he turned her bottom a hot, bright pink. Every inch of her flesh jiggled as the hard wood flattened her cheeks over and over again, searing her skin until he could feel the heat emanating with his hand. By now she was clenching and barely noticing the burn of the ginger, he was sure of it.

With a flurry of sharp swats to her sit spots, to ensure the lesson had been firmly driven home, Benedict finally tossed the hair brush aside and pulled the ginger from her bottom, eliciting a whimper from her as the finger moved, and placed it back in the bowl.

"Good girl," he murmured, rubbing her hot bottom, enjoying the way she writhed against his hand. "If you see the Baroness again what will you do, love?"

"Come find you and tell you," Christina said with a gasp as his fingers brushed over her tender anus. It looked a little swollen and quite pink from the ginger's effects, but none the worse for wear. Part of him ached to bury himself inside her there, but that was something else which would have to wait.

"Exactly," he said, helping her move so she was bent over the bed instead of his lap, his mind already moving from her discipline to a more amorous intent.

The little pink star winked between her rosy cheeks, the puffy lips of her pussy fringed with dark curls making an enticing view beneath. Benedict quickly undid the front of his pants, too desperate to be inside of her to bother with the rest of his clothes.

His cock was hard as a rock, fluid gathering at the tip in its eagerness to plow his wife. Benedict didn't think he'd ever tire of being able to release inside of her.

Grasping her firmly by the hips, he lined his cock up with her creamy sheathe, and mounted her with one smooth stroke that had both of them gasping with pleasure. The heat of her slick pussy was phenomenal, and she immediately shuddered around him, squeezing his cock as her bottom lifted, her hot cheeks pressing against his groin.

"Bloody hell... Christina..." He groaned, his fingers tightening on her hips as he began to ride her hard.

The pain was beautiful. Heady. Thrilling.

Christina moaned into the sheets, rubbing her breasts and nipples against them with every hard thrust of Benedict's cock into her, his body pressing her into the mattress. It wasn't enough. Her lower body was afire with pain... pleasure... she moved her hands beneath her to squeeze her breasts, almost as though she was trying to crush them with her fingers.

Her back arched, and she found her nipples, pinching the tender buds, pulling them hard as Benedict pressed into her from behind. He was fucking her so hard, so deeply, she could feel him all through her body. With his hands holding her firmly in place, she couldn't move back to meet him nor could she move away as his hard thrusts reignited the sensation of being spanked in her bottom.

As she tormented her own nipples, so needy, so achy for the jagged edges of pain to flavor her pleasure, Christina practically sobbed as Benedict's cock plundered her depths. She had no more room for doubts, for apprehension, for fear... he'd turned her into a *houri*, a siren, a creature there to pleasure him whether it was with her pain or her ecstasy.

"Oh yes... bloody hell... Christina... I love you..." His efforts doubled, his cock pounding into her hard and fast as it swelled. "I love you."

Christina screamed as her orgasm crested. Her fingers pinched the tiny buds of her nipples so hard they felt as though they were about to burst. Her body throbbed, shuddered, *shattered*, as undone by his heated declaration as she was by the physical sensations crashing over her. She released her hold on her breasts, overcome by the intensity of her climax, and grasped at the bed as Benedict surged within her.

She felt him swell, pulse, filling her with heat, his hoarse cry announcing his orgasm as she writhed before him in abject sexual bliss, a willing receptacle for his pleasure as he poured himself into her.

The grip on her hips relaxed, gentling as his fingers began to caress; the tender strokes of a man who had been quite well satisfied. With a little quiver, Christina slumped.

Her bottom burned, inside and out, and her lower body throbbed, but she no longer felt so wound up or so unsettled. Benedict's hands traced her curves, soothing her further, as if she were a sleepy kitten.

In the days to come she would apologize to everyone she'd been short with this evening, especially Lady Capell, and she would go to Benedict to be reassured if and when the Baroness made another appearance. There was no need to be so on edge.

She let out a little sigh as Benedict pulled himself free, leaving her lower body hot but satiated. The sounds of him undressing were recognizable as she muzzily tried to garner the strength to push herself up - or at least crawl fully onto the bed. Any moment now her muscles would stop feeling like limp noodles, she was sure of it.

A low chuckle made her lift her head, and she smiled sleepily over her shoulder at her naked husband. He shook his head, smiling back, before helping lift her up into the bed.

"Just lay there, love, I'll do the rest."

Christina was about to ask him what he meant, but he was already rolling her onto her back and spreading her legs wide, head lowering to her breast as she whimpered at the pressure of weight on her sore bottom.

It wasn't long before Christina was doing quite a bit more than just lying there; reciprocating touch for touch as Benedict made her burn, yearn, and scream all over again.

CHAPTER 14

"Welcome to the club!"

Blinking at this nonsensical greeting, Benedict's forward movement ground to a halt as he stared at Spencer. The man was raising a glass towards Benedict, a knowing grin on his face. Behind Benedict, Isaac jostled him forward, so he had no choice but to continue his advance into Spencer's billiard room. Darkly and comfortably furnished, the room was obviously a masculine haven; the air smelled faintly of liquor and cigars, and the furniture was heavy and well made.

"Keep moving, Benedict, and ignore Wesley," Isaac rumbled, pushing past him the rest of the way into the room. "The rest of us do."

Spencer, looking more piratical than ever without his jacket or cravat to give him even a smidgen of respectability, just chuckled as Isaac crossed to join him. Standing on the other side of the pool table, Felix leaned against the cue in his hand, while his brother Thomas lounged in a chair close enough to watch the game.

"What club?" Benedict asked, still feeling rather puzzled. Isaac had practically dragged him out today, as Benedict had spent the past week dancing attendance on Christina, asserting they needed some time together. Benedict, taking Isaac at his word, had reassured Christina they were merely paying a visit to Spencer's home, and had even hinted she should feel free to pay a call to Lady Spencer if she liked. She'd bitten her lip and shook her head no, although he was sure she was just trying to show she trusted him.

"It's not a real club," Thomas drawled, exchanging an amused look with Isaac as Benedict's brother crossed to a table laden with a decanter of amber liquid, several glasses, and a plate of biscuits.

"Alex says Wesley only wants to call it that because no real club will have him," Felix said, laughing as Spencer made a rude gesture at him.

"Alex?" Benedict asked, still feeling rather bemused as he followed his brother to the liquor.

"Greville," Isaac said, handing the first tumbler he poured to Benedict. A small smile played on his lips, and he looked considerably more relaxed than Benedict was used to seeing his brother, even in their friends' company. Although, prior to this, Benedict had only seen Isaac interact with these gentlemen at an establishment such as Whites or when they were accompanied by their wives. "We all call each other by our Christian names."

"Which we hope you will join us in doing so," Wesley said cheekily, giving Benedict a wink before he bent over and took his shot. Felix cursed when the ball Wesley had aimed for obligingly skid straight into the corner pocket.

As Spencer - Wesley - was the only one in the room whom Benedict had not already been close enough with to call by his first name, Benedict couldn't help but be curious. "Who else is in this club?"

"Petersham, Hyde, Greville, and Dunbury," Wesley said with relish. He shot Thomas a look. "Hood over here is actually not an official member, seeing as he's still a bachelor. So, you may assume any statements he makes about the legitimacy of my club to be pure jealousy on his part. We took pity on him today and offered refuge, as his mother is on a particular tear."

Thomas snorted, his lips quirking. "I won't need to be a member once I'm married, because *my* wife-"

"Oh, dear God, don't get him started on his list again," Felix said with a groan. "There isn't a woman alive who matches that damn list anyway, so he'll never be married at this rate." He looked at his brother. "If you're going to start in on that list, I'm never bringing you to another club meeting again, I don't care how bothersome Mother is being."

"Ah ha! So you admit we're a club!" Wesley crowed.

Scowling at his younger brother, Thomas opened his mouth - likely to argue, but Benedict started speaking again before he could.

"But what kind of club - real or fictional - is it?"

"It's a club for Spanking Husbands," Wesley said, knocking another ball into the pocket.

"Stop calling it that," Isaac said as he settled into one of chairs beside Thomas. Benedict hovered at the table with the whiskey; it gave him a good vantage point of the entire room, plus he had a feeling being near the liquor might be an advantage given the sudden turn of conversation. "It sounds as though we're the ones being spanked when you say it that way, not doing the spanking."

"You *all* spank your wives?" Benedict asked, dumbstruck. "All of you *and* the others?"

He'd known about Isaac of course, in the most general way, and Wesley had made more than one comment in Benedict's hearing which made his predilections no surprise, but Benedict hadn't realized *all* of them... Then again, there wasn't any real way to talk about such things in polite company.

"Yes, although Hugh only does it when Irene has actually earned discipline," Wesley said, almost sounding bewildered. As if to confirm his confusion, he missed the next shot. Grinning, Felix stepped up to the table as Wesley sighed and turned away. "Still, we have quite an accumulation of knowledge here, if you have any questions or any particular advice to dole out. Oh! And I have a wedding present for you."

"Now this is where you're really missing out," Felix said to his brother as Wesley retrieved a large box from a side table. "The wedding present really is quite something."

"But how did you all know..."

"Even if Isaac didn't know, it was fairly obvious your wife was sitting a bit gingerly at Lady Hampton's dinner last night," Felix said, giving Benedict a significant look. "Being husbands who spank our wives, we are all quite familiar with the signs."

Grinning like a mischievous young lad, Wesley returned to Benedict and set the box on the table in front of him. With some trepidation, Benedict put down his glass and opened the top. He blinked in surprise at the contents, all of which were carefully and securely laid out.

"Oils from India," Wesley said, pointing to the three well cushioned glass bottles encased within. "This one is for massages, this one for lubrication, and this one you only take a drop or two with a glass of wine if you'd truly like to be up all night. India's aphrodisiacs can pack quite a wallop."

"I actually already have this set," Benedict said, grinning as he tapped the familiar box of dilators. "On your recommendation, I believe."

"Ah yes, you'll find the lubrication oil quite useful for those, and the oils I only provide to members of our club," Wesley said with glee. The Earl seemed to have forgotten all about the game he'd been playing with Felix, but the other man didn't seem to mind as he'd begun chatting with Isaac and Thomas. "I have found there are different benefits to each one, depending on your desired outcome. Lately I've been experimenting with trying to create a strap to hold one in place, so Cynthia could walk about with it. What do you think about-"

As Wesley warmed to his topic, Benedict listened intently, thinking that such a club was not a bad idea at all.

Although Isaac was certainly correct about the name.

FORTUNATELY FOR CHRISTINA'S NERVES, she was not alone for long after Benedict and Isaac left the house.

Her anxiety didn't rise from a lack of trust, more from the feeling of being totally out of control. While she might enjoy a lack of control in the bedchamber, it didn't suit her temperament at all for everyday life - especially after so much time being entirely in control of her own life, including her emotions. Now she was not the only hand on the rudder steering her life; Benedict's was there as well, and while she found comfort in that, there was also fear.

Fear of losing him.

Fear of not being able to *keep* him.

Of course, she didn't really expect the Baroness to jump upon him the moment he left the house without Christina... but what if she did?

Benedict would turn her away, of course, she reassured herself.

But what if he didn't?

Of course he would.

But what *if he didn't?*

There was some part of her mind which refused to be reasoned with, much to her despair.

When Lydia arrived, accompanied by Arabella and Mrs. Hood, Christina felt almost faint with the relief of being rescued from herself and her destructive thoughts by her new sisters-in-law and Arabella's best friend. She'd told Mr. Jones she was only at-home to close friends and family, as she hadn't the patience for dealing with gossipy acquaintances while she was so overwrought with nerves, but she hadn't expected any to come by.

She'd asked Jones to show them into the drawing room, while Christina quickly looked herself over to ensure she did not appear as wild as she felt. After all, she'd noticed the ladies were always impeccably turned out and she did not want them to think less of her. Stepping into the drawing room to greet the beautiful bevy of women, Christina nearly sighed at how serenely perfect they all appeared.

Dressed in a beautiful mint and cream striped walking dress, Lydia looked every inch the perfect lady with every last hair tucked gently into place. She smiled wide at Christina's entrance, standing to greet her. Rising with her, Arabella and Mrs. Hood were also looking quite well, although they always seemed just a touch less self-assured than Lydia did. Mrs. Hood was wearing a rose pink gown which nicely suited her pink and cream complexion and light brown hair, while Arabella's pale yellow dress trimmed with pale blue was both perfectly respectable for a debutante and contrasted nicely with her dark eyes and hair.

After they exchanged greetings and Christina rang for tea, Lydia struck up a conversation with Christina about the new rose hybrid Mrs. Thomas would be displaying at Kew Gardens in two days. The younger two ladies pretended interest for all for two minutes before they fell to a whispered conversation between the two of them, which both Christina and Lydia ignored, although they exchanged a kind of knowingly amused look. It was very likely their conversation revolved around the various gentlemen who were competing for Arabella's hand.

Just after the tea arrived, a slight commotion in the hall had all the occupants of the room frowning and sitting up.

"No, because I know they are here... oh, fuss, just announce me and if Lady Christina wishes to turn me away, then I will go." The words were only slightly muffled by the closed door, and the voice sounded somewhat familiar to Christina, but Arabella and Mrs. Hood fell into fits of giggles, obviously immediately identifying the voice's owner without trouble.

A moment later, the door opened to admit a rather harried looking Jones.

"Lady Spencer is-"

"Here and most insistent on being admitted," Lady Spencer said cheerfully, bustling past poor Jones, who looked on the verge of apoplexy. A vision in red and gold, her dress' low neckline was just barely decent for making house calls, although her ample curves were part of what made it appear so. On a slimmer figure, the dress would barely cause comment at all.

"It's quite all right, Jones," Christina said, smiling at her poor butler. While she and Lady Spencer had met several times and she rather liked the young, brash, and occasionally haughty young woman, she had not included her on the list of those to be admitted.

However, she knew the young woman was an especial friend of Arabella and Mrs. Hood, and - despite Lydia's strict adherence to proprieties - that Lydia liked her a great deal as well. "Lady Spencer is most welcome to join us."

Sniffing his opinion, Jones nodded and closed the door, his stiff upper lip obviously sorely tested by the lady.

"Wonderful," Lady Spencer said, before greeting each lady in turn and plopping down on the chaise across from Mrs. Hood and Arabella. She beamed at Christina. "Please accept my apologies for barging in and interrupting your afternoon, I'm normally not so intrusive, but I am quite desperate. I originally called upon Gabrielle, but was informed she'd gone to see Arabella, and when I arrived at Manchester House I was told all the ladies had come here, and so I really had no choice but to follow."

Despite the impetuous manner in which she'd inserted herself - or perhaps because of it - Christina certainly didn't mind at all. If anyone could help distract her, it was the irrepressible, entirely Original and not entirely proper Lady Spencer.

"I hope your desperate situation is not entirely dire," she said, smiling as she poured Lady Spencer a cup of tea.

"Cynthia's situations are *always* dire, which is why I adore her," Arabella said, laughing. "What is it this time, dearest?"

"My house has been overrun, and I've been entirely cut out," Lady Spencer said dramatically, wrinkling her nose. She thanked Christina for the tea cup, taking it in hand as she continued. "The gentlemen have shut themselves away in Wesley's billiards room for smoking, drinking, and play. *And* Wesley set a footman to watch on the hall so I couldn't even listen to their conversation at the keyhole." All of this was said with utmost frustration. "Although I can guess what they're speaking of," she said rather darkly, as a scowl creased her forehead.

The others were all smiling at Lady Spencer's dramatic pronouncements, so Christina did not bother to hide her own amusement. It did not hurt that Lady Spencer's description was quite easy to picture and did much to set Christina's mind at ease. Even the most illogical side of her could not imagine a scenario where the Baroness might sneak into the Earl of Spencer's house, past a footman guard, and into the billiard room to steal Benedict away from his friends. For the first time since Benedict had left the house with his brother, Christina relaxed completely.

Lady Spencer would immediately be added to Jones' list of close friends and family she decided. The upright butler would probably not approve, but he would have to resign himself to her admittance.

"What are they speaking of?" Mrs. Hood asked, as Lady Spencer was obviously waiting for encouragement to continue her tale.

"They're having a spanking cabal!" Lady Spencer announced dramatically. Christina nearly dropped her cup of tea as her bottom suddenly tingled, her face flushing with embarrassed heat. Her eyes darted around the room, trying to avoid anyone's gaze. "Wesley says they've started a club! He told me so this morning when he informed me they were meeting."

Wait... but if the Earl of Spencer were forming the club and Isaac had taken Benedict there, then that meant... Christina's eyes darted between Lady Spencer and Lydia. The former was still scowling darkly, while the latter was blushing nearly as brightly as Christina was!

"Cynthia, this is not appropriate conversation for an unmarried young lady to be present for," Lydia said calmly, despite the two spots of color high in her cheeks. They became even brighter when she turned her gaze towards Arabella, but she did not lose her composure. Christina admired her fortitude.

"Oh, I already know," Arabella said artlessly, waving her hand. "Although I don't understand Cynthia's obsession with being spanked. I hated it when Isaac did it."

"I told you, it's different," Mrs. Hood said, sounding somewhat aggrieved. She elbowed her best friend in the side, practically rolling her eyes with the air of someone tired of repeating herself. "He's not going to spank you the same way your husband would."

"*My* husband won't spank me at all," Arabella shot back. "I'll just distract him by offering to pleasure him with my mouth."

"That doesn't-"

"*Girls!*" Lydia's shocked tones cut through their squabbling as Christina's jaw dropped open. The Duchess had now lost her composure, looking aghast and entirely at sea, struggling to decide what to say now that she'd ended their completely inappropriate conversation. "Arabella... you should not... you can't... where..."

"Oh, don't fuss, Lydia," Arabella said, shaking her head. "I assure you, I would not speak of such things in front of Isaac or Benedict, or ever in polite company, but it is just us."

"And we are not entirely polite," Lady Spencer murmured. She shrugged, looking almost apologetic when Lydia glared at her. "I do not approve in general of keeping young women in the dark about what the marriage bed holds, especially when they show themselves to be naturally curious. If you want to ensure she will avoid ruin, then she must know what being ruined actually entails."

Logically what Lady Spencer said made sense, but it was so backwards to common custom...

Throwing her hands up in the air, Lydia let out an exasperated sigh before glowering at Lady Spencer. "What am I supposed to do with you?"

"Hopefully keep my secrets from my husband," Lady Spencer said cheerfully. "While I might like being spanked, he is in possession of several tactics I do not find nearly as enjoyable." She turned her gaze to Christina, tilting her head to the side. "You've been very quiet, Lady Christina, have we shocked you out of all bounds?"

"I am a bit shocked, yes," Christina said, although her own sense of humor was quickly rising. After all, it *was* just a small, select group of ladies involved in this highly inappropriate conversation. A small, select group which apparently had something in common. "Mostly because I did not realize how commonplace such discipline was among our set."

Her previous husband and lovers certainly hadn't hinted at any such interest.

"I think it's the men we chose," Lydia said, with another sigh, as if resigning herself to the inevitability of discussion.

"*You* chose, I had chosen for me," Mrs. Hood said. A little smile curved her lips, her eyes suddenly looking far away. "It was not a bad bargain in the end, I suppose." Despite the lack of enthusiasm in her word choice, it was obvious from her tone and expression that she was happily content with her relationship, and Christina felt a spurt of envy.

Still, her curiosity over Lady Spencer's statement about enjoying her spanking and Arabella's assertion that the lady was obsessed with them overruled all other emotions. Christina focused on the lady in question, who was quietly sipping her tea as if she hadn't completely overturned the rules of polite society just moments before.

"Lady Spencer -"

"Please, call me Cynthia," the lady said, smiling widely. "I'm sure we're going to be quite good friends and I prefer not to stand on ceremony. Besides, we spanked wives should be close, don't you think? If we're going to speak of spankings, we should be able to call each other by our Christian names."

Pressing her lips together to hold back her laughter, as Lydia again gave Cynthia a reproving look, Christina marshaled her thoughts. She felt... good. Although she loved Daphne like a sister and the two of them often confided in each other, she'd never been part of such an open, warm conversation with so many different women before. She should certainly invite Daphne to their next gathering, it would be interesting to see if anything could shock Lady Cynthia Spencer - and if anyone could, it would be Daphne.

"Cynthia," Christina began again, and then hesitated. Despite her curiosity, she couldn't bring herself to be as brazen to ask the question she desperately wanted to ask. What if she had misunderstood? What would the other women think? "You... you said you found some part of a spanking enjoyable?"

"Oh yes," Cynthia said, her eyes sparkling wickedly. "Don't let Lydia's stuffiness fool you, she likes it quite a bit as well."

"Madness," Arabella mumbled, looking away, obviously uncomfortable hearing such a bald statement about her sister-in-law's relations with her brother.

"Not as much the actual spanking," Lydia said, protesting. "Just... what comes after is rather nice."

"Only if it's a playful spanking," Mrs. Hood said, speaking up again. Christina supposed she should start thinking of the young woman as Gabrielle, if they were going to be speaking of this. Cynthia was correct; it seemed silly to maintain formality when they were talking of such intimate matters. "I do not like the real spankings at all."

"But you still enjoy what comes *after*, even after the real ones," Cynthia pointed out.

The smile on her face almost made her cheeks hurt as the ladies began to argue the various merits of spanking. For once, Arabella was rather quiet, obviously both listening and disbelieving, but curious all the same, taking in all the information the ladies were now indiscreetly sharing. Yes, Christina would certainly have to have Daphne join them sometime. She also looked forward to getting to know the other ladies which were brought up during conversation - she'd had no idea so many of her acquaintances were so adventurous! Or required so much discipline!

WATCHING his wife whirling around the floor in his brother's arms, not far from where his sister was dancing with the eminently respectable Lord Charters, Benedict smiled. He could tell Arabella was bored to tears by Lord Charters, but to her credit he doubted anyone else outside his family and Gabrielle realized. Arabella really had been on her best behavior this Season, thanks in large part to Lydia's influence.

"You have the oddest expression on your face," Lydia murmured from beside him, going up on her toes to try and see what he was looking at. Being quite a bit shorter than him, with such a crush between their position and the dance floor, it was quite impossible.

"Just thinking about what a good influence you've been on Arabella," he said, smiling down at her. "This Season has been like heaven after last year."

Lydia shook her head, her blonde curls bouncing slightly at the movement. "Perhaps for you. I'm only relieved I never had to do this with Amy. Although, she would have been a good deal easier to manage than Arabella."

"How is Mrs. Tilding?" Benedict asked, a smile tugging at his lips. Amy and her husband had joined the Manchester household for Christmas, but had not come to London for the Season. Tilding, a cousin of the Duke of Kent, was restoring a manor estate to its former glory; he'd been promised to have it bestowed upon him if he could do so successfully. Although Amy had been curious about London, she'd wanted to stay with her husband, as they were only a few months wed at the time anyway.

Benedict was friends with Tilding, although not in the same manner he'd become friends with Wesley, Philip, and the Hood brothers, and from what he knew of the man he doubted they'd spend much time in London in future years either. Like Isaac, Tilding preferred the countryside; which suited both Lydia and Amy very well.

"Very happily helping Joseph with the restorations," Lydia said, smiling. "She's become much more serious as a result of all the hard work, but I think she's enjoying it. Amy always did love a challenge." Her smile slipped, just a touch. "Also... I believe the work helps to distract her."

Distract her from the disturbing revelations about her which had come to light at a house party in the late summer. The same house party where Amy's father's mind had finally snapped and the poor thing had witnessed it before being bundled into a carriage for an elopement in case her father had somehow escaped justice. The man had been blackmailing Lydia by threatening to marry Amy to a man who only desired a glorified nursemaid for his many children if Lydia didn't do everything he ordered.

Now they were both safe from him, but the younger sister still mourned the loving father who'd raised her.

Her husband kept her from being too melancholy though, and celebrating the Yuletide at Manchester House, where there were no memories to overtake the sisters had certainly helped. As Tilding's manor house was not far from Amy's old one, where the new Earl resided, Benedict thought it was probably beneficial for the young woman to have a project to focus on.

A hand suddenly grasped at his arm, on the opposite side of Lydia, startling him so badly he jumped as the feminine fingers closed about his elbow like a steel vise. He bit down on his lip hard to keep from shouting a curse in the middle of the ballroom, which certainly would have caused a scene.

"She's here," hissed an irate looking Lady Marley, clinging to his elbow like a limpet, barely glancing at Lydia who was now looking around Benedict curiously to see what was going on.

"Who?" Benedict asked, a little wildly, as he tried to convince his pulse to return to its normal rate. His mind felt a little bit slower than normal, as though all the blood had rushed away from it.

"The harlot," Daphne ground out harshly, making Lydia's eyes go wide. Immediately, both Benedict and Lydia began looking around. Which... Benedict doubted Lydia even knew who or what she was looking for, it was just an instinctive response.

"What's happening?" Lydia whispered back, her tone demanding, almost aggrieved. "Who is the harlot?"

"Baroness Alvenley," Daphne whispered back. "She's Christina's mortal enemy and she's sworn to make a play for Benedict, just to hurt Christina. The hussy probably actually believes she'd be successful too!"

It was a melodramatic pronouncement and yet entirely apt. The statement also had the effect of rousing all of Lydia's considerable protective instincts.

"Where is she?" Lydia asked, her voice full of suppressed fury, a mother bear whose protective instincts had been riled. She sounded quite a bit more aggressive than usual and Benedict couldn't help but wonder if her *condition* had something to do with her reaction. Were women who were increasing more volatile? She and Isaac still hadn't announced but Benedict really was quite sure she must be. "Point her out! I won't allow her near him!"

"Ladies," Benedict said, his tone quelling. "As much as I appreciate your stalwart defense, I'm not particularly worried about myself, although if you could keep her away from Christina..."

"There, there she is," Daphne interrupted him, completely abandoning all social manners and actually pointing across the room. "The petite blonde in blue with the frilly collar."

In his mind, Benedict had built up all sorts of ideas about what the awful Baroness might look like. While he supposed she must be somewhat attractive - for otherwise what man would abandon Christina for her? - he'd also been sure her selfish, cruel nature must show through as well. There would be something cold, something inherently off-putting about her, especially as he knew what she'd done.

He couldn't have been more wrong.

The Baroness was a Diamond of the First Water, a delicate English rose, and a pocket Venus all rolled up into one. Her smile was warm, welcoming, and flirtatious as she spoke to several gentlemen. The frilly collar of her dress did nothing to hide an impressive amount of décolletage, and the dress itself clung to curves just as rounded as Christina's. Her petite height made it possible for the gentlemen around her to enjoy a very fine view of her bosom, one which they were obviously enchanted by. All in all, she was one of the most stunningly attractive packages he'd ever seen.

But when she looked across the room and their eyes met, the repulsion he'd expected to feel finally rose up as she smiled flirtatiously and fluttered her fan.

His expression like stone, Benedict turned his head away without acknowledging her. It was not the cut direct, as she could not be *sure* he had even met her gaze, and no one else would realize what had just happened as they were so far distant from each other, but it was the least he could do. There was something rapacious in her gaze, acquisitively calculating.

He was honest enough to know if he had not met and fallen in love with Christina he likely would not have been repelled, but since he had and he knew what the Baroness was, he felt nothing but revulsion.

"Where is Cynthia?" Lydia asked suddenly, her head swiveling around.

The question was so abrupt, so off point, that Benedict stared at her in confusion. "Why?"

"Because she's the only one brazen enough to spill something on the Baroness' dress and force her to leave," his sister-in-law said matter-of-factly, before immediately setting off with a determined stride. Seeing her path, it was obvious she'd sighted Lady Spencer.

He should have remembered exactly how Machiavellian his normally sweet and gentle sister-in-law could be.

SOMETHING WAS WRONG. Christina knew it as soon as Isaac began leading her back towards Benedict, where Daphne had joined them. Her husband looked tense, and Daphne looked ready to burst.

"Where is Lydia?" Isaac asked, as soon as they'd reached Benedict, craning his neck around in search of his wife.

"Over there, speaking with Lady Spencer," Benedict said, nodding his head in their direction. Obviously seeing her, Isaac handed Christina off to Benedict and made his bow so he could go claim his own wife.

Holding out his arm, Benedict gave her a tight smile as she took it, his anxiety palpable.

"What is wrong?" she asked, looking back and forth between her husband and best friend. "Has something happened?"

"She's here," Daphne said simply, her green eyes glowing with protective fury. Ice washed over Christina, immediately dousing any enjoyment she'd been feeling. She tightened her fingers on Benedict's arm, prompting him to make a soothing, shushing noise as he placed his fingers over hers in comfort and reassurance.

Feeling sick to her stomach, she automatically began to look around, but Benedict pulled at her arm, leaning in towards her and drawing her focus back to him. His brown eyes were filled with warmth and love, a tenderness which made her catch her breath at the intensity of it.

"She doesn't matter, love," he said, his voice low but clear. "I will not leave your side for the rest of tonight, because I do not wish you to worry, but even if we separated for the entire evening you would have no cause to feel the slightest bit of anxiety. My heart, my body, my love is yours completely."

Her own words of love swelled up, just on the tip of her tongue... but Benedict deserved better than a declaration in the middle of a ballroom while she was obviously anxious over the Baroness' presence. Not once had Christina said the words, as though by holding them back she could keep from being hurt again. On the other side of Benedict, Christina could see Daphne, looking rather misty-eyed, obviously having overheard his bald statement.

"Mine is yours," Christina whispered back, her throat tight. It was the closest she could come to declaring her emotions without actually saying the words - although she would, later tonight in private. The happy joy, glowing from within, lit Benedict's face and was more than worth the tremor of anxiety threading through her.

On his arm, she could bravely face whatever trouble the Baroness tried to stir.

And she did try.

Benedict led Christina and Daphne to Arabella's circle of suitors, where Lydia and Isaac already were, along with the Spencers. Cynthia shot Christina a look which Christina couldn't interpret, winking at her as she raised a glass of punch in a kind of acknowledgement. Beside her, her husband frowned, eyes narrowed in speculation as he studied his wife suspiciously. She could only imagine the hoydenish Countess was up to some mischief.

From their spot in the circle, it did not take long for Christina to locate the Baroness. The beauty had gathered a whole coterie of gentlemen around her, although she constantly looked over where Christina stood, smirking and fluttering her fan. A triumphant little smile curved her lips when her eyes rested on where Christina's hand was clinging to Benedict's arm. Christina tried to tell herself she didn't care, but truthfully it irked knowing the Baroness was aware of how she affected Christina.

Once, she thought she saw the Baron moving through the crowded ballroom as well. She mostly remembered him for his kindness in the wake of George's death and the revelation of their spouses' betrayals. He had not seemed weak to her, nor unattractive, so she did not know why the Baroness behaved as she did. Mostly, Christina hoped the Baron did not actually love his wife, for she could not imagine how awful it would be to love a continually unfaithful spouse.

Benedict, for his part, completely ignored the Baroness' presence across the ballroom in a manner which Christina did her best to emulate. She was beginning to have some success, which was why she was so startled when the Baroness came swanning up to their circle on the arm of Mr. Walter Hood.

CHAPTER 15

Seeing Walter Hood moving through the ballroom towards their circle, the vivacious and flirtatious Baroness on his arm, Benedict wanted to curse.

He hadn't been able to warn his friends about the Baroness, not in the least because he couldn't imagine how to do so without rousing their curiosity over why they should avoid her at all costs, and Walter likely had no idea he'd been manipulated. From the triumphant gleam in the Baroness' eye as she came toward them on Walter's arm, she was planning on causing some kind of trouble. Brazen, really, considering Christina was surrounded by her own friends and family. Lady Daphne had been taken off to dance with her own husband after Christina had settled, but the rest of her allies remained in place.

Lydia, at least, was aware of the woman's existence and was willing to protect Christina - and bless her for not even asking why they were mortal enemies - and he was quite sure she'd managed to pass the message along to Cynthia at least. The gentlemen might be left floundering, but he was fairly certain his sister and Gabrielle would be immediately hostile to any lady Lydia and Cynthia were cold to.

The only question, really, was what he should do.

Take Christina away in retreat?

Cut the Baroness completely and end up also insulting Walter? He could do so, and explain to Walter later.

But he did not want to be so high-handed with making a decision for Christina, not in this. Obviously, he didn't mind being high-handed with other aspects of their lives, but here... there were too many possible missteps.

Leaning down to whisper in his wife's ear, he decided it was best to follow her lead. "The Baroness has managed to secure Walter Hood's arm and is headed in this direction, ostensibly for an introduction to everyone." He felt Christina's body stiffen next to his, tension gripping her tightly. Which only made him angrier at the Baroness, as Christina truly had begun to relax even with the woman present. "What do you wish us to do? We can retreat... I will cut her if you wish it... it is your decision."

⁓

To run...

Yes!

No. She wanted to, but why should she be chased away from her friends?

To watch Benedict give the woman the cut direct... his family would follow suit, but...

Christina looked towards the approaching couple.

The genial smile on Mr. Hood's face. The nasty, victorious one on the Baroness'.

Mr. Hood was a charming rogue, one whom Christina rather liked. It certainly wasn't his fault he didn't know about the animosity between herself and the Baroness. He didn't deserve to be another victim of the Baroness, embarrassed by his friends and family because the woman had used him. Giving her the cut direct would humiliate Mr. Hood as well, perhaps even damaging his friendship with Benedict.

Anger swelled up inside of her. For this was likely what the

Baroness had intended. She wanted to make Christina either retreat or hurt her friend. She wanted to make Christina uncomfortable, distressed. The same way she had been all night by sending little glances and fan flutterings Benedict's way even if he wasn't paying attention. But Christina had begun to manage to turn her focus away from the Baroness.

In fact, Christina's success in beginning to ignore the woman might even be what had driven her to up the ante.

Pushing down her emotions and her doubts, holding herself secure in her faith in Benedict as her champion, Christina shook her head and looked up at him.

"I am fine, darling," she said calmly, her voice sounding a little distant to her own ears, as if it were someone else's. "While I certainly will not be welcoming, I can manage to be civil."

"Then we will be civil," he said, pressing his fingers against hers before straightening up, just as Mr. Hood and the Baroness reached them.

Introductions were made, beginning with Isaac and Lydia of course. Lydia was haughtily cold to the Baroness, startling both her husband and Walter - the latter began to look a little unsure of himself. Also, unsure of his wife's motivations, Isaac nevertheless followed suit, greeting the Baroness properly but not warmly. Taking her lead from Lydia, Arabella was imperiously detached in her greeting as only a Duke's sister could be.

Christina didn't quite know how they had known - Lydia, at least, must know something after all! - but she found herself blinking back tears at their immediate support.

A slightly baffled expression on his face, which was quickly turning grim as he realized he must have made a misstep somewhere, Mr. Hood turned towards Benedict. As second brother of a Duke and still bearing the honorary title of Marquess until Lydia bore an heir, Benedict was the next highest-ranking member of the group. Which had not given Christina much time to steel herself, but after the rest of the family's cold reception of the Baroness, it was enough.

"How lovely to meet you," the Baroness said in a throaty, sultry voice she hadn't used until just now, fluttering her long lashes up at Benedict. "I've heard so much about you." Looking distinctly uncomfortable now, poor Mr. Hood looked very much as though he wished to dislodge the Baroness from his arm, but there was no way to politely do so. They could do nothing more than brazen on with the awkwardness the Baroness had created, and was now feeding with her obvious flirtation right in front of Christina.

Isaac looked horrified, Lydia infuriated, and Arabella was making some kind of wild gesture at Cynthia, who started forward with a wicked gleam in her eye before her husband's hand on her arm hauled her back for a heated, whispered conversation. The coterie of gentlemen who had been courting Arabella and were still waiting to be introduced looked distinctly uncomfortable, torn between setting themselves apart from the growing drama or watching it intently.

"I've heard quite a bit about you as well," Benedict said, but his contemptuous tone hinted none of what he'd heard was flattering.

Vicious indignation flared in the Baroness' eyes, but she let out a tinkling laugh. She gave Benedict a feeling look, glancing at Christine with the most appalling expression of sympathy on her face. "Oh dear... you make it sound so dire." She sighed, the very image of a misunderstood martyr. "It is quite lowering to know the things people will say out of jealousy or malice."

"Even more lowering to know the things people will do," Christina said, her voice low and biting. It was obvious the others were paying very close attention, aware of the undercurrents even if they didn't know the why of them, and debating whether or not to intervene.

But, despite the emotions roiling just beneath her surface, Christina felt rather pleased at the direct hit she'd just landed.

The Baroness looked more than a little taken aback at Christina's pluck and response, as if she'd truly expected Christina to just stand there silently while she flirted with Benedict. Or perhaps she'd thought Christina would erupt with anger, try to deny the Baroness' words or defend herself, all of which would make Christina come off rather badly to their audience.

She still smiled though, tittering as though Christina had said something particularly amusing, malice gleaming in her expression.

"It is *quite* shocking, isn't it?" the Baroness said, twisting the words around, and Christina realized she was referring to Christina's own flirtation and subsequent affair with Haversham... which had been motivated by the Baroness' interest in him. Heat flushed Christina's cheeks. She'd liked Haversham for himself as well! Otherwise she would have never been able to follow through with it. The Baroness batted her eyes at Benedict again. "Fortunately, I have quite an understanding husband, who is quite immune to the gossip of the envious."

"Not as understanding as you make him sound," Christina shot back without thinking, immediately biting her lip as she realized her impulsive answer had allowed her true emotions to show. Lydia and Gabrielle's small gasps as they realized what Christina's innuendo must mean were quite audible, and even the gentlemen widened their eyes.

Even if the Baron and Baroness did have some kind of arrangement now, they certainly hadn't when the Baroness had been George's lover, or he wouldn't have been killed while fleeing her husband.

"You-"

Whatever the Baroness had been about to say, it was lost as Cynthia suddenly stumbled forward, practically wrenching herself away from her husband, and the cup in her hand went arching through the air.

The Baroness let out a shocked squeal as cold liquid spattered against her backside. She spun around in outrage and Christina's eyes widened at the red liquid staining the beautiful blue skirts of the Baroness' dress.

"Oh my... look at what I did..." Cynthia said, tilting her head and attempting to look contrite. "I'm so clumsy!"

"You... you..."

"Yes?" Cynthia asked sunnily, smiling widely. Despite her friendly tone and expression, she somehow managed to look utterly terrifying. Behind her, Lord Spencer looked both resigned and amused at his wife's antics.

∽

BENEDICT COULD BARELY KEEP his mouth from twitching at Lady Spencer's audacity. She was barely bothering to pretend it was an accident - and it hadn't escaped his notice she hadn't really apologized for the spill either. Behind her, her husband seemed more amused than condemning, and Benedict remembered some rumors he'd heard about ladies who flirted with the Earl of Spencer often having sartorial mishaps. He now had a good idea exactly what might have happened to their dresses.

On his arm, he could feel Christina trembling, and when he glanced down he was pleased to see she looked as though she were holding back laughter. The tension which had gripped her from the moment the Baroness had entered the ballroom had now dissipated entirely.

The Baroness turned towards her escort, but Walter was looking at her with cold, contemptuous eyes; understanding he'd been duped and used by her, and he was unwilling to lend her any sort of assistance or alliance. The Baroness had vastly overestimated the strength of her charms.

Drawing herself up, she pulled her hand away from Walter's arm.

"If you'll excuse me," she said coldly, before turning on her heel and stalking away. They were all treated to the sight of her punch-soaked backside again as she did so. Benedict manfully held back his laughter, as Christina put her hand over her lips. Everyone was quite restrained actually, other than Lady Spencer who snickered, which then caused Arabella to giggle.

Gads he hoped his sister wasn't picking up too much from the Countess - although, given the result, he couldn't exactly feel upset. Looking around, he saw they'd been deserted by the gentlemen who had been dancing attendance on Arabella. He wasn't sure when they'd retreated from the dramatics, but he wasn't entirely surprised either. None of the upstanding, somewhat priggish nobles would have appreciated Lady Spencer's antics - not that they'd dare say a word against her either, but the scene would have taxed their sensibilities.

"Well baggage, you've chased off another one," Wesley said, stepping up to his wife and placing his hand on the small of her back to gain her attention. His tone was aggrieved, but not truly condemning, as though he was making only the most basic nod to reprimanding her for her behavior. If he'd actually been upset, his reaction would have been very different. "Are you pleased with yourself?"

"Very," Lady Spencer said impishly, smiling up at him and looking very pleased with herself indeed. Then she looked over at Christina and Benedict, tilting her head to the side as if in query. "I am also very curious, however."

Looking down to meet his wife's gaze, he pressed his fingers over hers in support again. While he would very much like to share what was going on with his friends and family, as he trusted them implicitly, this was also Christina's decision to make.

A feeling of warmth spread through him when she nodded. Looking around the circle at all of them, she cleared her throat. "Perhaps we could adjourn to a more private location and... I can tell you all everything."

Benedict didn't think he'd ever been more proud of her.

"Manchester House," Isaac said decisively. He smiled encouragingly at Christina. "Whatever your connection with that awful woman, I can safely say we are all on your side, my dear."

Sending a grateful smile to his brother as the group began to disperse, Benedict leaned down to whisper in Christina's ear. "Would you like to find Daphne so she may join us?"

She shook her head. "No, I will be fine without her. But I appreciate the thought."

The way she looked up at him, with unfettered warmth and what he hoped was love in her eyes, made him feel like a king. Earlier, when she'd repeated his declaration of fidelity and love back to him, although without saying the specific words, he'd dared to hope he was finally breaching the last of her walls. Now, that hope surged again, flickering through him madly and making him feel quite impatient.

"Come love," he said, lifting her fingertips to his lips. "Let us make our goodbyes then."

Not that he begrudged the others Christina's story to assuage their curiosity, certainly not after they'd come together for her so markedly, but the sooner they had their explanation, the sooner Benedict could have his wife all to himself.

TELLING all her new friends and family members about George and the Baroness was easier than Christina had thought it would be.

Perhaps because she knew some of their secrets as well. Or perhaps just because she was finally learning to trust again. Daphne had begun the process, but trusting someone she'd known prior to her marriage had been much less difficult than allowing new people into her citadel. It was Benedict who had truly broken through and made her start learning to trust again, who showed her it might be worth it.

Therefore she trusted those he trusted; and they were already showing themselves to be stalwart defenders.

Cynthia had thrown punch on a woman's dress without even knowing the full story of *why*.

Once Christina had told them all about her past with the Baroness and how George had died, everyone had expressed their shock and sorrow - except for Cynthia who mostly seemed aggrieved she'd allowed the Baroness to flee too easily.

"Ooooo, I just hope she approaches you again!" Cynthia had said, ire written clearly across her face.

"Now, baggage, as much as I love watching you terrorize the harpies of London, you know I can't allow you to step too far out of line," her husband had reminded her.

A glint in Cynthia's eyes said she hadn't cared. Christina thought she could learn a thing or two from the young woman. She doubted the Baroness would ever care to cross paths with Cynthia again; perhaps Christina would start taking a page from her book. A few more glasses of punch and the Baroness might learn to leave her alone entirely. Although, such a tactic would not guarantee the Baroness would avoid Benedict if she could catch him alone; but Christina did not worry anymore. Her husband's complete disinterest, even revulsion, despite the woman's beauty had been palpable.

Besides, even if he had found the woman beautiful, Christina realized she'd finally come around to feeling secure in his love for her, his commitment to their marriage vows.

The Baroness no longer had any power over her, and she had Benedict to thank for it.

Still, she might have continued to worry the Baroness would reveal the truth of Christina's first marriage to the *ton* at large, if it hadn't been for Lydia's parting words.

"Do not let her vex you," Lydia said, holding both of Christina's hands with hers, her grey eyes shining nearly silver with determined protectiveness. "After all, you have a Duke and Duchess on your side. Any gossip she tries to spread will be stymied by your connections, not to mention it would be folly for anyone to think you cannot fix a man's attention. Not after the manner which Benedict so publicly and determinedly courted you and has obviously reformed his rakish ways for you. Society loves a reformed rake and his wife, they are much less tolerant of those seeking to stir malice."

Unlike when George had passed away, with her family abroad and only Daphne a close enough friend to trust with such a secret, Christina now had a multitude of allies. It made the Baroness and her pettiness seem very small indeed.

By the time she and Benedict returned home, Christina felt as though she was floating lighter than air, free of the burdens and secrets which had been holding her down for far too long. They'd made the carriage ride in comfortable silence, with Christina resting her head on Benedict's shoulder, but as soon as they were alone in their bedroom, she could not hold back the words any longer.

"I love you," she said, practically flying into his arms the moment he shut the door, pressing kisses to his lips between her declarations. "I love you. I love you. I love you."

Half-laughing, her husband did his best to keep up with her assault, moving them away from the door and towards the bed. "I shan't complain, love, but may I ask what brought this sudden declaration on?"

"It wasn't sudden," Christina said, pressing her body against his as she pushed his jacket from his shoulders, looking up at him in earnest. "I've loved you... well for months. I left you, not just because my emotions were becoming too engaged, but because I had already begun to love you. When I saw you again, when you came for me, I hadn't stopped... I just wasn't ready to admit to my feelings."

"But now you are?" he asked, dropping a tender kiss to her lips, his hands moving over her body just as determinedly as her were his body, slowly disrobing her between caresses.

"I realized I was ready in the ballroom, when you said I held your heart, body, and love," she responded, sliding her fingers through his chest hair before stripping his shirt from his body. "But I wanted more privacy to finally tell you."

"I much prefer this," he murmured over her lips before kissing her thoroughly, a sweet, drugging kiss which nonetheless felt like a claiming on his part. Christina moaned against his lips, her body on fire with need, and yet... she realized there was one more thing she wished to offer him. One more way she wished to be claimed.

Pressing her fingertips against his bare chest, she pushed him away gently, ending the kiss so she could speak. Heat rose in her cheeks, causing her to blush before she could even state her scandalous desires.

"I... I would... Tonight..."

"Yes?" he asked, his brow drawing together in confusion. Taking her hand, he wrapped his fingers around hers, holding their joined hands against his heart. "What is it, love?"

Her voice dropped to a whisper. "Tonight, I want you to-to-to take my, um, bottom."

The immediate heat and lust which flashed in his eyes, the way his fingers tightened around hers, his body pressing closer, made it very clear exactly what he thought of her proposition.

"Are you sure?" he still asked, making her love him all the more.

She nodded her head, lips curving up in a tremulous smile. While she was a bit scared and quite a bit nervous, she also wanted him there. Wanted him to have all of her.

LOWERING his lips to his wife's, Benedict kissed her ravenously, passionately, his desire pounding through him like a gale wind. His cock, which had already been hard, now felt as though he could drive it through steel after her shy, scandalous request. Instinctively, he knew she was trying to show him how much she loved him, trusted him, with the gesture.

It was not a necessary demonstration, and yet he would certainly not be declining the offer.

His hands moved over the fabric of her chemise, down the supple muscles of her back to the rounded curves of her bottom, and he groaned as he squeezed the soft flesh, holding her buttocks tightly as he ground his cock against her front. Little whimpering noises, aroused and yet anxious, escaped from Christina's throat as he kissed her, his hands massaging her plump cheeks. The fine fabric of her chemise was barely a barrier, but he wanted it off of her anyway.

Pulling away, he spun her around and tugged it off over her head.

"Onto the bed," he ordered, his voice coming out more harshly than he intended in his lust, but Christina didn't hesitate or seem upset. Completely naked, she stepped forward immediately and climbed onto the mattress. As Benedict finished undressing, she sat and watched, eyes wide but aroused.

Coming forward, ignoring his bobbing erection for the moment, Benedict arranged the pillows for her to place herself over, and Christina immediately draped her body over them. The position left her bottom high up in the air, her hips supported by the pillows, with her pert breasts hanging below. With her legs slightly parted, the pink shell of her cunt glistened in the candlelight, vulnerable and enticing.

A wry grin on his face, Benedict reached under the bed for their wedding present from the Earl of Spencer.

"What is that?" Christina asked curiously, peeking over her shoulder as Benedict set it on the bed.

"Something to help," he said, picking up the bottle of oil and the second smallest of the little rubber dilators. As her virgin hole had been previously stretched by the bullets, as well as his fingers, ginger, and her hairbrush, he didn't feel the need to start at the very beginning. He also doubted he'd make it all the way through to the largest.

Christina's pupils dilated, and her face flushed as she saw what he was holding, obviously recognizing it. When he climbed onto the bed behind her, her head snapped back around away from him as he straddled her lower legs, trapping them between his. Her creamy bottom practically begged for color, but all his focus was currently the little star winking between her cheeks.

Dripping some of the oil onto his finger, he pressed his digit to her narrow aperture and pressed in.

"Oh!" Her muscles clenched around his finger as he quickly delved deeper, knowing he wouldn't hurt her as she'd taken his fingers more than once. Mostly he wanted to spread the oil around inside of her a little, although he also enjoyed the heat of her interior and the way she squirmed as he pumped his finger.

But he didn't allow himself to enjoy it for too long before he removed his finger and pressed its replacement to her opening.

"Oh!" She gave a little cry this time as he pushed the thick rubber in about halfway before halting its forward momentum. "It feels too big"

He couldn't help but chuckle. "There's going to be much larger things in there soon."

Christina moaned at his blunt statement, her buttocks quivering, and he was sure she'd just clenched again. Working the dilator back and forth, he admired the sight of the dark rubber disappearing into her virgin hole, stretching the tight ring for his entry. Of course, he could do this with his fingers, but he had to admit he rather like the contrast of the black rubber plugging her milky white bottom.

Besides, with the dilator, he could leave it in her to do its work while he turned her cheeks a brighter hue.

"Time for the next one," he said, breathing a little hard as he pulled the first from her body. Christina let out a little whimper, but didn't protest. The whining noises she made as he pressed the thicker, longer dilator into her rear entry were conflicted, as if she didn't know whether she was more uncomfortable or more aroused. It was the largest thing he'd ever pushed into her virgin hole, but it wasn't as large as his cock. Watching it slide into her, stretching the entryway further, had his cock practically pulsing with the need to replace it. "What a naughty girl you are, letting me play with your ass like this."

She moaned again, a tremor shaking her body, and Benedict pressed the dilator securely into her tight hole. Her panting breaths were coming faster, and the cream of her pussy was beginning to coat the tops of her thighs from her arousal.

"Such a naughty girl," he repeated. "I should give you a spanking."

SMACK! SMACK! SMACK! SMACK!

Crying out, Christina arched her back, thrusting her bottom up as he began swatting her creamy buttocks with the palm of his hand, hard enough to sting but not truly hurt.

"Oh! Oh, Benedict!" Her hips were moving up and down now, as if her swollen pussy was seeking some kind of stimulation, the spanking only increasing her needy arousal.

SMACK! SMACK! SMACK! SMACK!

"That's right, love, I'm going to turn this little bottom pink and then I'm going to claim it," he said, almost fiercely, spanking her even harder as her cheeks turned a blushing pink under his hand. The base of the dilator seemed to move with her bottom as she squirmed and writhed, pressing her thighs together and rubbing to give her clit the pressure and stimulation she craved. "And you're going to love it."

SHE WAS... she truly was...

Christina already loved what he was doing to her; she felt both wild and submissive simultaneously. Something about the perverseness of having that tight hole stretched, the shameful intimacy of feeling so full there – more so than ever before – made her feel completely owned in a manner she'd never experienced. She was giving herself over wholly to Benedict's dominance, allowing him to master her completely.

The spanking didn't hurt as much as it excited, the slaps of pain an erotic counterpart to the throbbing in her pussy. She wriggled, practically sobbing with the need growing inside of her as she tried to rub her thighs together, to hump herself against the pillow, and satisfy the clawing craving of her body.

"Oh please," she begged, sure she couldn't take another moment of waiting, needing to feel him inside of her. "Please, please, please Benedict! Please, take me, I love you, please!"

She was babbling but she couldn't stop, not until she felt him sliding the cool, hard length of the dilator from her ass. Then she froze, panting, waiting.

The hot, blunt head of his cock pressed against the tiny ring and pushed. Christina whimpered. The final dilator had been large and uncomfortable at first, but easily managed after a few moments. Benedict's cock felt much larger. His hands curled around her hips, his legs pressing against the outside of hers as he groaned and pushed, sliding the first few inches of his cock into her virgin hole.

She cried out. It felt so odd... her pussy pulsed in envy as her tighter channel burned with discomfort. The heat of his cock was entirely different from his finger or the cool, slick dilators; it did not burn the same way the ginger had, but neither was it entirely pleasurable. Of course, for Christina, the slight hurt spurred her arousal and pleasure to greater heights in counterpoint.

Slowly, so slowly, he sank into her. It seemed as though his cock went on forever, moving deeper and deeper, until she was sure she couldn't take anymore, and then deeper still.

"Oh... oh... Benedict... oh... oh no...." Her hole clenched and squeezed, making him moan and his fingers flex as she unintentionally massaged his cock.

"There, love," he rasped finally, his groin coming to rest against her warm bottom, his hands caressing her hips lovingly. "There now, you've taken it all. I'm going to give you a moment to get used to it, and then I'm going move."

She felt so full. So empty. So conflicted.

And when he began to move, his cock pulling back through the sensitive channel he'd just stretched open, the sensation was indescribable. Christina whined, her fingers scrabbling at the bed, trying to pull away from the strangeness of being emptied, and then she cried out as he thrust back in. The fingers on her right hip moved, seeking out the swollen nub of her clit, and confusing her further as to whether she wanted him to withdraw immediately or if she wanted him to never stop.

The slick glide of his fingers over her clit made her squirm as he began to thrust, gently riding her backside with his cock, her tight furrow feeling incredibly, rawly sensitive as he deflowered it. Christina moaned and writhed, gasping for breath as her need to orgasm warred with the shocking sensation of his cock moving inside the wrong hole.

But her husband knew her body, and he rubbed and circled in just the right way, melding the pain with the pleasure until his cock began to feel good. Incredibly good. Christina moaned and pressed back against his thrusts, easily taking them now despite his movements growing faster and harder. His fingers strummed over her clit as she bucked beneath him, her ecstasy beginning to spiral, her body quivering from the overload of sensations.

When she came she screamed, tears sliding down her cheeks from the force of her orgasm. It felt like her entire being was splintering apart, the pain and pleasure so intermingled it all felt the same, and she was so full, so hot, so rapturous. Behind her, from a great distance away it seemed, she heard Benedict shout and then felt the hot spurt of his cum as he filled her, claiming her complete submission and the whole of her body for his own.

CHAPTER 16

*C*hristina woke to tender kisses covering her brow.

"What time is it?" she mumbled, wincing slightly as she turned onto her back to look towards the windows. Sunlight was already trickling in, but she still felt completely spent.

"Nine o'clock, love. I need to run an errand, but I did not wish you to wake up to an empty bed without knowing where I'd gone."

"Oh." Smiling sleepily up at her husband, she was muzzily pleased at how handsome and thoughtful he was. "That is most considerate."

Chuckling, Benedict pressed another kiss to her brow. "You're still sleep befuddled, love. I'll try not to be too long."

Winding her arms around his neck, Christina drew her husband down for a proper kiss before releasing him, snuggling back into the warm bed sheets. It didn't even occur to her to ask where he was going or why, or even worry about what he might be doing. Later, she would be quite proud of herself for her unthinking, instinctive trust - and she would also be well rewarded for it.

BENEDICT'S COMMANDS

DESPITE THE EARLINESS of the hour for town, there were already some gentlemen haunting the clubs (although, for a few of the most disreputable it was a very *late* hour), and it only took about half an hour of asking around to obtain Baron Alvenley's town address.

On the outskirts of Mayfair, the rented house was on the fringes of the fashionable neighborhoods but still in a perfectly respectable area. Well maintained but modest, there was nothing especially noteworthy about the house.

It was before calling hours, but as Benedict was still ranked as a Marquess for now, his prominence did call for a certain amount of privilege; rather than being forced to leave a card, the butler immediately showed him into the library to wait while he went to see if the master of the house was available. Benedict wondered how much of a mark the Baron had put on the house; after all, they were well into the Season. He must have left some mark on the interior of the house, although it wasn't apparent from the pristine state of the library.

The door creaked open and Benedict turned to look.

"Good morning," said the man entering, distractedly tugging at his shirt sleeves as if he had dressed in a hurry. Benedict felt a fleeting spurt of guilt for having harried the man from his morning toilette, but not much. "I don't believe we've been introduced; to what do I owe the honor of a visit from a Marquess?"

Taking a moment to study the man before him, Benedict didn't find anything remarkably offensive about him - certainly nothing which would immediately cause a wife to seek out other gentlemen's favors. The Baron was fit, only a few inches shorter than Benedict so still quite tall, and his attire was fashionable but unremarkable. He had sandy blonde hair that was combed back from a fairly handsome face (at least, handsome as Benedict judged such matters) and warm blue eyes which seemed to reflect the kindness Christina remembered him with. His voice betrayed a small note of worry - after all, it wasn't every day an unknown Marquess appeared on a Baron's doorstep with no warning.

"I apologize for the early call," Benedict said, coming forward to shake the man's hand. He did not want to begin by antagonizing the

Baron; Christina remembered him rather fondly and if he was unaware of his wife's antics then Benedict was willing to be somewhat forgiving. After today, however, his forbearance would be much harder to come by. "I do not know if you heard, I recently married Lady Christina Rowan, formerly the Marchesse of Stanhope."

The man's face softened with something very like pity at Christina's name, and then veered into concern.

"Is the lady well?"

"She is, however..." Benedict hesitated for just a moment. The Baron of Alvenley seemed like a nice enough chap and it was not a pleasant thing to have to tell a man his wife was misbehaving. "I hope you will excuse my forwardness, but we had a bit of a... an unpleasant encounter last night with the Baroness."

The Baron's face hardened, both frustration and resignation evident in his expression. He cursed. Sighed. Looked away from Benedict as though ashamed. Looked to the ceiling of the library. Sighed again. And re-met Benedict's gaze.

"My most heartfelt apologies," he said, moving away to go and sit in one of the chairs, gesturing for Benedict to do the same. Obviously, he felt a quick conversation was not in order. Curious about this man, and also his perspective, Benedict was content enough to settle himself down in one of the comfortable leather seats. While he did want to hurry back to his wife, he also wanted to extinguish the headache of the Baroness once and for all. "My wife is... well, to be perfectly honest I don't entirely understand my wife. She promised to be on good behavior if I brought her with me to London for the short time I had to be here." He rubbed his forehead, still frowning. "What did she do?"

"Ah... I don't mean to be indelicate..." Benedict groped for the adequate phrases which would explain the Baroness' aims without being overly insulting to her husband.

"Do not worry about my being offended," the Baron said rather dryly. "While I am quite fond of my wife, as much as she allows me to be, I am well aware of her personal failings."

Since the man seemed altogether sensible, Benedict took him at his word.

"She seems to be going out of her way to provoke my wife," Benedict said, his mouth twisting in a bit of a grimace. Talking so bluntly, to someone who may be hurt by the revelations he shared, left a nasty taste on his tongue. "They encountered each other by happenstance, at which time she told Christina that her aim was to seduce me away from Christina. Such a goal is impossible, but last night she did her best to make us both very uncomfortable."

To his surprise, the Baron's eyes glinted with something like amusement. "Ah, is that why Mathilde returned home with punch all down her dress? I admit, I wouldn't have thought Lady Sta - that is, Lady Dearborn now isn't it? - had the gumption."

"She didn't," Benedict said, relieved that the Baron seemed so affable about the entire situation. "A friend of ours did, however. I believe it's the Countess of Spencer's preferred manner of deterring flirtatious females."

"Well, hopefully it did Mathilde some good," the Baron said. "I haven't seen her yet this morning, however, so I can't be sure." He sighed, the amusement leaving his face and, with it, the energy holding him up. He seemed rather defeated. "I'm sure you are here to request my assistance in controlling my wife, and I wish I could be more so but... may I be quite frank, Dearborn?"

"If you wish it," Benedict said solemnly. "My Christina remembers you with a great deal of fondness and I assure you I would keep any of your secrets the way you've kept hers."

Alvenley's mouth curled up on one side, an almost sad smile. "Poor thing. She was so devastated. By that time Mathilde and I had our arrangement. I'd once hoped for a more meaningful marriage but once she'd borne our two sons she desired the more conventional *ton* marriage. Ours wasn't a love match to begin with, so I was a bit put out at the time but certainly not stricken by her preference as long as she was discreet."

"I take it she wasn't with the late Lord Stanhope?" Benedict asked, now curious as to how an accommodating husband such as Alvenley came to be chasing down Christina's late husband when the fatal accident occurred.

The man's mouth twisted with unhappiness. "Mathilde brought him to our home. I was quite furious with her - and with him. Of course, he paid for it, but his death only seemed to depress Mathilde for a short time." He sighed again, resignation in every line of his body. "Since then I've tried everything I can think of to bring her in line. I cut off her spending, she goes to her father to beg for money, and then her parents come to berate me for my hard-heartedness - all the while rendering the tactic useless as they give her everything she asks for. I send her to the countryside, where she creates enough havoc to cause the servants to quit and throws scandalous house parties. The best I've been able to do is keep her constantly where I am able to watch over her, but - as you have experienced - she cannot be under my eye all of the time. The only time I've ever met with success was Stanhope's death, by threatening that if the truth around his death became known, I could divorce her for adultery. And I would, if I'd heard a whisper of gossip and she knows it. It was the only thing I could do to protect your wife at the time. I don't know why Mathilde is so malicious about other ladies and acquisitive when it comes to their husbands; she's quite agreeable otherwise."

The man looked so defeated, Benedict felt rather badly for him. He really was in a difficult spot if his wife's family and friends undercut every action he took to try and curb the Baroness' bad behavior.

Leaning forward, Benedict rested his forearms on his knees. "Alvenley, you've been frank with me and now I shall return the favor. If you do not feel up to my suggestion, you certainly need not feel any obligation but I hope you will keep our conversation in confidence. Have you ever heard of domestic discipline?"

WAKING up to find her husband was still out was rather disappointing, but did little to damper Christina's rather dreamy mood. Her bottom was a bit sore, mostly on its tender interior, but, overall, she felt wonderful.

She'd faced down the Baroness, had confessed her love to her husband, and given herself to him completely. While she did not fool herself into thinking life would be perfect from now on, at the moment she certainly had nothing to complain about and really felt rather grand.

When Daphne arrived at tea time, full of apologies for not being present when the Baroness confronted Christina, she could only laugh and hug her friend, assuring her she was fine. Of course, then Daphne wanted to know what had happened word for word, as all the accounts being relayed by the gossips were purely speculative.

By the time Christina got to the part where Cynthia had smiled prettily while deliberately not even pretending to apologize for spilling her punch, Daphne was in stitches.

"I'm so sorry I missed it!" she said in between fits of giggles. "I would have paid to see that shrew's expression!"

"She looked ready to explode," said Christina, giggling as well. Part of her felt badly for her amusement over another's misery, but another part of her felt the Baroness had gotten her just desserts. After all, if she had not insisted on tormenting Christina, Cynthia would not have poured punch on her. "I must confess, I feel so much better. If she dares approach us again, I shall merely hold up my cup. And if she approaches Benedict on her own, I'm sure I won't be the only one descending upon her with a full glass!"

"I know I should like my chance!" Daphne exclaimed, a combative light in her eye even as she burst into more laughter, holding up a pretend cup as though she were hoisting a banner aloft.

It was upon this merriness that Mr. Jones knocked on the door and entered, standing stiffly as he announced, "The Countess of Spencer and Mrs. Hood have called, my lady."

"Lovely!" cried out Daphne. "The heroine of the hour is here!"

The two ladies stood to greet the new arrivals. Cynthia and Gabrielle were both dressed in pink, although Cynthia's pink was dark enough to border on red and Gabrielle's was more of a rosy hue.

Together, with their dark good looks, they were quite the attractive pair. Daphne was effusive in her greeting, and Cynthia took the excessive praise in stride, although she did seem quite pleased with herself.

"I hope you didn't get into trouble with the Earl," Christina said, as they sat down. From what she could tell, Cynthia was sitting just a touch gingerly, which surprised Christina as Spencer had seemed more amused than upset by his wife's actions.

"No real trouble, he just used the incident as an excuse to spank me, which he was likely going to do anyway. But he prefers to pretend I've been naughty sometimes," Cynthia said cheerfully, making Daphne choke on her tea while Gabrielle snickered.

"Do you deliberately try to shock everyone you find in my drawing room?" Christina asked, highly amused both by Cynthia's brazenness and Daphne's sputtering.

Cynthia shrugged, although she looked a little guilty. "You said she knew about the spankings and things."

"Mine, yes, but I didn't tell her about anyone else," Christina chided. "Those are not my secrets to share."

"Well, I figured if she knew about yours then it couldn't be too shocking to know about others."

"To know, no," Daphne said, her voice still sounding a little choked -Christina was quite sure she was holding back more laughter. "However, I don't believe I've ever discussed such matters in a drawing room during tea before."

"Oh?" Cynthia cocked her head curiously. "Where do you normally discuss them?"

"Give the woman a few minutes to get to know you a little," Gabrielle admonished as Daphne choked again, blushing furiously. Christina was fascinated; she'd expected Daphne to shock Cynthia, not the other way round! But her conversations with Daphne about their predilections *had* always been whispered, in complete privacy, accompanied by half-scandalized giggles as they made their confessions. Cynthia's particular brand of brazen conversation did take a bit of getting used to. "Not everyone wants to discuss their marital life immediately - or ever."

"Which is really too bad," Cynthia said, picking up a biscuit. "I think it would improve conversation immensely among the *ton*. At least it wouldn't be boring."

Sitting up a bit straighter, Daphne looked as though she were trying to pretend to match Cynthia's casual bluntness, but the color in her cheeks still revealed her embarrassment. "What would you like to know?"

Cynthia's eyes lit up as Gabrielle leaned forward curiously, obviously completely willing to take advantage of her friend's nosiness. Christina found herself also curious, wondering if Cynthia might coax extra details from Daphne that would be new to her.

"What's the most shocking thing you've ever done?" Cynthia asked. And then grinned. "I can go first if you like."

Clearing her throat, Daphne seemed to draw herself up even further, determined to show herself just as bold as Cynthia.

"Anthony and I once had sex with an entire room full of people as an audience." The haughty tone she used was entirely at odds with the scandalous statement.

Already knowing the Marleys' penchant for exhibitionism, Christina had heard the general gist of the story, but she did enjoy seeing Gabrielle's eyes go wide as saucers, bulging in a rather comedic manner, and Cynthia's hand fly up to her mouth in complete shock. True to Cynthia's brazen nature, however, her hand only remained in place momentarily before it lowered and she was leaning forward with fascination.

"Were you... were you completely unclothed?" Cynthia asked, her voice a hushed whisper. The wild look Gabrielle gave her friend said she couldn't believe her audacity in asking - but the look she turned towards Daphne proclaimed her desire to hear the answer. Christina was curious as well - she hadn't even thought to ask.

Daphne sat even straighter if that were possible, her cheeks now a flaming red blush which was spreading down towards her neck. "Yes."

"Where did you get the audience from?" Cynthia asked, as always, eager to know more.

"We belong to a... a kind of club," Daphne said. "It's very private, but the other club members made up the audience."

"How does one become a member? Is having sex in front of the audience part of being a member? Do all the members have sex in front of each other?"

The color in Daphne's face was slowly receding as Cynthia peppered her with questions in a matter-of-factly curious tone. Even though Gabrielle was obviously shocked into silence, there was just something about Cynthia which made it possible to speak of the most scandalous subjects as if they were engaged in perfectly acceptable conversation.

"Are you thinking of joining?" Daphne asked, sounding both amused and a little relieved.

"Not if I have to have sex in front of other people," Cynthia said frankly. "But I would like to watch."

This bald statement was too much for Gabrielle, who whooped with laughter and collapsed into a fit of hysterical giggles, setting off the other three women as well. Suddenly all of them were giggling, harder and harder, and no matter how Christina tried to stop, the moment she caught someone else's gaze, it set her off again.

It was this scene of merriment which her husband returned home to see. The door opened, making all of them shriek and jump, and then start giggling again. Well, blushing and giggling as soon as they all saw Benedict. Gabrielle actually grabbed a pillow and pressed it to her face, as if trying to hide from him, which only made Cynthia laugh even harder.

"Stop!" Christina gasped out, pressing her hand over her aching abdominal muscles. "We have to stop!"

"Don't stop on my account," her husband said grinning, one hand still on the doorknob. "I enjoy hearing the sound of laughter echoing through the halls. I'll leave you to your friends now, love, but I'd like to take you out riding in a few hours."

Helplessly nodding, Christina waved her hand at him as he grinned and closed the door.

Catching Daphne's eye again, tears sprang to her own eyes as she dissolved into another fit of giggles.

"Would you *stop!*"

"I'm not doing anything!"

THREE HOURS LATER, Christina was the perfect picture of tonnish elegance as Benedict steered his phaeton into Hyde Park. No one would have ever guessed that she'd spent her afternoon gossiping with friends about scandalous subjects until they were laughing so hard they couldn't speak any more. He'd been highly amused by the foursome's unconstrained hilarity when he'd returned home.

Christina wouldn't give him any of the specific conversation details about what had set them off, only that the Countess of Spencer had - as usual - managed to both scandalize and amuse.

Glancing over at his wife as she nodded to a passing carriage, Benedict felt incredibly puffed up over having her by his side at the fashionable hour in Hyde Park. It was such a small thing, but a highly enjoyable one.

Possibly even more enjoyable today than ever.

Benedict hadn't told Christina why he'd felt the sudden urge to join the throngs of Society about the park, in large part because he was unsure whether or not it would be worth it. There was every chance the Baron would not make an appearance. However, if he did...

Benedict casually tooled around the pathways, occasionally slowing for conversations with others who were visiting the park. The Dowager-Countess of Spencer, a formidable woman who intimidated even the current Earl and Countess, motioned them over and spent a good five minutes interrogating Christina. His wife bore up well under the questioning, and her ladyship's haughty lines soon fell into a smile.

Lydia and Arabella were also in attendance, unsurprisingly, although Isaac was nowhere in sight. His sister looked very pretty but quite bored by all the company surrounding their carriage and Benedict decided keeping their distance would be wiser. Otherwise, Arabella might very well insist he and Christina stop for a while, which would not suit Benedict's plans at all. They acknowledged each other from a distance, and he ignored his sister's scowl as he urged his horses onward.

"You don't wish to speak with Lydia and Arabella?" Christina asked in surprise, turning towards him with a curious expression on her face.

"Not today," he said cheerfully. "Let's say we move closer to the water, shall we? It's a lovely view today with the clouds on the water."

With a little laugh, Christina leaned into him slightly, a small press of her shoulder against his for just a moment before she straightened again. "Yes, let's. If we are going to avoid your family, we might as well be thorough about it."

As he steered down towards the Serpentine, he finally saw the Baron, sitting beside his wife in a stately barouche, also headed towards the Serpentine. A small smile curved Benedict's lips as he took in the picture the couple made. There was something indefinably more confident about the way Alvenley held himself, more self-assured. Beside him, the Baroness was looking decidedly more downcast than she had the previous evening, almost as though she'd shrunk into herself.

"Ah, good," he said, nodding towards the barouche. "Just who I was hoping to see."

Beside him, he felt Christina stiffen. "Benedict?"

"Yes, love?"

"I don't want to talk to her again," she hissed at him, unable to speak any louder as they drew nearer to the Alvenley carriage. The coachman looked straight ahead, as if his mind were entirely elsewhere as he slowed his horses, allowing Benedict to come alongside them.

The Baroness was staring at the floor of the carriage, her hands fidgeting on the lap of her demure blue skirts. Beside her, Alvenley smiled warmly.

"Good afternoon, Dearborn, my lady. Well met."

"Hello again, Alvenley," Benedict said cheerfully, drawing a sharp look from his wife.

"Good afternoon, Baron Alvenley," Christina said, her voice strained. "Baroness."

The Baroness Alvenley did not immediately respond, but kept staring at the floor. Beside her, her husband cleared his throat, one long finger tapping against the thigh closest to her. She squirmed and raised her head, and Benedict could see the puffiness of her eyes, as if she'd been crying before their outing. Her cheeks were slightly flushed and her expression almost confused, anxious. In other words; she was the very image of a well-chastised woman who had received discipline she'd never expected.

"Good afternoon," the Baroness said, averting her gaze slightly, as if she was uncomfortable actually looking at either Benedict or Christina.

Benedict gave Alvenley a rather congratulatory look, which the man returned with one of gratitude.

CONFUSION AND A NIGGLING suspicion filled Christina as she stared at the Baroness Alvenley. The woman's attitude was nothing like she'd expected. When Benedict had first noticed the Alvenley barouche, Christina had thought he'd meant to confront the Baron and Baroness right here in Hyde Park, but Benedict had said 'hello *again*' and he and the Baron kept exchanging looks as though there was some kind of understanding between them.

Not only that, but the way the Baroness kept fidgeting on her seat, the puffiness of her eyes and nose, the way she seemed subdued, the anxious manner in which she watched her husband from the corner of her eye, Christina could almost think...

"Don't you have something else you'd like to say to Lord and Lady

Windham, Mathilde?" Baron Alvenley asked, his voice mild but stern and very firm.

Clearing her throat, either anger or shame coloring her cheeks - or perhaps both - the Baroness lifted her head. She wasn't quite able to look either Benedict or Christina in the eye, but fixed her gaze somewhere about their shoulders.

"I apologize for my behavior and remarks last evening," she said, sounding almost defiant and yet there was a small ring of sincerity to her words. "It will not happen again." That last was said more firmly, as if making a vow.

The Baron smiled and reached out to take his wife's hand, patting it. "There, my dear, well done."

Despite the confused and angry expression on the Baroness' face as she turned away, dropping her gaze back to the carriage floor, Christina thought she saw a small flash of pleasure as well.

"Thank you," Christina said, a bit belatedly. "I accept your apology."

"As do I," Benedict said congenially.

A few more minutes of polite social chatter - with no further conversation from the Baroness - and the two carriages parted again, leaving Christina feeling rather dazed.

She knew it was dreadful of her, but there was something so, *so* satisfying about knowing the Baroness had been spanked. At least, she was fairly certain that was what had motivated her change in attitude. While Christina didn't like to think of herself as the kind of person who enjoyed another's pain or misery, she felt so incredibly vindicated - as well as relieved. It looked as though she no longer had to worry about the Baroness's vendetta against her.

Turning to her husband, who was looking quite cheerful as he steered the horses to the path along the Serpentine, Christina laid her hand on his thigh. "Did you... Were you..."

Smiling cheekily, Benedict winked at her. "I made an early morning call today. It didn't go quite the way I foresaw or even intended, but I do think it made for the best possible outcome."

Not caring who saw, not caring how indecent the high-sticklers would find such a display of public affection, Christina leaned over, grabbing Benedict's face between her hands, and kissed him soundly on the lips.

"I love you," she said.

"I love you too," he said, chuckling and apparently not at all upset by her impulsive act. "But you do know I'm going to have to spank you for that when we return home."

"I know," she said, leaving her hand on his thigh. Might as well truly earn her punishment.

In love again, with her husband. It was everything she'd hadn't wanted ever again, and yet she'd never been happier. A bubble of warmth filled her chest as Benedict placed his hand over hers, using only one to guide the reins of his - fortunately - well-behaved horses. The future looked brighter than ever.

EPILOGUE

Coming into the dining room, Thomas was surprised to see only his mother and her protégé Miss Mary Wilson at the table having breakfast. Normally his father was the earliest riser in the house, and he enjoyed lingering over his meal while reading the paper and pretending he wasn't listening to the conversation. There was a plate at the head of the table, the paper neatly folded beside it, but the seat was empty.

"Good morning. Has father gone out already?" he asked, giving Mary a nod of greeting. Blushing, she nodded back. He wondered if she would ever stop blushing when he or one of his brothers or any other gentleman within twenty years of her age addressed her. So far the only men who didn't cause her to blush upon mere acknowledgement were his father and those old enough to be her grandfather.

His mother was looking over a small stack of invitations, holding a piece of toast which remained uneaten in one hand.

"Hmmm? Oh, he wasn't feeling quite the thing this morning," she said, unconcerned as Thomas dropped a kiss on her head as he headed towards the sideboard, intent on filling his plate with the delicious smelling bacon. "He's having a bit of a lie in."

Unusual but not unheard of.

"What are the plans for today?" he asked, knowing his mother would already have a full schedule laid out.

Under the guise of escorting Mary about and establishing her creditably this Season, Thomas had been looking over the herd for an acceptable bride. It was marginally easier to do so when it was not immediately obvious that was his goal. The matchmaking mamas were uncertain if his appearance at so many events was for his own benefit or if he was doing so at the behest of his mother in order to provide an escort to his cousin. Then too, there were those who wondered if perhaps his cousin would end up meeting him at the altar. The situation did not entirely deter the matchmakers, but neither were the young ladies pursuing him in earnest.

All in all, Thomas was rather glad of the excuse to meet so many young ladies and yet be able to take his time about choosing a bride. He did have rather exacting standards after all.

His brothers and friends might mock the list of qualities he'd made up in order to assist him with his decision, but marriage was a serious business.

It was for life.

He didn't want to be stuck in a miserable union for the entirety of his existence, which meant his bride must be enjoyable company, intelligent, but not too demanding of his time and attention, and be able to - at the very least - appreciate his favorite activities. Since he would one day be the Viscount, she must also bear his heir, which meant she must be virtuous (he had no interest in raising a cuckoo in the nest) as well as attractive enough for him to do his duty. As a viscountess she would also need to be trained to run a household, responsible, fiscally conscientious, and command respect from the servants. As the mother of his children, she must also be warm, caring, and attentive. He didn't want a wife who would neglect their children in favor of balls, shopping, or the social rounds.

His own parents had always been very involved in his and his brothers' rearing, although of course they'd also had nannies and tutors as well.

Thomas had seen his friends secure such relationships with

women who fulfilled nearly every item on his list, so he didn't understand why they acted as though it would be impossible.

So far he'd met several candidates, in fact, whom all seemed as though they might meet the qualifications. Now he just needed to narrow them down, although he was by no means closing himself off to any other young ladies whom he had yet to meet, as long as they also fit his needs. This was not a decision to be made hastily.

"Mary and I are shopping this morning," his mother said as he filled his plate and came to sit down. Mary, of course, had no comment. While she fit quite a few of the items on his list, she would never do for a wife. He liked how demure she was, and that she was perfectly able to entertain herself, not demanding much in the way of attention from anyone, but he needed to at least be able to carry on a conversation when he married. Besides, his appetites in the bedroom... well, it's not as if he could test future brides for compatibility there, but Mary's frequent blushes and delicate sensibilities were clearly no match for his vigorous and exotic appetites. "This afternoon there's the tea at Lady Blakely's, and then -"

A distant shout, upstairs but still loud enough to be heard, had his mother frowning and looking up without finishing her sentence. Thomas frowned as well, setting down his fork and knife.

"What do you think-"

"Help! *Help!*" The shouting grew louder, clearer. Scared. Panicked. Horrified. "It's his lordship! Someone call for a doctor! Oh, help!"

Thomas and his mother were moving before he could think, his heart pounding in his chest. He had no idea how Mary reacted, all he could think about was getting to his father, nausea churning his stomach as he ran, his mother panting and hot on his heels.

ARABELLA RUSHED to Hood House practically as soon as she received the message.

Her hair was not quite done, strands already coming out of the simple, too-loose chignon she'd managed on the trip over. Her dress was askew, two of the buttons done incorrectly, making the skirt hang awkwardly and showing off the mismatched slippers she'd shoved onto her feet in her rush.

During her mad dash, neither she nor her eldest brother Isaac had noticed any of these details, but the moment she stepped into Hood House and came face to face with Lord Thomas Hood, *he* noticed immediately. His dark eyes swept up and down her person, a frown crinkling his brow as he gave her a slightly condemning look.

"You may want to look in a mirror," he said, his tone faintly contemptuous. As if she couldn't feel the strands of hair on her neck or look down and see her dress and slippers for herself. Arabella wanted to stomp on his foot and scream at him. His father might be dying and he was critiquing her appearance?!

Sometimes she wondered how she'd managed to fall in love with such a stuffy, patronizing prig.

"Where's Gabrielle?" she asked (demanded really), giving his comment all the attention it deserved - none.

"The drawing room," he said gesturing.

Arabella started to hurry past him when her brother spoke up.

"How is your father?" Isaac asked, his voice deep with concern. Her steps slowed, because she wanted to know the answer. Dread twisted through her as she waited for the answer. Her best friend Gabrielle was an orphan, like Arabella, but one without siblings; her parents-in-law had welcomed her with open arms, and she would be devastated by the loss of either of them.

"Still alive," Thomas said grimly, his voice strained as if he were in pain. Arabella had to resist the urge to turn about on her heel and hug the poor man. She decided to forgive him his presumptuous comment. Obviously he wasn't currently quite in his right mind. "The doctor said it's his heart. He seems to have made it through the initial crisis, but he's going to be weak and at risk for future problems, and this attack will necessitate some changes in his lifestyle."

Isaac clapped Thomas on the shoulder, and Arabella picked up her pace again, heading for the drawing room.

Gabrielle was there, weeping on Felix's shoulder. For his part, her husband was stoic faced, but, unlike his eldest brother, his eyes were shiny with unshed tears.

"Oh, sweetie..." Arabella rushed forward, hands outstretched.

With a wail, Gabrielle launched herself from her husband's arms to her best friend's, her sudden renewed sobs obviously shocking Felix. He even looked a little hurt at being abandoned so quickly, but mostly concerned at his wife's distress. Standing, he looked like he wanted to move forward, but since his wife had just left his arms, he seemed unsure if his presence would be welcome.

Hugging her tightly, Arabella shot him a helpless and apologetic look. She didn't know why Gabrielle had reacted this way either.

"Gabrielle, sweetie, it's going to be okay," she said, even though she knew there was no guarantee, but Gabrielle sounded very close to hysteria. "Thomas said the Viscount is alright now." Which wasn't exactly what Thomas had said, but it was close enough to the truth.

"I can't stop crying!" Gabrielle wailed, hugging Arabella tighter, her words slightly muffled by the way her head was turned into Arabella's shoulder. Fortunately, she was a bit shorter than Arabella, which made for a more comfortable position than it would have otherwise been. "And he's Felix's father not mine, but Felix has had to comfort *me*, and I can't comfort *him*, because I can't stop crying, and I'm a horrible wiiiiiiife!"

"Oh, Gabrielle, darling," Felix said, coming forward to place his hands on Gabrielle's shoulders as they shook with the force of her sobs. His dark eyes were warm with sympathy as he and Arabella exchanged a look over Gabrielle's head. "I did not - do not - mind comforting you at all. I know you love my father, and comforting you has helped me."

"Really?" Gabrielle asked, lifting her head to turn and look at her husband. Her eyes were red-rimmed, her face blotchy and wet with tears, but Felix looked at her like he'd never seen a more beautiful woman. Arabella would have sighed with envy if the current circumstances weren't so awful. While she'd been unconvinced of Gabrielle's happiness with Felix as a husband when the couple had first wed, it was now obvious how much they loved each other and how well suited they were. Who wouldn't be envious?

"Yes, sweetheart," Felix said tenderly, and he stepped forward to enclose her in a hug which involved Arabella as well. His arms were long enough to close around both of them, trapping Gabrielle between them and lending her both their support. It was odd to feel so included and yet so on the outside simultaneously, but Arabella was just glad she could be there for her friend.

Gabrielle was the best friend she'd ever made, and had led her to other good friends like Cynthia, Eleanor, Lydia, Irene, and Grace. All women who Arabella could be sure liked her for herself and not just because she was the sister of a duke. Such friendships were not to be taken for granted.

After they broke apart, Gabrielle much calmer now, they rang for tea and Felix filled Arabella in on everything they'd heard since they received the initial message. The Viscountess was currently with the doctor in the bedroom. Walter was in the library getting drunk - Arabella imagined that's where her brother and Thomas had probably gone to since they hadn't followed her in here. Felix wasn't sure where his cousin Mary was; quite likely hiding in her room, he supposed. They began speculating on whether or not the Viscountess would decide to finish out the Season in London with her husband ill and what would happen to Mary's Season if the Viscountess decided to make the move back to the country.

They hadn't even finished their first cup of tea when Arabella noticed Gabrielle was beginning to droop, her shoulders slumping and her hand constantly coming up to cover her lips and hide a yawn.

"Did you not sleep well last night?" Arabella asked, keeping her tone innocent since Felix was in the room. After all, he didn't know his wife had been occasionally very indelicate in how much information she shared with Arabella.

He didn't look suspicious at all, however, he actually beamed, wrapping his arm around Gabrielle and pressing a kiss to her temple as she blushed furiously.

"No, I did," Gabrielle said, blushing - but not with embarrassment.

She and Felix exchanged another one of those loving looks which made Arabella feel a bit on the outside. "We aren't making the announcement yet, but..."

She placed her hand on her stomach and gave Arabella a significant look. The adoring, worshipful expression on Felix's face made him look wonderfully sappy.

Arabella squealed as Gabrielle's meaning became clear, clapping her hands with delight! "You're increasing!!! Oh, how wonderful!"

Smiling ruefully, Gabrielle laughed. "It is! But I tire so quickly, I've found, and with all the emotions of today..." She sighed as she waved her hand in an encompassing gesture. "Please don't say anything. As soon as Papa is well enough we're going to tell the family, and then we'll start letting our other friends know." Gabrielle's smile widened. "However, seeing as the topic had risen, and since we were going to ask you to be godmother anyway..."

This time it was Arabella's turn to launch herself at her best friend - it was much nicer to do so in happiness rather than misery.

Seeing as how Gabrielle was obviously worn out, once Arabella had gotten over expressing her joy and accepting the honor, she insisted Felix take Gabrielle up to bed. She needed to rest! Arabella would find Isaac and they could be on their way - she would be hard pressed to keep from blurting out her joy, but somehow she would manage.

TAKING ISAAC INTO THE LIBRARY, Thomas sighed when he saw Walter, already disheveled looking and slumped in a chair. None of them were dealing well with his father's sudden malady.

His own emotions felt as though they were seething just below the surface of the facade he'd erected. With his father out of commission, even temporarily, he became the de facto head of the family until his father recovered. So, as much as he wanted to drink himself three sheets to the wind as Walter appeared determined to do, he could not.

Isaac clapped his hand on Thomas' shoulder, steering him towards a chair.

"Come, sit. You look like you're about to fall over," Isaac said firmly. Thomas almost started to argue, but he would like to sit.

Isaac apparently wouldn't think any less of him for doing so.

Indeed, his friend had a very sympathetic expression on his face, and somehow Thomas knew it wasn't just because his father was ill, but also because Isaac knew what it was to have the burdens and responsibilities of a title suddenly thrust upon him before he was ready. Both of them should have years, even decades, before it became a concern, and yet Isaac was already a duke, and Thomas could very easily have inherited his viscountcy this morning.

He was so very relieved he hadn't, but he couldn't deny his reality still felt entirely altered.

"How much have you had?" Isaac asked Walter, who looked up at him morosely.

"Not enough," Walter replied, slurring the words.

"More than he should," Thomas said, slumping into his own chair.

He decided not to protest when Isaac handed him a snifter of brandy. At least he gave Walter a glass of water, which someone had thoughtfully left a pitcher of next to the bottle of brandy. Walter hadn't actually touched it, but having it on hand was good. Thomas should have thought of that. He was already failing his brother.

"I take it Felix is with Gabrielle?" Isaac asked.

"Yes, she and Mother cried on each other when they first arrived, but when the doctor called Mother back into Father's room, Gabrielle became quite overwrought so Felix took her aside." Something else to feel guilty about. Thomas hadn't had the slightest idea what to do for his sister-in-law, whom he doted on, nor had he been able to assist Felix in any manner.

Looking at his snifter, Thomas decided one glass wouldn't hurt. He would still have his wits about him.

"Arabella will help," Isaac said consolingly as he sat down across from Thomas. "She adores Gabrielle."

"Yes, I'm sure her presence will comfort Gabrielle greatly,"

Thomas said, feeling a little better. That had been one thing he'd been able to do - when Gabrielle had said (between heaving sobs) that she wanted her best friend, Thomas had dashed off a message immediately.

Isaac's sister was a hoyden - over-dramatic, mouthy, far too bossy, spoiled, and strained the limits of Society's conventions, but she was also a very loyal, trustworthy, and protective friend to Gabrielle - and by extension to Gabrielle's family. Walter liked her, but then, Walter did like audacious personalities in general. She was certainly beautiful, and could be charming when she bent her mind to it, but eventually her true self would emerge. More than once, Thomas had wished he had charge of her - while Isaac had mentioned he'd spanked her on occasion, she obviously wanted for more stern discipline than she actually received. She had both her brothers wrapped around her slim fingers and they didn't even seem to notice.

Still, if she could help Gabrielle today, he would be grateful.

He'd had the oddest moment when she'd first arrived, cheeks flushed, hair falling from her coiffure, dress slightly askew, as if she'd just risen from bed - an image of what she might look like after being thoroughly pleasured - and he'd actually felt a stirring of arousal when he looked at her. It had been completely inappropriate of course, not only because of who she was but because of the circumstances, and Thomas could only conclude his body's responses were completely thrown off kilter by the morning's events.

"Is Miss Wilson with them?" Isaac asked.

"No, she's retreated to her room," Thomas said. She'd looked very upset but she hadn't cried - at least not in front of anyone. He supposed he should send a maid to check on her eventually and be sure she didn't require anything. Heaven knew the too-shy chit would never speak up and ask if it were left to her.

A long silence stretched between them, before Walter asked after Lydia. Thomas grimaced. He hadn't even noticed Isaac's wife's absence. Had his wits completely abandoned him? Isaac answered that she was feeling under the weather, which led to a general discussion of the various maladies going around the *ton* currently. No one mentioned the obvious one, happening upstairs.

"Do you think Mother will want to go home?" Walter asked suddenly, a question which made them all pause.

Mother had been overjoyed to throw herself into the Season, especially with a protege to establish. Cutting Mary's Season short by a month would not be entirely detrimental, but it would cause their mother a certain amount of guilt. On the other hand, since she and their father were a truly loving couple, unlike so many in the *ton*, she would also wish to remain with her husband.

"I think it will depend on what the doctor says," Thomas said slowly. "He did say Father shouldn't strain himself-"

"Or eat so much bacon, drink so much wine, or smoke so much," Walter said with a snort. Those were certainly going to be some uphill battles for their mother.

The corners of Thomas' mouth twitched. Except, he shouldn't be smiling considering the seriousness of the situation, so he pushed the impulse back down. "If the doctor says Father *can* remain, even if the recommendation is not to, Father will probably want to out of pure stubbornness, and Mother will end up not fighting him too hard since she'll feel as if she's neglecting her duties by not giving Mary a full Season. Although, perhaps we can hire a chaperone, so my parents can retire to the countryside, and Mary can still finish out her Season."

"With you as escort?" Isaac asked, raising his eyebrows and then tilting his head, thinking it over. "As long as the chaperone resided here as well, I don't think it would cause much comment. Although, you'll certainly raise the odds on those who think you'll offer for her by the end of the Season."

Thomas couldn't help his snort of laughter. "Not likely. She and I would not suit at all. But I must admit, she is very helpful as a shield when it comes to my own quest."

A quest which had now taken on so much more importance.

Logically, intellectually, Thomas had known his father wouldn't live forever. He'd known he would need to marry and bear an heir, because one day his father would pass and he would be the Viscount. But he'd never imagined his father wouldn't be there to see him marry, to meet his grandchildren and dandle them on his knee.

This morning, his father's mortality had smacked him square in the face, harder than any blow he'd ever taken while boxing at Gentleman Jim's. The realization had completely changed the way he viewed the world, his goals, and his timetables.

He no longer felt so blasé about taking his time to choose a bride and start a family, not if he wanted to ensure his father would be there to see him do both.

After this morning, he'd be taking a much more serious look at the candidates he'd already had in mind.

"The quest for the perfect wife!" Walter said, raising his glass and hiccupping. "Thomas' personal Holy Grail."

"The grail was fictional," Thomas pointed out.

Walter gave him a sardonic look.

"I already have several possibilities in mind," Thomas said haughtily. "With father's health in mind, I've decided I will spend the next few weeks ascertaining which lady is most suited to me, and make an offer by the end of this Season."

"Don't suppose my sister might be one of them?" Isaac asked almost hopefully. "I'd really prefer not to suffer through a third Season with her as a debutante."

"Absolutely not," Thomas replied firmly. He had no wish to be rude, but neither did he want Isaac to hope for the impossible. "We would not suit at all."

"Why not?" asked Walter, with a drunken chuckle, while Isaac sighed and slumped back, already defeated. "She's beautiful, accomplished, knows how to run a household, is actually an experienced hostess unlike the other debs, and can carry on an intelligent conversation - something else which is in short supply."

"She's also brazenly outspoken, prone to melodrama, often insultingly direct, far too used to being the center of attention, demanding, hoydenish, and spoiled," Thomas said succinctly, with a shrug of apology to Isaac.

"Here now," Isaac said, although he didn't sound especially defensive. "She's gotten quite a bit better this year, especially with Lydia steering her Season. She's barely made any real waves at all."

Thomas rolled his eyes. "Marginal improvements are better than none I suppose, but I barely saw a difference in her behavior. She still goes galloping through Hyde Park in the morning, doesn't she?"

"Well... yes."

"And she asked Lady March if she'd stuffed her bosom with cotton?"

"Yes, but only after-"

"And called Lord Charters a dunce in his hearing?"

"The man isn't exactly-"

"Barged into the Marley box without an invitation?"

"That was for-"

"I caught her speaking to the Marquess of Hartford myself."

"She wouldn't have normally, but-"

"And those are just a few of her antics this Season," Thomas said, shaking his head. "I won't count her appearance this morning, since it's to her credit that she rushed to Gabrielle's side, but really she should have taken the time to put herself to rights in the carriage over here."

Isaac grimaced. "Well, she did what she could. She actually put her hair up herself on the ride."

Hearing that, Thomas didn't know whether he felt guilty for disparaging her efforts which, after all, were made in an attempt to reach Gabrielle with all speed, or condemning because she'd tried to put up her own hair. Either way, it didn't really matter. She obviously wasn't the woman for him. Not only did she not come close to meeting all the qualifications on his list, she was the very opposite of quite a few of them.

"At any rate, she and I decidedly would not suit."

"So what paragon of pedestrian plainness are you planning to marry?" asked Walter, who then giggled at his own witty alliteration. At least, Thomas assumed he thought his alliteration witty and that was why he was giggling.

"Miss Priscilla Bliss is currently the forerunner," he said. "Although I'm also considering Lady Winifred Bellmont and Miss Charity Sawyer. They've both attended a finishing school I'm told is well recommended, so they should be exemplary hostesses. I'm sure Miss Bliss has been trained as well, and she has a very soothing presence, and she is probably not aiming as high as Lady Winifred or Miss Sawyer."

Although Miss Bliss' parents were perfectly respectable, Lady Winifred was the daughter of the Duke of Somerset and Miss Sawyer was the niece of the Duke of Marbury. By all rights, Miss Bliss couldn't hope to aim as high as either of them. Not that a landing a viscount was anything to sniff at, but it truly depended on the lady's preferences. None of them seemed averse to his suit, but he was a realist and knew Miss Bliss would be grateful for his attentions while the other two might take it as more their due. Especially Lady Winifred, but as she seemed to fit his qualifications, he had not struck her from the list.

"*Not* Lady Winifred," Isaac said, making a face. "I remember her from her debut last year. She was determined to catch a duke; from what I understand, though, she's perfectly happy to keep other titled gentlemen on a string. I suppose in case she fails to succeed in her goal."

Thomas was not too disappointed to strike her from the list.

"As I said, she was not my first choice."

"I have met Miss Bliss," Isaac said, musing. "I remember her being quite sweet."

"Sweet," Walter said, snorting. He pointed at Thomas. "You're going to end up miserable and you're going to thoroughly deserve it."

HE MOST CERTAINLY WAS!

Furious, unable to bring herself to listen any further as her brother started to describe his impression of the boring and sweet Miss Bliss. If she recalled correctly, last summer her brother had described the young woman as having the same personality as a sheep. The debutante actually simpered. *Simpered!*

And somehow that nodcock, Thomas, found her attractive?

She was at the top of his mind? *She* fit his infamous list of qualifications?!

While Arabella had confined herself, cribbed herself in, done her best to show she could fit the list. She'd dampened her spirits, made herself behave, bit her lip more times than she could remember, and all in the name of showing Thomas she *could* be his perfect wife. Because for some reason, she actually liked him.

Oh... bother and damnation.

Arabella knew the reasons. She didn't want a husband whom she could run right over, and Thomas never let her push him around, not even the way her brothers did. She couldn't manipulate or cajole him, and she found that strength of personality rather attractive.

Add to that his honor, his occasional wry sense of humor, the debilitating charm he could conjure when he chose, his sense of duty to his family, and his acceptance of a woman's intelligence - what wasn't there to love?

Well, his priggishness for one thing.

Arabella hadn't realized exactly how far it ran.

I won't count her appearance this morning.

Ha! And she'd been going to forgive him for his supercilious attitude!

Careful not to stomp down the hall, no matter how much she might want to, Arabella hurried for the front door. She embraced her anger, because it was much preferable over embarrassment and hurt. Granted, not all the changes she'd made to her behavior this Season had been necessarily bad; Lydia had been right about many of the corrections she'd gently made, but Arabella had felt more and more stifled as she'd tried to show off for Thomas.

The bloody numbskull hadn't even noticed.

Telling herself the tears in her eyes were from righteous fury, Arabella stormed out the door - she was far away enough from the library that they wouldn't be able to hear her. Wearing slippers, she could only make so much noise anyway, no matter how heavily she tread.

Of course, walking home in mismatched slippers and her hair slipping every which way - even if she had fixed her buttons - without an escort was rash. Even as early in the day as it still was, she had a good chance of being seen as the *ton* began to leave their houses.

Good, she thought grimly.

Thomas thought she was an unmanageable hoyden on the edge of scandal anyway. Why should she bother to continue trying to prove him wrong?

He could have the perfect, simpering, undemanding, boring Miss Bliss as his bride, and Arabella could finally have some *fun* this Season.

I HOPE you enjoyed Benedict's Commands! Arabella and Thomas finally get their chance at happily-ever-after next - CLICK HERE to read Arabella's Taming and watch the sparks fly.

If you'd like a free historical spanking romance from me, CLICK HERE to sign up for my newsletter and receive an exclusive freebie!

ABOUT THE AUTHOR

Golden Angel is a *USA Today* best-selling author and self-described bibliophile with a "kinky" bent who loves to write stories for the characters in her head. If she didn't get them out, she's pretty sure she'd go just a little crazy.

She is happily married, old enough to know better but still too young to care, and a big fan of happily-ever-afters, strong heroes and heroines, and sizzling chemistry.

She believes the world is a better place when there's a little magic in it.

www.goldenangelromance.com

bookbub.com/authors/golden-angel
goodreads.com/goldeniangel
facebook.com/GoldenAngelAuthor
instagram.com/goldeniangel

OTHER TITLES BY GOLDEN ANGEL

HISTORICAL SPANKING ROMANCE

Domestic Discipline Quartet
Birching His Bride
Dealing With Discipline
Punishing His Ward
Claiming His Wife

The Domestic Discipline Quartet Box Set

Bridal Discipline Series
Philip's Rules
Gabrielle's Discipline
Lydia's Penance
Benedict's Commands
Arabella's Taming

Pride and Punishment Box Set
Commands and Consequences Box Set

Deception and Discipline
A Season for Treason
A Season for Scandal

Bridgewater Brides
Their Harlot Bride

Standalone

Marriage Training

CONTEMPORARY BDSM ROMANCE

Venus Rising Series (MFM Romance)

The Venus School

Venus Aspiring

Venus Desiring

Venus Transcendent

Venus Wedding

Venus Rising Box Set

Stronghold Doms Series

The Sassy Submissive

Taming the Tease

Mastering Lexie

Pieces of Stronghold

Breaking the Chain

Bound to the Past

Stripping the Sub

Tempting the Domme

Hardcore Vanilla

Steamy Stocking Stuffers

Entering Stronghold Box Set

Nights at Stronghold Box Set

Stronghold: Closing Time Box Set

Masters of Marquis Series

Bondage Buddies

Master Chef

Dungeons & Doms Series

Dungeon Master

Dungeon Daddy

Dungeon Showdown (Coming 2022)

Poker Loser Trilogy

Forced Bet

Back in the Game

Winning Hand

Poker Loser Trilogy Bundle (3 books in 1!)

SCI-FI ROMANCE

Tsenturion Masters Series with Lee Savino

Alien Captive

Alien Tribute

SHIFTER ROMANCE

Big Bad Bunnies Series

Chasing His Bunny

Chasing His Squirrel

Chasing His Puma

Chasing His Polar Bear

Chasing His Honey Badger

Chasing Her Lion

Night of the Wild Stags

Chasing Tail Box Set

Chasing Tail… Again Box Set

Made in the USA
Coppell, TX
27 July 2021